MW00834176

SPIRIT OF FEAR

a novel

Dr. Jeff S. Pate

LifeRich PUBLISHING

Copyright © 2022 Dr. Jeff S. Pate.

All rights reserved. No part of this book may be used or reproduced by any means, graphic, electronic, or mechanical, including photocopying, recording, taping or by any information storage retrieval system without the written permission of the author except in the case of brief quotations embodied in critical articles and reviews.

LifeRich Publishing is a registered trademark of The Reader's Digest Association, Inc.

LifeRich Publishing books may be ordered through booksellers or by contacting:

LifeRich Publishing
1663 Liberty Drive
Bloomington, IN 47403
www.liferichpublishing.com
844-686-9607

Because of the dynamic nature of the Internet, any web addresses or links contained in this book may have changed since publication and may no longer be valid. The views expressed in this work are solely those of the author and do not necessarily reflect the views of the publisher, and the publisher hereby disclaims any responsibility for them.

Any people depicted in stock imagery provided by Getty Images are models, and such images are being used for illustrative purposes only. Certain stock imagery © Getty Images.

Scripture quotations taken from The Holy Bible, New International Version® NIV® Copyright © 1973 1978 1984 2011 by Biblica, Inc. TM. Used by permission. All rights reserved worldwide.

ISBN: 978-1-4897-4133-2 (sc)
ISBN: 978-1-4897-4132-5 (hc)
ISBN: 978-1-4897-4137-0 (e)

Library of Congress Control Number: 2022907717

Print information available on the last page.

LifeRich Publishing rev. date: 04/13/2022

People are seldom truly afraid of the dark. They're actually afraid of what might be in the dark. So then, what is it that *might* be in there that scares us? What is it about the bump in the night or the closet door cracked open that makes us so uneasy? What do we think will *get us*? Maybe, if we believe in such things, what's *really* coming after us is a...

PROLOGUE

Summer 1992

"You guys are so lame!" Tim proclaimed trying a little too hard to sound at ease. "I don't have to go to some stupid *haunted cabin* in the middle of the woods to prove I'm not afraid."

It was true, of course, but it still came across as a flimsy excuse not to back up his bold claims. Tim had been insisting he wasn't scared of anything or anyone which instantly began the goading and mocking from his fellow sixth-grade campers. Bugs, snakes, lightning storms, even the spooky tales of an old haunted cabin didn't bother Tim. Never had, really. But now his insistences earned him the challenge to sneak out of his cabin, leave the campground, walk to *the cabin* alone, and bring back a piece of it as proof. All at the magical hour of midnight. How cliché.

The cabin in question was about a mile into the woods off of the old trail around the pond. Until the late 70s, it was used as a place for serious hikers and fishermen to lodge for the night, back when the fishing was good in these parts. Unfortunately, there hadn't been any use of it since they recovered the dead bodies in the lake. Fourteen of them in all.

Hiking and camping in these parts stopped almost immediately. The pond was never really the same attraction after they pulled the bodies out. They drained a good five feet of shoreline that never quite filled back in. The local fishing industry pretty much dried up after that, too. The sad fact was that the only good thing to happen in these parts in the last fifteen years or so was when a family sold the land to the little Baptist church up the road to start a boy's summer camp.

It was called Camp Muscogee, after the local Native American tribe that used to inhabit most of the South Georgia land in the area. Kids could paddle canoes, ride horses, learn to shoot a bow and arrow, all the good camp stuff. After the first summer, the ghost stories about the cabin started. It was said that that's where the killer tortured and dismembered the boys and then threw the disfigured bodies in the lake. If you went there alone at night, then the ghosts of the mutilated boys would drag you into the lake so you would share in their watery torment...*forever.* (Cue scary music.)

Camp Muscogee was only in its third year since it took a couple of years to raise the money and build the camp. The camp catered more to middle school-aged boys because those were the ages of the boys killed almost fourteen years ago. Kinda sad, kinda creepy.

The current challenge was simple enough, anyone who was brave enough to get there and back, *alone,* simply had to rip a piece off the dilapidated walls to prove to the others that you had, in fact, visited the cabin. It was made of a type of birch which was rare in these woods so a chunk of it served as satisfactory proof. Only one boy had ever dared to try it. And he was never... seen... *again!* Yeah, right. It had a flair for the dramatic, but what good ghost story didn't? Seeing as how this was only the third year that the camp was in existence Tim was convinced all the stories were pretty much bull anyway.

But that's how the story went as told to Tim and that's when he chimed in with his now famous, "Well, I'm not scared of anything" line. The "yeah, rights" and "puh-leases" were quick to follow. But Tim adamantly insisted that he was scared of absolutely nothing. Why had he done that, he wondered? He knew it would only lead to a series of taunts and dares that he would eventually have to back up or else look like a lying sissy.

Tim was smart enough to know that if a boy had gone missing from the camp that he, or better yet his dad, would've heard about it before coming. His dad wouldn't put up with that kind of nonsense. No, it was a made-up story to scare kids and get them to think twice about sneaking out of their cabins at night. Still, was he willing to go there? Alone?

"I'm just saying that it's dumb to think that some ghosts of some dead kids are waiting to come get us, is all." He tried to sound as nonchalant as he could but now the gauntlet was about to be thrown. And by the one kid who knew just how to get under Tim's skin better than anyone.

"Timid Timmy is too scared to go," got it all rolling. Timid Timmy. Not an altogether *un*clever nickname but one that could destroy a boy's self-esteem and social image if not eliminated immediately. Del knew just what to say. Del *Whatever-his-last-name-is*. Who cared, really? He was as mean-spirited a person as Tim had ever met and now he could potentially ruin his first summer at camp with this idiotic nickname.

"Forget you, man," was Tim's unwitty retort.

But Del just pouted out his lower lip and in his best baby voice said, "Timid Timmy's too afwaid to go. Him thinks da boogeyman gonna get him."

This brought all kinds of laughter from the other boys. Great, now he had to step up to the plate or he was toast. Tim had never backed down from a challenge before. He was an only child and often had to prove himself to other groups of kids for the simple reason that his family moved a lot making him the perpetual "new kid." His dad was a contractor and they had to go where the money was. Tim was only twelve but had moved six times in his life. He longed for a home but at least he was well-liked... most of the time.

Every once in a while, he would have to do some stupid stunt to get "in" but he always did it and this would be no exception.

"Fine," was all he said.

"Fine what? Fine you'll go or fine you're a sissy?" Del just wouldn't quit.

"I'll go. Tonight. Midnight. No biggie." Tim knew that once he did this he would be the camp stud and Del would be calling him 'sir'. "Wanna tag along? Or are *you* too scared?" Tim knew the rules he just wanted to do some of the tauntings for once.

"You have to go alone, Timid Timmy. Or do you need me to hold your wittle hand?"

"No, no. I prefer to go alone that way I won't have to drag your dead body back when the pond boys take you out for being such a little punk." Score one for Timmy. The other boys seemed to like that as well because a cacophony of "oh mans" and "he told you's" followed. But Del just smiled his creepy smile and said, "We'll see."

Midnight came at a snail's pace. The boys had lights out in the cabin at ten so two hours crept by for Tim. He couldn't explain it, but he had a sort of dread about going. He knew it would be a piece of cake. He even planned out some elaborate practical jokes to pull on the boys upon his return. Scratching on window screens, moaning outside the door, stuff like that.

Their cabin leader was a seventeen-year-old kid who slept like a rock so sneaking out wasn't really a challenge. He knew when the time finally came, he'd be stealth enough to get out and back in without detection.

But as he lay there awake his mind started down a road he wasn't prepared to travel. He was almost glad when midnight came so he could get out of that place and get going. His watch alarm beeped its faithful chime and he eased out of bed so as not to wake anyone.

"They're gonna get you, Timid Timmy," came the first of many hushed taunts. So much for not waking anyone. The others were as worked up about this as he was. He could hear Del above the others, almost as if he were whispering the words into his mind, *"they're gonna get you."*

Only one boy, Gabe, whispered an encouragement.

"Tim."

"Yeah?"

"Be careful, ok?"

"I will, Gabe. Don't worry about me. I'll be back in half an hour."

And with that, he eased out of the cabin and began his journey. He felt like a character from a story or something. Off on this eerie adventure with no one else around. There was no band of brothers on this trek. There was no Samwise to his Frodo.

Man, he would give anything right now to make this story a comedy. Goofy music would play as he walked. Maybe he would get to the cabin and it would be decorated for his birthday or the cute girl who lived down the street from his new home would be there to welcome her hero with a sweet kiss.

Well, his birthday was in November, and this was an all-boys camp, so those weren't the most likely scenarios to be played out. And this didn't feel like a comedy in any way. The Georgia summer night was muggy and thick. This was the stuff all good horror movies were made of and he knew it.

All the plans of meandering over there, grabbing a handful of birch, and heading back for some pranks were out the window now. He just wanted to get there and get back as soon as his Nikes would let him. This was so dumb.

What had his father told him about trying to prove himself? "It takes a man to walk away, son," Easier said than done sometimes, Pop. His dad was always trying to get him to be a little more by-the-book, a little more *military* if you will. His dad had never actually served in the military, but you wouldn't know it. *All business* summed him up pretty well. Tim's creative approach to life caused some unrest between them but he knew his dad loved him and meant well.

He got his creative side from his mother. Music and acting lit his fire and he was a pretty gifted musician, by any twelve-year-old standards. His dad had become a lot less tolerant of Tim's "hippie ways" as of late. This last move was supposed to be the jackpot for them. "No more moving for a while," was his father's promise. "But I expect you to buckle down in school and find yourself a good paper route or something to earn yourself some money for your extra-curricular activities."

Extra-curricular activities? Paper route? Who talked like that? Tim's dad did, that's who.

"This summer I want you to get your head out of the clouds and take life more seriously," he told him at the close of the school year.

"You do realize I'm twelve, right dad?" was his smart-alec response.

This got "the look" from the old man and a chuckle from his mom. She shouldn't encourage him, but she did. It was her idea to let Tim go to camp in the first place. "Let him be a kid," she said with pleading eyes.

The old man caved every time with her and that was cool. He loved her and Tim knew it. So really, it was his mom's fault he was in this mess with the stupid haunted cabin by the lake. "Thanks, mom," he said sarcastically to the trees.

He figured it would be about a fifteen-minute walk each way. No dilly dally and certainly no stopping to look inside or anything. He had seen enough cheesy horror movies to know what not to do in situations like this. Grab the wood and haul butt back to camp. Fifteen, nothin'. He might make it back in five.

With each step, he grew more anxious and worried about what might lie ahead. Strange thoughts like, "what if somebody lives there and really does kill anyone who dares to trespass?" and "what if I'm attacked by a wild animal?" began to plague him. He could see Del's mocking face in his mind's eye. That kid was evil.

The cabin was within site now. Flashlights were against the rules so Tim took this one by moonlight. Lucky for him it was nearly a full moon. Was it waning or waxing? He could never tell. The cabin looked extremely uninviting with the moon's pale light hitting it through the leaves. "Here we go," thought Tim.

He was about ten feet away when the niggling fear that had been nipping at his mind began to take bigger and bigger bites. He was reaching out to touch the wood when the fear began to feast on him. His mind was becoming a buffet of terrifying thoughts and it took every ounce of courage he had to reach out and rip off a piece of the wood.

Done. He did it. This was almost over.

As he held the wood in his hand the fear subsided for a moment. Timmy turned to jog back to camp with his prize and SMACK! He was knocked on his butt by... by what? Was that a tree? No, it couldn't be a tree! There were no trees this close to the cabin. Timmy looked up and his throat seized shut. Looking down at him was a beast of a man with hate and darkness etched so deeply in his face that it was nearly enough to stop his heart.

Tim tried to scream but couldn't. He wanted to get up and run away but couldn't. He could only sit there and look into the face of evil. The dirty, cold hand of the large, old man reached down as his fingers laced around Tim's throat. Was this the end of his story?

A mile away Gabe lay there crying softly in his pillow while Del sat in the dark with a twisted smile on his face. His lower lip came out as he whispered loud enough for Gabe to hear, "Timid Timmy found a new fwiend."

PART ONE

"your enemy the devil prowls around like a roaring lion looking for someone to devour."

1PETER 5:8

CHAPTER ONE

The drive home was usually the best part of the workday. Windows down, music blaring, and walkie-talkie off. Tim almost always took back roads for two reasons: one, because he hated traffic, and two, because he loved the outdoors—most of the time. He had grown accustomed to the smell of it. He took the family camping at least twice a year up in the Blue Ridge National Park. He was an outdoorsman, up to a point. He fished and hiked, but he wasn't an avid hunter. It wasn't that he was opposed to hunting or had some moral hang-up about it, he just preferred doing other things.

Things like spending time with the wife and kids, for instance. He was, in every sense of the word, a family man. Tim fully enjoyed a day of golf or the occasional football game, but he also didn't mind turning down a day on the links for a day at the park. His wife sure didn't mind either. Tim was no saint, but no one could ever say that his family wasn't top on his list.

Still, he loved taking these back roads. It was a good time to unwind after a day of micromanaging a construction crew. Three crews, technically. His uncle's business was doing well in the suburbs north of Atlanta. That was, in no small part, due to Tim's people skills. He could communicate with people in a way that was authoritative but not condescending. The crews respected him, and therefore they would give the extra 10 percent when asked.

The only reason he wasn't the head of McDaniel Construction was that before his father died Tim made it well known that he didn't want it. That was a source of tension at home, which reared its ugly head all too often. Tim was a musician at heart. In college, he chose the more general major of fine arts, but it was mostly music that floated his boat.

"So, you have no interest in the family business?" His father often asked with a tone that reeked with disdain.

"No, not really. But thanks though," was the response that got his father's blood boiling. Why did he have to goad the old man so much? He regretted making statements like that for a long time.

Tim worked on sites with the business every summer since he was fifteen, but he didn't want to run it, own it, or anything. He just wanted to make some extra cash for dates and guitars. That all changed the summer before Tim's senior year in college. His dad had a massive heart attack. He died on the spot. Tim was on a site with his uncle when he got the news.

The will was simple, Uncle Frank got the business. Tim got the house. It seemed his dad had gotten the point after all. But the kicker was Uncle Frank leaned way too much on Tim's dad to be an effective leader, and Tim was stuck having to be that support for him. The irony was that after college graduation he went to work full-time for his uncle doing the very thing he told his dad he wanted no part in. His dad had won again.

It wasn't the first time Tim's dad, or Bill, as everyone else called him, would somehow manipulate Tim to get what he wanted. For years after Tim's mother died, his dad would say things like, "You know your mother would have wanted *so and so* for you," and "this would sure have made your mother proud." Tim wanted to hate him for saying things like that, but he didn't. He knew his dad loved him, even if he had a hard time saying or showing it.

Driving home, Tim would think about these things and laugh. He missed his parents, especially his mom. He worked hard, and he knew his dad would be proud of him for sticking with his uncle for so long. His afternoon escape from the dread of spending the rest of *his* life living his *father's* life was John Denver, at least on this ride home. Other days it was Kansas or the Eagles. When he was particularly *emo* he chose Twenty-One Pilots or My Chemical Romance. He would get lost in song and his troubles would fade out for a while.

Right in the middle of *Country Road*'s chorus, he caught sight of the lone work truck ahead on the road. It had flashers on and a sign blocking the road. Great, he takes the back roads to avoid traffic and now he gets stuck all alone by a truck taking up the whole road. After sitting there for about five minutes he thought he'd better call Liz.

Ah, Liz. Sweet Elizabeth Anne, his blushing bride. He knew she wouldn't worry or fuss if he wasn't home at five-fifteen on the dot. But he was a pretty considerate guy, most of the time, and it would be nice to hear her voice. As he sat there he said, "Hey Siri, call home." She did.

"Hello?" came the voice of a five-year-old angel.

"Hey, baby girl. Lemme talk to Mommy."

"Are you almost home, Daddy? I want to show you what I found today!"

"OK sweetie, I can't wait to see it. But lemme talk to Mommy real quick." He loved the excitement that Hannah brought to the world. A precocious five-year-old who found the beauty in everything. She was the perfect balance for her older brother, Caleb. He was the cynical eight-year-old who was learning that life was more than Legos and recess. He was introduced to the world of homework this year.

In the sing-song tone that kids do so well, he could hear her bellow into the house, "Mo-ommy it's Da-addy." He heard Liz pick up the cordless phone in the kitchen. In the world of cell phones, she insisted on having a landline so she could stay "grounded." He loved her for silly things like that.

"Hey, babe. It looks like I might be a few minutes late today. I'm stuck out here on Route 16 and there's some small road crew doing something, though I don't actually see anybody working." He felt strange. He realized it was odd that he didn't see any workers, but he was sitting at the Road Closed sign diligently. "I'm the only one out here but they have a truck blocking the road and the drop-off is a bit much to go around."

"Too much for the Tahoe? I thought you were a real man," she said teasingly.

"Of course, I could just drive through the woods clearing my own path, but I thought it best to obey the traffic laws on this one," he answered back. "Anyway, I'll find somebody and see what the hold-up is. t I just wanted to let you know it might be a few minutes if this road is closed all day and I have to backtrack."

"That's fine. I know you—" she stopped short. "Very funny, smart guy," she said with a tone that implied she figured out his secret.

"What?" he asked ignorantly.

"Oh, like that's not you pulling into the driveway now." She sounded dead serious.

"Uh, no. I told you I'm out here on Route 16," he responded with a measure of annoyance in his voice.

"Well, then it must be someone else with a black Chevy Tahoe." She thought she had him now.

"I guess so because I'm still ten miles away," he stated honestly.

"OK. So then that's not my adorable husband getting out with a cell phone in his hand and flowers in the other?" she sounded so convinced it was him that it started to scare him a little.

"Babe, I'm serious. I'm out on Route 16 stuck at a roadblock. This isn't a joke. Who do you see?" he asked curiously.

"Let's see, he's about 6 foot 2, around 235lbs, ruggedly handsome with short brown hair and that awful soul patch thing." It was him to a "T," even down to the soul patch he'd sported for the last few years just to bug her. "Yep, that's my husband."

This was freaking him out more than a little. "Listen, Liz, I am not kidding. That is *not* me. I'm —"

"Give it up, Tim. I see you plain as day walking to the front door. Now hang up and give me my flowers." And with that the line was dead.

What on earth was happening here? Who was this guy that looked so much like him that it even fooled his wife? Was she in danger? Tim cursed at the stupid roadblock!

He hit send again hoping to get his wife and find out something more about this. Surely when she got to the door and saw that it was, in fact, not him she would call him back, he just didn't want to wait.

"Excuse me!" he yelled out. "Hello?!"

The sound of his voice filled the air. He heard no sounds of work or people anywhere. He honked his horn and waited for a beat to see if that summoned anyone. Nothing.

There was no answer on the phone so he began to feel uneasy about this. If there was a need to do some work out here, he couldn't see what it might be and there was no indication of how long the road would be closed. That was it, enough was enough. He was going home.

Tim hit the gas and went far-right onto a bit of a dip off the road. He pushed the four-wheel-drive button and prepared himself for some bumps. He bounced and lunged on the uneven ground past the roadblock. Strange, there was nobody at this whole site. Not one worker. He made a mental note but was far more concerned with getting home to his wife and kids right now. There was some guy that looked like him and drove the same car as him about to give his wife flowers and he didn't like that one bit.

As his Tahoe found the road on the other side of the roadblock, he switched off his four-wheel drive and hit the gas. He would be home in less than ten minutes if he obeyed the speed limit but this was no time to be a boy scout. He had to get there as soon as he could. His dread built up with each passing moment.

As he pulled onto his street, he noticed that there was no stranger's car in his driveway. There were no police cars or neighbors outside to tell him what had happened. His mind relaxed a bit, but he wasn't home yet. He wanted to feel the warm touch of his wife and the reassuring hugs of his kids before he started shutting down from rescue mode.

He screeched the tires to a halt in the driveway and ran out to the front door. He half expected Liz to run out laughing at the prank she had pulled on him. She didn't. He walked into the house and was greeted by an eerie silence. The only sound was Buckley barking in the backyard.

Tim ran to the back door and opened it. Buck, his Husky-Shepherd, was happy to come in but Tim could tell something was bothering him.

"What is it, boy? Where is everybody?" Tim knew this wasn't an old Lassie episode where his dog could fill him in on what went down, but he was getting more anxious by the second.

"Honey?" he yelled into the emptiness. "Babe, are you here?"

His heart began to sink. Where were they? He was about to call her cell phone when his phone chirped to life. He looked at the number. Paul. His best friend since high school and then some. Out of desperation, he opened it.

"Paulie, you heard from Liz?" was the only thing he cared to discuss right now.

"Well hello to you, too," he feigned hurt feelings.

"Not now, man. Liz and the kids are gone and something weird is going on. Have you seen or heard from her?" It was a long shot since Paul lived over an hour away.

"No, man, I haven't. What's so weird?" he asked sincerely.

"I don't have time to explain but I'm freakin' out a little here."

"Deep breaths, man. I'm sure it's all good. Did she leave a note or anything?" Good question. He hadn't thought to look for a note. Maybe they went for a walk or something.

"Yeah. Good idea. Lemme check the kitchen table." Paul could hear him making his way to the kitchen and then the sound of a piece of paper being picked up. "There's a note but..."

"Tim." No response. "Tim!" he tried again.

"Oh my God," Tim said with panic in his voice. "Something's wrong."

"What is it? What does it say?" Paul practically begged.

Paul half expected a ransom note or a "dear John" letter, but he knew better than that. Liz would never leave Tim and who in their right mind would kidnap a woman and her two kids from a blue-collar guy who made like 45k a year? There had to be something pretty bad to make Tim sound so scared. Paul repeated himself, "What does it say?"

"It just says... 'did you miss me?'"

The last two hours were surreal. Tim called the police out and tried to file a report. The problems started snowballing there. There was no sign of forced entry or struggle. There were no indications that anyone was taken against their will. When the neighbors were interviewed one saw nothing but the other, Mrs. Jenkins, was positive that Tim had come home and picked up the family.

"They all left together," she smiled. "They are a sweet family. The kids were laughing and smiling. He seemed in a hurry though."

When the police tried to explain that it was Tim trying to find his family, she was very confused and just said kept saying, "That poor boy. That poor, poor boy." When the police informed Tim of his neighbor's account, he tried again to recall the occurrences that led to this moment. The road work, the phone call, the Tim look-a-like. It sounded ridiculous to Tim so he could only imagine what they were thinking.

"Look, I know this is bizarre. I'm as confused as you guys. I'm sure this is some whack job that wants to make me look insane and he's doing a bang-up job." Tim was not sure how to come off as sincere without sounding like a loony.

"Listen. All I'm saying is that I was on the phone with my wife when she was convinced that I was home. Somebody was dressed up like me with the same car as me, maybe even looked like me but it *WASN'T ACTUALLY ME!*" He didn't mean to sound as angry as he came across. He was about to explain again but one of the two officers spoke up.

"Sir," the condescension was thick, "do you hear yourself? As of now, there is no missing person because your neighbor says that it was you who took your wife and kids away. Not by force, mind you, but laughing and smiling. There is no evidence *at all* that this is a kidnapping." The officer was polite but annoyed. "I mean, are you trying to play some kind of joke or something? Because we're not laughing if you are."

"Joke? No! What about the note?" Tim asked with the last ounce of hope he could muster. "That's evidence, isn't it?" At least he hoped it was.

"We'll take it in and have it analyzed, but it doesn't ask for anything or make any threats and for all we know you wrote it or your wife might have left it for you." Tim went to object to that but the officer held up his hand and continued. "You need to understand that if this turns out to be a missing person case then *you* are our top suspect at this time. We have witnesses who have stated that you took your family. I advise you to stay in town as we might need to talk to you some more about this." The other officer didn't appear happy about him saying that, but he didn't step in just yet.

This was getting nowhere fast. Tim was physically shaken and emotionally worn out. He was to the point of telling the police to take their accusing eyes and pointing fingers and shove 'em right up —

Just then Paul drove up. Thank God for Paul. He could help, couldn't he? He would tell these guys the deal. Come on Paulie, make this go away.

"Officer, can I be of any assistance?" He was always sincerely polite, not at all fake or manipulative in his kindness.

"Who are you?" came the unfriendly response from the unfriendly officer.

"I'm Paul Thibodeaux. I'm a close friend of the family." Paul explained.

"Paul Tibba who?" the so-far-unfriendly officer asked with his eyebrows raised.

"Tib-uh-doh," he sounded it out and spelled it. Out of habit, he offered, "It's cajun."

Both officers nodded like that was all he needed to say.

Paul continued, "I work with Brunson University up in Toccoa and came down here when I heard there was some trouble. I spoke with Tim right when this all happened, and I rushed down here as fast as I could to help."

"You're a professor or something?" the officer asked.

"No, I'm a Campus Minister. Like a Chaplain, kind of. I work on campus with the students, but I'm not employed by the school so I'm not faculty, per se." Paul walked over to the car with the officer to talk out of earshot of Tim. Tim knew that Paul would never say or do anything that wasn't helpful, so he didn't follow.

"I see. Well, unless you can provide this man an alibi then he's the one we're watching. When did you say you spoke with him?" the officer didn't sound very hopeful.

"Well, I called him just after five o'clock. He was in the house looking for them. I was on the phone when he found the note." Paul knew it was no alibi, but he tried to make it sound as if it were. It didn't work.

The other officer spoke up for the first time. He was clearly the senior officer and his badge said *Detective* but he had been letting the other guy do most of the talking thus far.

"So, you can't corroborate his story either then? Listen, here's the deal. Your pal seems genuinely concerned about his family, but currently, all fingers point to him. He called us. He's sticking to his ludicrous story like glue. Either he's a real bonehead of a kidnapper or there's something else going on here that is beyond us. Personally, my gut tells me he's telling the truth, or at least he thinks he is. I'm waiting on a call that will either help him out or tear his story to shreds right now. Either way, I suggest you go talk to him and let him know not to leave town for a few days."

Paul went to talk with Tim. He explained what the officer said, and Tim looked frustrated beyond belief. Paul was sure that Tim was innocent but even he could see the officer's point. Paul noticed the senior officer on the phone frowning and shaking his head while he was speaking with Tim. This probably wasn't good.

"Sir?" the officer called to Tim.

"Yes?" was all he could muster.

"I'm afraid there's yet another hole in your story," he started.

"What hole?" Tim demanded.

"It seems that there is no road work happening anywhere on 16 today or in the last three months. There are no city trucks out there today."

This was more than he could bear. Tim felt his knees going weak, but he forced them to hold him. He had to know what was going on.

"Then who was out there?" his voice was shaky with emotion. "Who stopped me long enough to take my family? It must be a setup or something. I thought it was strange since there weren't any workers out there, but I just wanted to get home and make sure my family was ok." He sounded weary but found his resolve.

"I swear to you I did not do this. I love my family more than anything and if you go around convinced that it was me then you won't be looking for the real kidnapper. Please, don't just assume it was me!" Tim was desperate now. "I know I'm a suspect. That's fine. Watch me, follow me, interrogate me but please don't stop looking elsewhere. Please find my family." Tim was breaking down.

Paul put his arm around his best friend. He had never seen Tim like this, and it made his heart ache for him. He prayed in his heart that God would help him through this and that Liz and the kids were ok.

"Mr. McDaniel, we will do everything we can to find them. I promise," the senior officer assured him. The other officer seemed annoyed that they didn't just arrest Tim on the spot but there was no evidence of a crime yet and it was Tim who had called them out in the first place. They piled back into the police cruiser and headed out. With the window down the senior officer offered one more cautionary word.

"Try to think about anyone who would want to hurt you or your family. If this is some elaborate setup, then we need all the help we can get to find this guy."

But who would want to hurt Tim? Who could hate a man so much that he would take his wife and children? Who was so evil that he would take delight in another man's misery? Not since childhood had Tim known a person who would fit that description. It had been thirty years, but Tim could think of only one person that took such joy in Tim's pain. Those were thoughts long buried, but never truly forgotten.

CHAPTER TWO

Down at the police station Detectives Sean Peters, the senior officer, and John Calloway, the snippy one, were discussing the McDaniel case. It was still a mystery to either of them but they were certainly taking opposite sides on this one.

"It's obviously him, Sean," John insisted. "The guy's either lying or nuts but he did it. Eye witness puts him at the scene and his only alibi was proven to be non-existent. There were *no* workers out on 16 *all day.*"

The facts were certainly stacked against him but sometimes facts are misleading. Sean Peters had been a detective long enough to understand that things weren't always what they seemed. Too many perfect facts were as suspicious as none at all.

"Listen, I'm not saying he's innocent here but I have a feeling—"

"A feeling? You've got a feeling?"

"Let me finish, please," the detective said, emphasizing each word for effect.

"Sorry," Calloway said sheepishly.

"I've got a *feeling* that this guy is either telling the truth or he really believes it is the truth. It's not so far-fetched to assume that some guy could have it in for him and want to make him look nuts in the process."

"Yeah, but that's a long shot," Calloway interjected, "I don't buy it."

"Sure it is. But long shots are what detective work is all about, John." Peters knew full well that Calloway longed to be a great Detective but had just recently gotten his break. Reminding him of this was a subtle way of reminding him who was really in charge of this case. Calloway took the hint and began to sulk out of the room.

"I'm getting some coffee. Want some?" Calloway offered.

"Nah, thanks. Hey, John."

"Yeah," he said halfway out the door.

"Sorry about pulling rank on you. You've got a good head on your shoulders, you just need to consider all options in a case before you go fingering someone as guilty. I've seen some strange cases in my day. Cases you wouldn't believe without the evidence or the confession to back them up. Don't be in so big of a hurry to close the case that you don't work the case from *every* angle." Sean didn't enjoy hurting people's feelings and he knew Calloway didn't mean any harm.

"It's cool," was his only response. He needed time to lick his wounds but he would be all right. And if not then he wasn't cut out for detective work. Either way, this case was a doozy.

"What's your story, Mr. McDaniel?" Peters wondered out loud. "Who would want to stick it to you *this* bad?"

Tim and Paul were at the kitchen table trying to make sense of this. Tim had called everyone he could think of to double-check that Liz hadn't taken the kids somewhere without telling him. Of course, her car was still in the driveway and her cell phone was on the kitchen table but he was very willing to overlook those details to have her safely home.

The tough one was calling her mom to see if she had spoken with her today. He didn't want to alarm anyone yet so he had to sound all carefree and loose while asking if she had called today.

"Why what's wrong?" were the first words out of Mrs. Stroud's mouth.

"Nothing," he lied, "just checking." This was hard. Maybe he should have just told her the truth but then she'd be on her way here freaking out the whole time and Tim wouldn't be able to help at all. It was better this way. If there were no strong leads by tomorrow, he'd call her back and tell her what was going on.

After lying to his in-laws and most of their friends he was stuck here at the table with Paul wondering what his next move should be. Paul was the intuitive type so there wasn't a need to "be strong" around him. Still, Tim seemed distracted by something so Paul took a shot.

"There something you're not telling me, buddy?" he gently inquired.

"Waddaya mean?" he tried to convince himself there was nothing to be said but deep down he wanted to scream it out.

"Come on, dude. It's me. You can talk to me. What is it?"

"All right. But you are gonna put me in the whacko category just like that cop did when you hear this," he warned.

"Try me. I believe a lot of weird stuff. I'm a Christian Minister, remember?" he said teasingly to ease his friend's tension.

"Well, ya know when that one cop asked me to think of anyone who could want to hurt me or my family?"

"Yeah."

"I was suddenly blown away with a flood of memories from my childhood. It's like a closet door in my mind flew open and a butt-load of skeletons popped out. I remembered this kid from camp for some reason." He knew it sounded dumb but he valued Paul's opinion and wanted to hear what he would say.

"Why him?" was all he asked.

"He was a demented little dweeb, that's why. He got his jollies off on making kids cry and stuff, ya know?" He hated even thinking about that night.

"I know the type," Paul admitted.

"Well, this kid was pretty much responsible for about a year of psychotherapy for me and for getting an entire summer camp shut down for good."

"Wow! Sounds like a real winner. You were in therapy?" Paul was a little shocked to hear this after so many years of friendship.

"Real wiener is more like it. And yes, I was in therapy. That's another story. But this kid, Del was his name, he was always getting other kids to do dumb and dangerous stuff. A kid almost drowned one time because of him. He lied and told him the lake was only two feet deep and he could just stand up. He convinced him to take off his lifejacket and hop out of the canoe. The poor kid believed him. Scared us all to death!"

"Ok, so what's he got to do with this?" Paul wondered.

"I have no idea. Probably nothing. But ever since the cop asked that question I can't get this kid out of my mind."

"That was a pretty long time ago, right?" Paul asked trying to piece Tim's thoughts together.

"Yeah, like almost thirty years ago or something. Why?"

"Have you seen or heard from this Del in all this time?" Paul asked with a logical tone.

"No."

"So, I repeat, what do you think he has to do with this?" Paul was trying to help Tim bring this notion into focus.

"What I'm about to tell you has only been heard by my parents and my therapist when I was twelve." He paused for what seemed like dramatic effect but it was really that he wasn't terribly comfortable talking about this. "I had a traumatic accident as a kid at that camp and Del was a big part of it."

Paul seemed to be unfazed by it but he was always an even keel kinda guy. "The psychotherapy happened after that?"

"Yeah."

"Must have been a doozie of an accident to have to get therapy for a year. Personally, I feel you could still benefit from some therapy from time to time." Paulie was a real morale booster but his sarcasm was a welcome relief to the tension Tim was feeling recounting this story in his head.

"You finished?" he asked.

"I am," he said with mock shame and his head bowed.

"Good. Like I was saying, this Del kid was always daring kids to do stupid or dangerous stuff and one day I became his target. He set me up from the beginning. I wished, for once, I had taken my dad's advice and walked away."

"Hey, Hero! Where's your cape?" Del bellowed from the stack of life jackets on the ground. Some nerve this guy had. Gabe had almost drowned and he was making jokes.

"What's your problem, Del? What the heck were you thinking telling Gabe to jump out of the boat?" Tim knew Gabe couldn't swim and was quick to grab him when he went under. He had a good mind to stroll over there and pop Del in the chops one good time.

"That's not my problem," he stated so casually you would think he was referring to laundry. "He said he was scared of being out in the boat so I told him he could just go back to shore. No biggie."

"He said he was scared because you were tipping the boat and he told you he couldn't swim, you jerk! You told him it was shallow enough to walk back. How's that not your problem?" Tim was getting ticked now.

"Like I said, I just told him if he didn't want to be in the boat, 'cause he was such a big ole baby, then go to the shore." How could a kid be so callous? Gabe was petrified and would most likely never step foot in a boat again. "Good thing you were there, huh?" he said with mock concern.

"You've got problems, man." Tim left it at that. He could have tried to get him to see how irresponsible his actions were but he wasn't the camp counselor, he was a kid. And this wasn't his fight. Gabe was safe, Del was a psycho. Life goes on.

"You're so brave, Timmy. Pulling Gabe out like that took real courage. I bet you're not scared of anything, huh?" Del was using that fake sincerity junk again. Tim wasn't really in the mood but something inside of him, pride maybe, didn't let this one go.

"As a matter of fact, butthole, no." It felt good to stick it to Del, even if only a little.

"You mean," Del was drawing the other boys' attention now, "there's nothing in this whole world that scares you? You are, in fact, without fear?" He was pouring it on thick and Tim was falling right into his trap. "Not rats, or zombies, or werewolves, or anything?"

"Can't think of anything... except maybe your face." The boys had a good chuckle and Del seemed to take it in stride. He had bigger fish to fry and wouldn't be sidetracked by a digression into "yo momma" jokes and "I'm rubber, you're glue" comebacks.

"Well, there's a way you can prove what a stud you are, ya know?" Oh no, what was he doing now? "You know the story of the old cabin in the woods, don't you?" he asked.

"Can't say I do. This is my first year here." Tim was sure there would be the typical ghost stories circulating this camp. Heck, it wouldn't be Summer Camp without them. But this one wasn't just spooky old witches and goblins. No, this one was based on truth and, as everyone knows, that's the worst kind.

"Well, let me fill you in," Del began with a twisted smirk. "You know how the lake is like half the size it should be?" There was a huge ring around the lake where its old borders were. It was a little like a marshy beach now and it gave it a strange look but Tim hadn't thought too much about it. The camp had built an extra-long dock that extended into the water. The lake had, at one time, jutted off deep into the woods and came within about fifty feet of an old, abandoned cabin. The dirt road trail was a bit grown over but you could still get to it pretty easily if you wanted.

"Yeah, so?"

"That's because they had to drain the lake to remove all the bodies." Del let the phrase 'all the bodies' linger in the air for a moment before continuing. "Fourteen of them, to be exact."

"Whatever." Tim hoped Del was full of it but the boys' response wasn't reassuring. They joined in with a chorus of "uh-huhs" and "it's true, man."

"Everybody knows it, dude. Even the camp workers know it. Anyway, it doesn't matter if you believe it because no one has ever gone out there alone at night and lived to tell about it." Del knew he had Tim now.

"Oh, really? Spare me the melodrama."

"That's right. The first year the camp opened this kid thought he was brave," Tim just rolled his eyes at that, "but now he's with the other fourteen boys."

"You are so full of crap!" Tim was a hard nut to crack.

"The boys were all tortured with these huge fishing hooks and old hunting knives before they had their throats slit from ear to ear. They were all about twelve or thirteen, just like you. It happened almost fourteen years ago back when this place was nothing but a good place to fish. Whoever the killer was cut out their eyes." Del seemed to enjoy retelling the story. It didn't occur to Tim at the time to ask how he knew all of this.

Another boy Tim knew only as "Elvis" chimed in with his slow Georgia accent, "It's all true, Tim. I'm from around here and my uncle had just become a deputy when it happened. He says it was the most awful thing you ever did see. He said that all of the boys had their stuff cut off, too." He made a circle with his finger around his crotch to illustrate what "stuff" was. I guess it was his strong southern accent or maybe his propensity to walk around singing old hymns that earned him his nickname, but either way his corroboration of Del's story made Tim wish that Elvis had left the building.

"So? That sucks for them but I don't believe in ghosts." Why was he trying to sound so brave? He knew he should back off with the machismo but he just didn't want Del to get the best of him. Truth was, this story was freaking him out a little.

"So, this other brave kid went out there at night, without a flashlight, to get a piece of the cabin —" Del was explaining.

"Why did he want a piece of the cabin?" Tim was curious.

"Well, the cabin's made of White Birch," Del answered matter-of-factly like that was supposed to clear things up.

"So?" Tim wasn't satisfied with that.

"That tree doesn't grow in these woods, genius! That's the only way to prove that he was really there." It made more sense now. Tim probably couldn't tell a White Birch from a Carolina Pine but there was no need to flaunt his ignorance further.

"He never came back and his body was never found. They got him."

"Who? The dead boys? Gimme a break." Tim wasn't fazed.

"Well, the camp tried to spin the story of his disappearance by saying he ran away cause this camp used to be for little poor boys with broken homes and stuff, but everyone knew what happened. If you're so skeptical then you won't mind going out there tonight and proving us all wrong?" Del brought the other boys in on it now. They were a unified front and it was Tim against the world.

The more Tim thought about it the dumber it sounded. A little creepy, but dumb.

"You want me to sneak out of the room after the camp counselors are asleep, hike like a mile into the woods to some old dump that's supposed to be haunted, tear off a piece of it and bring it back here to prove I'm not scared? Please, don't be ridiculous." Tim hoped it convinced the others how silly it was, but it didn't.

Everyone was egging him on now. The banter lasted another minute but eventually, it came to a climax with one final exchange.

"I'm just saying that it's dumb to think that some ghosts of some dead kids are waiting to come get us, is all."

"Timid Timmy is too scared to go."

There was no backing down now.

"Fine," was all he said.

"Fine what? Fine you'll go or fine you're a sissy?"

"I'll go. Tonight. Midnight."

And with that, the nightmare began.

CHAPTER THREE

Paul listened with interest as Tim began recalling the worst night of his young life. Just when he came to the part where he was sneaking out of the cabin his cell phone came alive to the chorus of Peaceful Easy Feelin' by the Eagles. An ironic ringtone at the moment. He snatched it up hoping it was Liz or someone with some good news at least.

"Hello?" came his desperate greeting.

"Mr. McDaniel? This is Detective Sean Peters."

Tim's heart sank a little.

"Any leads?" Tim fought the pessimism in his heart and asked a question he knew the answer to already.

"Not yet, sorry. Listen, I was wondering something."

"What's that, Detective?" Tim wondered what it was now.

"I was wondering if you and your friend would meet me downtown. I have a few more questions I want to ask you."

"Downtown? What questions? Can't you just ask me now?" Tim didn't like this game of hurry up and wait. He wanted to start trying to find his family now.

"It's not something I want to do over the phone. It would be best if you could meet me at 8:30 at Maggie's. You familiar with that café?"

"Yeah, I know it. But —" Tim started to object again.

"Good. I'll see you boys at 8:30 then." And with that, the conversation was over.

Tim couldn't understand why on earth the detective wanted to talk to both of them at a little hole-in-the-wall diner but he didn't have a choice at this point. He filled Paulie in on the plan.

"Maybe he has something he has to tell you and didn't want anyone else around?" Paul guessed, but he didn't have a great feeling about this meeting.

"So, instead of coming back by the house, we meet in a public diner?" Tim poked a hole in that theory.

"Good point. I dunno, man. I guess it's best if we just go and see what the deal is. Couldn't hurt, right?"

Tim was used to Paul's loyalty as a friend but a thought occurred to him.

"Don't you need to be heading back soon? I mean you have almost a two-hour drive home." Tim was glad for his company but he didn't want him to lose his job over this or anything.

"Are you kidding? It would take wild horses to drag me away from this. Liz and the kids are my family too, ok?" Paul was almost hurt by Tim's suggestion that he leave.

"Hey, I'm glad you're here so don't get me wrong. I just want you to be ok."

"I'm fine. Before I left to come, I briefed my intern and let him know that I would be gone a few days at least. I'm pretty much my own boss there so I decided to give myself a vacation. The higher-ups love me so it's all good. Besides, you're more important than a job any day." It didn't sound cheesy coming from Paul and Tim knew he meant it.

"Thanks, man," was all that needed to be said.

"Now let's go see what the good detective wants with us."

Twenty minutes later they pulled into Maggie's parking lot. They didn't notice a police cruiser and weren't sure if they should just go in and wait or stay outside. The place wasn't a dump but it wasn't exactly the best part of town either. Tim had eaten here a few times in the mornings when he needed to go over some blueprints with his uncle.

They had your typical greasy spoon menu complete with coffee that could strip paint off a wall. In college, Tim and Paul ate many a late night in dives like this one. Nothing was better after binge drinking and puking your guts out than eating hash browns smothered, covered, and chunked. Those days were long gone now for both of them, each for different reasons.

"Nice place." Paul's the kind of guy who would look for the pony in a pile of manure.

"Yeah, a real breath of fresh air, Tinkerbell. Where do you think he is? This is wasting precious time." Tim was a little annoyed by the detective's apparent lack of concern for the time-sensitive nature of the situation.

"I'm sure he's on his way. Let's go in and get some coffee. I have a feeling this is going to be a long night." Paul wasn't trying to be prophetic but he also knew his friend would not rest until he found his family.

They went in and sat in a booth near the front so they could keep a lookout for the detective. Once they ordered their coffees Tim's cell rang again. Tim could see it was the same number as before, presumably the detective's cell number.

"Where are you?" was Tim's greeting.

"Around back. Tell your friend to stay put and you come out the side and meet me at the dumpster." This was getting strange and silly.

"Look, enough of the cloak and dagger stuff, ok? What's the deal?" Tim had a bad feeling about this. Paul didn't seem to like it much either as he sipped his coffee with a frown.

"Just come out back." And with that, the conversation ended abruptly again.

"Look, he says to come out back to the dumpster alone. Just sit tight and I'll fill you in."

Tim was getting up from the table when Paul pulled at his shirt sleeve.

"Hey, I'm not so sure about this. What kind of detective wants to discuss your missing wife and kids at a dumpster behind a diner at 8:30 at night?" Paul had a good point but Tim was committed at this point.

"I know but hey, if he can help then I need to hear what he has to say."

And with that Tim slipped out the side door and made his way around back. It was what you would expect to find behind a diner. Two rusted dumpsters side by side reeking of old grease and rotted food, one lonely street light that barely lit the alley, and the back entrance of a biker bar named *Hog Heaven* across the way. Where was the detective?

As Tim was scanning the alley for some lone cop in the shadows the back door to the biker bar flew open. Out came a man who surely had the nickname "Tiny" or "Killer." He was a beast of a man standing at least six foot four and he had to tip the scales at 350. A leather biker vest, black leather boots, and ripped jeans were all he wore. He had tattoos on both arms and up the sides of his neck. Tim couldn't make them out in the dark and honestly didn't desire a closer look.

Tim was going to give the cursory nod that implied "hi there, please don't eat me" but the man locked eyes with him first. They were cold and dark. And vaguely familiar. Tim felt very uneasy now.

"Hey there, Timmy," came his deep, gravelly voice. How did he know Tim's name?

"Do I know you?" was his unsteady response. Now would be a good time for the detective to show up with a gun and badge in hand.

"Your wife tastes sweet, like honey." His voice hung in the air for a moment.

Caught off guard, Tim could only respond, "What did you say?" Tim was scared that he heard him correctly. What did he have to do with his wife?

"I've missed you, Timmy. And now we're gonna play the game we never got to finish." The man-beast had a grin on his face while he talked that made ice water run through Tim's veins. What was happening? Had the detective found out about this guy and wanted Tim to know or could he be in on it? And what game was this guy talking about?

"Look, fella, I don't know who you are but if you have any idea where my family is I suggest you tell me right now." Tim wasn't afraid to get physical, even with a brute like this. He was no ragdoll at six-two, almost 240. Still, a couple of inches and a hundred pounds could make a difference. Tim worked out regularly but this guy looked like he could bench press a city bus.

"Tiny" parted his lips with his tongue and let out a shrill whistle. Five more guys, a few pretty similar to his description, filed out the same door he had exited and began to cut off the only exit to the alley, besides the door Tim stood by, which went back into the diner. These odds were not so favorable.

"I'm not afraid of your goons, where's my family?" Tim wasn't sure why he was trying to sound so brave. The truth be told, he was more than a bit frightened at the moment.

"I know, Timmy's not scared of anything. Well, that's all about to change. I'm gonna make you *tremble*." The big man seemed to take delight in his advantage. The others were poised to attack at any minute. There was something familiar about what this guy was saying that bore a hole in Tim's brain. He knew he didn't recognize the guy but could swear he knew him somehow.

"I don't want any trouble. I just want my family."

"And I just want you to suffer, cower, and beg like the pathetic coward you are." There was something familiar about his eyes. They were so cold and vacant and yet they pierced the heart. He had definitely seen eyes like that before.

Tim ran to the back door of the diner and yanked on it. Locked. He knew it would be one of those doors that didn't allow access from the outside, but he hadn't planned on having a meeting like this when he came out. He pounded on it a couple of times but he was pretty sure no one would hear it over the noise of the diner. This was getting scary.

Tim's mind began to fill with images of him being beaten to death and thrown in the dumpster. His ribs broken, choking for air. The pain of being kicked and punched again and again. His heart was racing.

Just then, he realized he had his phone in his pocket. He wondered if he would have enough time to get a call off before Armageddon broke out back here. But who should he call? He wasn't sure he could trust the cops anymore. Paulie! Could he dial the ten digits fast enough? Time to find out.

He yanked his phone out and before he started dialing remembered that he had talked to Paul earlier so he tried to hit redial on the number. But immediately the crew of bikers closed in. Fists started flying as Tim heard Paul say, "What's up, man?"

"Paulie help!" was all Tim got out before the phone was knocked out of his hand and his face was smashed in by a fist that could drive nails in a wall. Tim tried to get in a few good punches but he either missed because he was being pummeled or the blow did little damage. His fears were surfacing as reality. Tim knew the odds of him beating five guys at once, each having a slight strength advantage, was highly unlikely even if he was a tough scrapper.

He covered his head and dropped to one knee. From this vantage point, he threw a punch at the most vulnerable part of any man. One of the hulks was at least momentarily stunned. One on four was better but still not great. Just as Tim was yanking the feet out from one of the other guys, he felt the pounding to the back of his head stop. Paulie!

He looked up and saw that Paulie had caught one guy off guard and was able to slam him back into one of the dumpsters, knocking him out cold. The odds were improving. The next thirty seconds were not like the Jackie Chan movies or Bruce Willis flicks everyone has seen. There was no witty dialogue or catchy one-liners. No motivational soundtrack. No spinning back kicks. There was blood and grunting and pain.

Paul was a tough cookie in college. That is before he found religion. He wasn't a big guy by any means. Five-foot eleven and a good bit lighter than Tim at 190. He was a runner but he had a good jaw and a great uppercut. He and Tim had taken on, and whipped, many a challenger in their day. Granted, most of the fights had been in a drunken stupor, but they still counted. Those days were gone but thankfully not forgotten. They were throwing punches and kicks like two men whose lives depended on it. Of course, they did.

To Tim's amazement, he and Paul had kind of won. They were able to knock the remaining guys over and run out of the alley, past the biker bar, which was like a victory in itself. They rounded the corner back to Maggie's and made it to Tim's Tahoe and Tim stopped in his tracks. "My phone!"

"Ah, man. Are you kiddin' me? We have to go back there?" Paul had a trickle of blood in his nose and his left eye was already swelling a little.

"Not empty-handed." Tim was in his domain now. He popped the back hatch of the Tahoe and there were dozens of tools for the job. Tim grabbed a claw hammer and Paul snagged the tire iron then shut the hatch.

"Let's go," Tim felt a little better about the odds now.

When they rounded the corner, they saw that the one guy Paul had slammed into the dumpster was still out and the other four were standing there a little dumbfounded. When they saw the hammers one spoke up.

"Hey man, hold on! This is gettin' out of hand!" His southern accent had the tone of fear in it.

Tim noticed that "Tiny" was nowhere to be found. "This all got out of hand when you jumped me! Where's the other guy?" Tim wanted some answers.

"What other guy?" the spokesman of the group answered looking around wonderingly. "There's only the five of us." *Only the five.* Tim found it hard to believe that he was still alive. "We came out here cause a minute ago a dude came in and told us some other dude had trashed our bikes out front. He said he saw the guy that had done it and that he was in the back alley. We came out and you were standin' there all scared lookin' and talkin' crazy, fit the description so we figured it was you." That explained their fury, but not the disappearance of "Tiny".

"I had nothing to do with your bikes and I'm willing to bet it was him in the first place. He was standing right there when you came out," Tim pointed to the back door, "how could you not have seen him? In fact," Tim was recalling, "he whistled for you and we all stood here talking before you jumped me!" Tim was not sure if they were lying or if something weird was going on again. What were they hiding? Did they truly not see him?

"Someone took my wife and kids tonight and I want some answers! You're telling me that you didn't see that big guy when you came out? It was him who told you about the bikes, wasn't it? Now I want some answers or somebody's gettin' a cracked skull," Tim raised the hammer up for effect.

"Like he said," the guy on his left chimed in, "we didn't see no guy. I wish we could help ya but that's the truth. It was a little guy with gray hair that told us about the bikes. We're sorry 'bout the misunderstandin' but don't go swinging no hammer at my head, dude. Our bikes are all beat up now and we still have no idea who did it."

Tim was utterly confused. Gray hair? Detective Peters? Then who was this other guy and why the façade? These guys were just pawns in his game. It was time to get some answers. Tim wanted to whack these guys one good time out of principle but he had priorities.

"Let's go," Tim looked over at Paul.

"You sure? We could try to beat a little more info out of these guys." Paul raised his crowbar now.

"Aren't you a minister? What happened to turn the other cheek?" Tim asked with a twisted smile.

The bikers had a strange look at that one, too.

"Hey, don't think that a Christian can't kick some butt now and again if the need arises," he said with false bravado. "Plus, I did turn the other cheek. They hit that one too. Once I was out of cheeks, I figured it was time to take action." His logic was impressive. "But always remember to forgive those you have to whoop," he said in a ministerial tone.

Paul smiled at the bikers. "I forgive you guys and hope that you learned a little lesson tonight about flying off the handle. If I hadn't shown up you guys might have beaten my buddy here senseless for no reason." Leave it to Paul to turn a back-alley brawl into a moral lesson. Tim doubted that these hardened individuals gave a flying leap about Paul's forgiveness, not to mention the lack of concern they surely had for beating Tim to death.

"Sorry. Hope you find yer wife and kid," one of them spoke up to Tim's utter shock.

"It's *kids*, but apology accepted, I guess." His jaw and right eye wouldn't be so forgiving in the morning.

With that, they left the bikers to ponder the meaning of life and headed back to the Tahoe after picking up Tim's phone. Tim desperately wanted to find this guy but had no idea where to start. He did, however, have some unfinished business with detective Peters, it seemed.

"You ok?" Paul asked as they pulled out of the parking lot.

"No," came his honest reply. "Something bad is going on and I can't get my head around it. Peters calls me and tells me to meet him. I go to meet him and this hulk comes out and starts in about Liz and some game we started and that I'm gonna "*tremble*" and all kinds of junk that doesn't make any sense to me at all. And then these guys come out and start wailing on me but they don't even see the guy who called them out?! And now Peters is setting me up? This is crazy!" Hearing it all laid out like that Paul had to agree, it was crazy. There had to be a logical explanation but what?

"So, you're gonna do what?" Paul was curious.

"I'm gonna find Peters and beat some answers out of him!" Tim was angry and confused. Paul knew Tim wouldn't normally beat anybody with a hammer but he wasn't willing to take the chance that under these extreme circumstances he might act out of character, and beat an officer of the law with said hammer.

"Not such a good idea," Paul had to be the voice of reason. "One, he's a cop. Two, you don't know that it was him back there so you shouldn't assume anything."

"Of course it was him. He called me. He told me to go to the alley. He has gray hair!" Tim was sounding a bit desperate.

"Lots of people have gray hair, Tim. Don't go hammer happy until we know something for certain, ok?" Paul wasn't going to let him do something stupid that might land him in jail instead of finding his family.

"Fine," he said tossing the hammer into the back seat, "but we're going to talk to him now." Tim was already driving towards the police station.

They pulled up and went in. They both failed to realize what a sight they must have been post-brawl. Blood and bruises made a man seem on the edge. It didn't help that Tim walked right up to the front desk and said, "I need to see detective Peters immediately."

"Is there a problem, sir?" The female officer behind the desk wasn't intimidated by his blood or his bruises.

"I need to see Detective Peters." Tim over-enunciated each word as he repeated himself.

"One moment, please. I'll see if he's still here."

Tim doubted he was in. He was probably out setting people up for beatings and helping some lunatic hide his wife and kids from him. He mainly wanted everyone here to know that.

"Sir, you have a Mr. —" she looked up at Tim for a name.

He was there? The nerve!

"McDaniel. Tim McDaniel." He wondered if he would be man enough to face him.

"A Mr. McDaniel here to see you. Yes, sir." She waved them back. Well, well. Looks like this was going to get interesting.

"How can I help you, Mr. McDaniel?" The guy seemed a little shocked by their appearance but he had a pretty good poker face.

"Where's my wife?" Tim got straight to the point.

"That's what we're trying to find out." He said with concern on his face.

"Don't give me that. Where's the big guy? You set me up!" Tim was worked up and Paul knew he had to step in.

"Sir," he interrupted, "please understand that he's under a lot of stress. What he's asking is why didn't you meet us at the diner?" This got another confused look from the detective.

"Diner?" Peters' confused look remained. Tim was about to pounce. "Am I supposed to be psychic? Please explain to me what you're talking about. You're upset and you're not making any sense. And what happened to you two?"

"You called me and told me to meet you at Maggie's Diner. You called me again and said to meet you in the back. Then we were jumped by some bikers because you told them I trashed their bikes. Sound familiar?" Tim's voice was rising.

"Mr. McDaniel, I assure you that I did no such thing. I haven't called you at all and I certainly haven't been talking to any bikers." He sounded honest enough but Tim wouldn't let this one go without a fight.

"Oh no? Well, then why is your number on my cell phone?" He pulled out his phone and showed him the number.

"That's not my number." He said flatly.

"Ok, then let's call it and see," Tim responded as he hit *send*. Instead of ringing the sound was the familiar tri-tone alert that was followed by the recording, "*You have reached a number that is not in service. Please check the number and try again.*"

This was getting nowhere fast. Was it or wasn't it Peters? Tim didn't know anymore. He felt honesty was the best policy at this point.

"Look, a guy called saying he was you and it sounded like you. The bikers that jumped us said that a guy with grey hair told them it was me. You do the math."

"Someone claiming to be me called you? Well, I assure you I was here all night working on your case so you can take me off your most wanted list." He was taking this whole accusation thing in stride.

Tim was more confused than ever. Who was the guy on the phone? Who was the big guy who knew about his wife? Why was all this so strangely familiar?

"Look, Mr. McDaniel, I think you need to go home and get some rest. We are doing our best to follow any leads we have about your family but look at the facts. An eyewitness saw you drive them away. You say you were stuck at a roadblock that didn't exist and now you're claiming I called you and set you up." It didn't sound very promising. "You might reject this idea on the surface but deep down… under that exterior, you might want to prepare yourself for the possibility that *you* had something to do with this." His words hung in the air like a hummingbird at the feeder. Tim knew what he was saying but could he really believe that?

"I've told you nothing but the truth from the beginning. I want my family back. I had nothing to do with this. I'm being set up by somebody. I don't know who or why but somebody's doing a great job at making me look crazy."

"Right now, the only person making you look crazy is you, Mr. McDaniel. Get some sleep. Let your mind and your nerves unwind so you can think and do some soul-searching." Peters looked sorry for Tim but Paul wasn't sure about all this. "You've done nothing but fly off the handle and make absurd accusations since you called us out. I'm no therapist, but I would say that you need to calm down and think long and hard about any involvement you might have in this case. Perhaps there's something under the surface that you aren't willing to see."

"Detective Peters, I assure you that Tim would never hurt his family. I've known him and Liz for a long time. They love each other deeply. Tim's a great husband and wonderful dad. Please keep looking into what he's telling you, no matter how crazy it sounds. I was with him when the phone rang so obviously somebody called." For the third time that night, Tim was glad Paul was here.

"We're doing everything we can. In the meantime, may I *strongly* suggest that you two go home and get some rest? I'll call you in the morning and we can see if there is any new information, ok?" Peters was a good guy and Tim felt bad for accusing him like this. He decided to take the detective's advice. Sheepishly, he nodded and turned away.

"I'll go by this biker place and ask around a little since you say one of them mentioned your wife. I'm not sure why my name was used but if this is all some elaborate game at your family's expense, I'll leave no stone unturned."

And with that Tim and Paul walked out of the police station and headed home. Paul was uncharacteristically quiet on the drive home. Tim was afraid of what might happen if Paul lost faith in him, too. He was a desperate man hanging by a thin cord right now and he needed to know that someone was on his side.

CHAPTER FOUR

"So, am I crazy or what? If you tell me I'll believe it." Tim wasn't sure of anything right now. He felt helpless to find his family and everyone was looking at him as the bad guy. Paul would be honest and that would either set his mind at ease or cause him to take the few remaining steps to insanity. Either sounded like a winner right now.

"I'm trying to go over it all in my head," Paul began, "but no, I don't think you're crazy. Unless you're *really* crazy."

"How's that?" Tim wasn't following.

"You know, crazy as in paranoid schizophrenic, multiple personalities, sees little green men in his Cheerios, crazy. Though mental health professionals don't really like that word anymore. Still, you're probably not." Was this a pep talk?

"Thanks for the vote of confidence." Tim was deflated. Even he began to ponder through the events of the past six hours. "I guess if I'm honest my story isn't so believable," Tim confessed, "but I swear it's all true."

"That's the thing. If you are, indeed, insane then it will seem completely true to you and you wouldn't know the difference." Paul was so matter-of-fact that Tim wondered if he was entertaining the thought that he was seriously mentally ill. He knew Paul had his Bachelor's degree in Philosophy with a minor in Psychology so he could be pretty clinical at times.

"Seriously, man. What's the deal?" Tim was desperate to hear that he wasn't insane.

"Come on, man. Let's look at the facts. Your family is missing, somebody called you 'cause I heard the phone. We were, in fact, jumped because somebody told those guys you trashed their bikes and that's real. They confessed that much. My face knows it's real. Something funny is going on because things that you say happened to you seem to just vanish like the roadblock or the guy you said you talked to in the alley. I have no idea what's going on here, but you've got to hold on until we find Liz and the kids, ok?" Turned out to be a pep talk after all.

"All right, sorry. I just feel... bewildered. Much like I tumbled down the rabbit hole but I'm not sure I'm even done tumbling yet. Ya, know?" Tim hadn't felt so fragile since that night over thirty years ago. He still hadn't explained all that happened that night to Paul. He wondered if it would sway the crazy vote or help him to establish a motive for why someone would want to do this to him.

"You know what we were talking about when we got that first call?" Tim continued.

"Yeah. Your camp story. Let's get back to that 'cause you seem to think these two events are somehow related, right?" Paul didn't miss a beat.

"Somehow, but I have no idea how yet. Let's just say that I've got some serious déjà vu going on." Tim was about to reopen a scar that had been closed for most of his life and he was scared. He took a deep breath and started with his exit from the boy's cabin. He recalled the irrational fears that seized him as he got closer to the old cabin.

"The moonlight hit it through the trees so it was pretty washed out. Everything had a blue-gray tint. I decided then that I would just grab a piece of it and go. My heart was racing. I could hear it beating in my ears. As I took one last step, I could hear voices whispering...all around... in my head... from the trees. They weren't loud enough to understand but they were definitely voices."

Paul swallowed hard. This was scaring him a little and he wasn't even there. Tim went on.

"I kept thinking that someone would jump out of the cabin and grab me or that some wild animal was about to pounce from the shadows. I had thoughts like a horror movie or something. But I wasn't just scared, it's like I *knew* something bad was gonna happen. My hands were shaking and I couldn't stop my thoughts from running wild. Finally, I grabbed a chunk off the corner and everything stopped." Tim paused for effect. Paul looked eager to hear what happened next. Would he even believe it?

"And?" Paul finally said.

"I turned around to go and walked smack into someone. He was big, tall, and smelled like old roadkill. I wanted to scream but nothing would come out. He slowly stretched out his arm until his hand was around my throat. His skin was cold and rough. I haven't thought about this for almost thirty years but I can still remember every detail like it was yesterday.

"I wasn't sure what was happening, but then he lifted me so we were eye to eye. *Oh my God*, his eyes were awful. I know it was dark but his eyes were a pale, milky white. He had almost no color to them at all except for some bloody lining where his pupils were. His face was ashen and expressionless. He didn't speak but his mouth hung open and his breath was rancid. It didn't even occur to me to kick or punch or anything. I just hung there for what seemed like an hour until I noticed that there were others around me."

"Others?" Paul raised an eyebrow.

"Yeah. Kids. Fourteen of them. I didn't count but I knew. They were circled around me like a game or something. They were all kinda bluish and bloated with their hair matted to their heads with mud and dried blood. But, unlike the tall man who held me, they were missing their eyes completely. Only the blackened sockets remained. They were smiling a sickening smile.

"They were all naked and had deep cuts all over them with a huge, deep slit across their throats. They were castrated, but there was no blood as if it had all drained out. They inched in together tightening the circle until I felt I couldn't breathe." Tim had to stop to catch his breath.

As he took a deep breath Paul asked him, "You think it was the ghosts of the fourteen kids and the killer?" He sounded opinionless, like a psychiatrist asking his patient something like, *"and then the pink elephants flew you home to the mushroom village?"* Tim wasn't sure how to answer but he knew Paul wasn't judging him.

"No idea, honestly. I guess it could have been. I've never been the ghost and ghoulie type... until then. You know how sometimes in a bad dream you sort of realize it's a dream? Well, that didn't happen. I knew I was awake and I knew what I was seeing was not just my mind playing tricks on me. I don't know what they were, but all I know is that as they inched in and my breath started to leave me I could hear guttural, gurgling laughter. And that's when I noticed him." Tim's face was in a scowl like he was putting together the pieces.

"Him who?" Paul was scowling too, but it was more pathos than puzzlement.

"I could have sworn that while that... mob of mutilated children closed in on me and this hideous man held me in his hand, I saw Del laughing on the porch of the cabin. I even tried to scream for him to help me but... he just looked over at me and said *'scared now?'* My mind was racing and then I felt the cold hands of the kids touching my face. They were touching my eyes and mouth and then they started grabbing at me harder and harder.

"I could hear Del whispering in my ear. He was saying that I deserved to hurt. That I was just a coward. Freaked me out."

"How did you get out alive?" Paul seemed to be going along with this, for now at least.

"That's the crazy part. I was so scared that I eventually blacked out. The next thing I remember was hearing my dad talking to the camp director while I was in an ambulance the next morning. I guess the cabin leader woke up and found me missing. One of the kids, Gabe I think, told him where I was and he said he found me passed out in front of the cabin in the woods. I was told later that the camp was being shut down due to negligence. Thanks to my dad. He was pretty ticked." Tim finished.

"So, you have any physical proof of the attack?" Paul inquired.

"Well, that's one of the weird things. I had some bruising on my neck and I had some scratches and bruises on my face but they said that they must have been, *'self-inflicted'.*"

Paul frowned and nodded. He was being too analytical and it worried Tim. As the story poured from Tim, even he brooded about the pure insanity of it all.

"So, then the therapy?" Paul wanted to know what Tim's take on it was.

"My dad insisted. I was having nightmares – oh, excuse me," he used his official-sounding voice, "*night terrors and post-traumatic stress.*

Everyone just thought that spending the night in the woods by myself freaked me out. It was like no one was even remotely open to the idea that I was literally attacked out there. Lack of evidence.

"I tried to tell the therapist the truth at the beginning but I could tell he was having none of that. Basically, I figured the only way to end the god-awful sessions was to get 'cured'. It took me about six more weeks of agreeing with the therapist that it never happened and that it really was my mind playing tricks on me, yadda yadda yadda, I surely must have clawed my own face up, blah blah blah. Then after about another six or seven months I was finally pronounced healed of my 'mental infirmity.'

"In retrospect, I know my dad was trying to help but I felt like it was just his way of dealing with his loony son. It was shortly after that when my mom finally gave up the battle with cancer." There was a hint of bitterness in his tone.

"You were, what, about fourteen by then?" Paul figured.

"Almost, yeah. It was a very tough year after that, but then I started high school and met you. It's been sunshine and roses since then," Tim faked a big smile, "until now." The reality of the situation was closing in on him again.

"You really loved your mom, huh?" Paul had heard him talk about her several times in their friendship but he wanted to offer a happy memory to Tim right now.

"She and I were so much alike. It drove my dad nuts. We would gang up on him all the time. Once she was gone, me and the old man kind of drifted a little. When he died I had a lot of regrets," Tim lamented.

Paul was intrigued by the story. He wanted to ask some more questions but he didn't want Tim to have to relive too much pain in one night. Still, they were looking for answers and Paul might be able to help.

"You mind if I grill you a little? You might be surprised to hear this but I don't *not* believe you. I would just like to pick your brain a bit."

"Pick away." Tim wanted to hear Paul's opinion.

"So, if the therapy didn't help you deal with the nightmares and stuff what did?"

"My dad kind of helped with that."

"How so?" Tim's dad wasn't the real nurturing type so Paul was interested in hearing this.

"Well, right after I got back from camp was when they decided to tell me that our last move was actually to have mom closer to Atlanta for her treatments. They had known about this for a few months but were just letting me in on it. I think that my dad letting me go to camp was supposed to give them time to figure out how to tell me or something. They didn't want me worrying about it, though," he said, imitating his father's tone. "You just be good and get better so your mother won't worry about you."

"Heavy for a kid who just had a pretty traumatic experience," Paul admitted.

"Well, mom was cool about everything with me. She was supportive and didn't seem to mind me hopping into bed with them in the middle of the night when I woke up screaming now and again. Imagine, a kid about to be thirteen having nightmares so bad he couldn't sleep alone." Tim sounded ashamed of himself. Paul wanted to comfort him but knew Tim didn't want to be comforted.

"So, what did your dad do to help you?" Paul couldn't imagine Tim's dad being the one to guide Tim back to emotional health but you never really knew.

"Well, I was figuring out the game with the therapist but I was still having a time of it at night. One day my mom was in a lot of pain. Bone cancer is bad news. Well, I was having a rough day myself. I was seeing things around the house." Tim waited a moment to see if Paul had any comment on that. He didn't. "So, I come running down the hall because I'm scared senseless that something is chasing me and my dad grabs me by the arm and drags me outside.

"He takes both of my arms and makes me look him in the face. He wasn't crying but I could see the trail where he had been earlier. His eyes were swollen and sad... and angry. He tries to sound all understanding but he says to me 'Son, you've got to stop this. Nothing is trying to get you. There is no one under your bed or in your closet. You are safe. Now for Pete's sake, stop getting into bed with us at night and running around the house like a maniac. Your mother is *very* sick and you're making it worse! There is nothing to fear so *grow up*.' And with that, I did the same thing I did with the therapist. I acted better.

"It took a while for me to stop wetting the bed but I learned how to do the laundry so my pop wouldn't know about it. I never bothered him or mom with my fears again. I tried to just turn it off. I convinced myself that there was nothing to fear." Paul never knew any of this about Tim. He was always so full of life and was generally happy. Who would have guessed that there was so much pain inside all this time?

"So, you just kind of swept it under the rug and moved on? That's kind of a major occurrence to just forget about." Paul was concerned. Could there be something under the surface with Tim that his friendship blinded him to? He never knew about the camp or the therapy and they met not a year and a half after all this.

"I just grew up, I guess. I self-medicated from time to time. Weed, porn. You and I would both do some heavy drinking on the weekends, as I recall." As a minister, Paul was ashamed of his wild past but he knew it was a part of who he was and that God had forgiven that a long time ago. Still, he and Tim both tied it on quite regularly until their junior year in college.

"Whatever happened that made you quit drinking anyway? What did Liz say to you that made you stop?" Paul never knew about this mystery either. He knew why *he* had quit drinking. A drunk driving accident that nearly killed a fellow student got his attention and he went to the Baptist Campus Ministries building the next day with a guilty conscience. They were having a lunchtime Bible study and a guest speaker was preaching through Romans. It was there that he heard the Gospel for the first time and shortly after that decided to give his life to Christ and become a Christian. He got pretty active in the BCM after that and, to his surprise, felt a call to ministry shortly thereafter.

Tim hadn't been in the accident but seemed to be supportive of Paul's conversion experience. He always referred to it as "getting religious" but he didn't mean it in a derogatory way. He was a "to each, his own" kind of guy, and if Paul wanted to stop drinking and go to church, good for him. Coming from an alcoholic mother was rough for Paul. Tim knew he would either stop one day or get a new liver in his fifties. Might as well find religion and get straight. It wasn't long after that Tim met Liz and they started dating. He was in the fall of his junior year and she was a freshman.

"It wasn't anything she said at all." Tim's response caught him off guard. "In fact, we met at a party where we were both drinking." Tim was about to share another dark secret about himself that could alter Paul's perception of him, but the truth was the truth, wasn't it? "I was talking to her at the kappa sig pool party. We had only had a few drinks because the night was young but I was impressed with her. She was a music major, loved the mountains, and had piercing blue eyes, you know the story. I decided then not to get so wasted that I would puke on her later."

"Good call," Paul agreed.

"She was there with some girlfriends and you were out of that scene by then, so I just shot some pool and threw some darts for a while. I wasn't really in a swimming mood that night.

"So, about midnight I go out to find her again because I couldn't get her off my mind. I saw one of her friends, drunk as a skunk, and she pointed over to the house. I asked her who she was with and she shrugged. I went in and started looking around downstairs. I took a gamble and opened the bedroom door.

Tim seemed to steel himself for what came next. He set his jaw and began.

"She was half-naked begging this guy to stop and get off her. He was *raping* her right in the middle of the party!" Tim hated recounting this. Paul looked shocked. "He balled up his fist and punched her right in the face! He told her to shut up and went back about his business. He looked up at me and said 'shut the door, will ya Tim?' Shut the door? Shut the door!?

"I lost it, man. I beat that guy until somebody pulled me off. I took her to the Campus Police station but they said that if alcohol was a factor for both of them then it would be very hard to press charges, you know the song and dance. She was already humiliated and just wanted to get home. I still don't know how he knew my name but I guess we had a class together or something. I wasn't Mr. Popular but I made it through the party scene enough I suppose."

Paul was genuinely moved. "I never knew about that man. I knew she had the scar above her right eye but she just said she got it in college. I never assumed it was from a punch." Paul felt sick that this had happened to Liz. He understood the secrecy and wasn't hurt by it. This was hardly dinner conversation. He knew it was really hard for Tim to tell him even now and he appreciated it.

"It was then and there that I gave up binge drinking. For a while there I barely drank at all anymore. Liz, too. We have an occasional glass of wine or beer or something now and again on special occasions, but we exited the party scene altogether. If alcohol abuse leads to that then count me out." Tim had a strange recollection bouncing around his head like a BB but he couldn't figure it out. "There's something about that night that is so familiar. Something about the guy that attacked Liz."

"What is it?" Paul was eager to hear a connection.

"His eyes. His eyes were almost identical to the Big guy I saw in the alley. It was like they were enjoying the fear and pain of someone else. Like Del." Tim knew it sounded far-fetched but he might as well go for it. "You think there's a connection?"

"I'm not sure. I kinda doubt it." Might as well be honest. "There are a lot of sick people out there, Tim. Are you suggesting they're the same person or something?"

"No, not the same person. None of them look anything alike except for the eyes. I'm just trying to figure it out." Tim didn't have any answers, only questions.

"Well, you only saw this Del as a kid, right? Who knows what he might look like as an adult. I was a fat kid and now I run five miles a day. People change is all I'm saying." It was a good point but Tim wasn't convinced.

"I'll give you that but I know that the guy in college and the guy in the alley aren't the same guy, trust me. I beat that little punk to a pulp. He was no beast like the guy in the alley. And Del had sort of a dark complexion. Dark hair, dark eyes, olive skin. The guy in the alley was a purebred, pale-skinned redneck. Same dark eyes, but that was it." Tim wanted the pieces to fit together, but they didn't. "Even if the college perv had hit the weights with a vengeance, he wouldn't grow five inches in the process. Not only that, but I saw that guy on campus again about a year later and he didn't even recognize me. He looked young and stupid, and kind of scared of his own shadow but not like a rapist. A real shell of the person he was that night."

"How do you mean?" Paul wondered.

"Well, I kinda figured that it was the alcohol that gave him his tough-guy courage, but I don't know. He was more than sober... he was scared." Tim hadn't thought much about it until then.

They were pulling into Tim's driveway when Paul said, "Well, at least you're getting some old wounds out in the open." Old wounds. They were all starting to feel fresh again. He had saved Liz in college but what about now? He was powerless and it scared him. Somebody wanted him to play a game. Was he up for it? He just hoped they would call again.

Tim flicked on the lights in the living room and went to the answering machine to check for any calls. Just one about his car warranty, no surprise, and one from Liz's mom calling back to check up on everybody. He would call her in the morning and let her know the truth. He wouldn't keep her family in the dark. Tim knew that Paul must be tired and he wanted some time with his thoughts to sort through some of this mess that was uncovered from the basement of his mind tonight.

"You can crash in Caleb's room. Hope you like Star Wars." Tim missed him so badly right now. He wanted to pick him up and hold him tight. He wanted to smell that great mix of dirt, sweat, and shampoo that created the "little kid" smell he loved so much. And Hannah. Oh, how he would spin her around until she begged him to stop through her giggles. Liz would warn of the "dangers of horseplay in the house" in her best mommy tone, but she loved it too.

"Star Wars, huh? The good stuff or the new junk?" Paul was an avid fan of the entire series, but he had to appear hardcore for old school. He *was* in his forties now.

"Mostly Mandalorian, but I might be able to find you a Jar Jar Binks blanket." Tim knew the game.

"Fine, it is. Comfortable I will be," Paul did his best Yoda voice. "As long as there are some Baby Yoda squishy pillows."

"Weirdo. I'll be out here for a while if you need anything."

And with that Paul went out to his car to grab his overnight bag and Tim sat down at the kitchen table to think. He heard a whine and a clawing at the back door. Buck! He had forgotten about his poor, hungry dog. He hopped up and opened the back door. Buckley barreled in and made a mad dash for his food bowl. He normally came in for the night after dinner but this had not been an ordinary day, not by a long shot.

"Sorry, buddy." Tim went to the fridge to get him some lunch meat to make up for his negligence. After a few pieces of ham, there wasn't a trace of a grudge being held. Dogs were forgiving like that.

Buckley was part Alaskan Husky, part German Shepherd and he had the ice-blue eyes that made people go *awwwww*. He was gray and white and was great with the kids. He was a pretty smart dog, thanks to the Shepherd in him. Tim had him trained pretty well and all it took was time and lots of hot dogs.

"Go to bed," came Tim's command. Buck trotted over to his doggie bed by the couch and curled up on it. Once he had eaten something and was safely in the house, he was glad to oblige.

Paulie could have crashed on the couch in the playroom slash office slash guest room but he was more like family and deserved a comfortable bed. The house used to be a three bed, two bath but after Tim inherited it from his dad, he decided to do some remodeling. It used to be a split floor plan with the master bedroom on the left and the two other bedrooms where the kid's rooms were now on the right.

Tim didn't mind the layout of the house but it was his parent's master bedroom that bothered him. He had basically watched his mother die in that room and then watched his dad fade away every day since. Once the house was his, paid in full thanks to his dad's insurance, he decided that he did *not* want to sleep in that room, so he built on a master suite and turned that room into the aforementioned playroom slash office slash guest room.

Since his uncle owned the company, he got it done pretty cheap and Liz loved it. The house sat on an acre and a half lot so there was plenty of room to expand backward. Tim planned it out and oversaw every detail. They built a 600 square foot master suite with a California King-sized bed, a huge walk-in closet, a bathroom with a Jacuzzi tub, and a stone tile shower that has shower heads on every wall, all for basically what it would cost a customer to remodel their kitchen. The best part was the French doors that open up to the wrap-around deck in the backyard.

A fresh coat of paint, a daybed, and some kid's furniture removed almost all of the bad memories from the old bedroom. Liz had a knack for remodeling. Now Tim could walk by it and think of happy times and good memories instead of…well, you know.

Tim decided to go into the bedroom and think. He would call Detective Peters in the morning and see if there was any new news. He would also apologize for his behavior today. He knew that he was under great stress but he still didn't want to take that out on good people trying to help him. Buck would stay in the living room for the night.

As Tim flicked off the dining room light he started down the hall. He noticed that the door to the playroom was open. He didn't think too much of it except that he remembered going through every room of the house earlier with the police checking for Liz or the kids. He could have sworn he shut all the doors as they left the rooms.

A low moan came through the crack and Tim nearly jumped out of his skin. It sounded like a woman's voice but gravelly and strained. He thought that it might be Liz for a moment and pushed the door open. His mind was seized with fear as he saw not the playroom that they had designed, but his mother's room, exactly as it had been years ago…and she was on the bed staring back at him.

The moonlight through the window gave the room a pale glow. It shone on her face like a weak spotlight. She was disfigured from the late stages of bone cancer and her skin sagged on her weakened frame. Her lips were thin and pale and spittle hung on the corners of her mouth. Her eyes were dark and angry, not at all the loving eyes Tim remembered. She lay there staring at him and moaning in pain.

"*Tiiiimmmmmyyyyyy,*" she finally spoke his name. It came out in an almost whisper.

"Mom?" Tim knew this wasn't really his mother, was it?

"*Timmy, why did you leave me? Why did you hurt me?*"

"I never left you, mom. I love you."

"*You did this to me! You were a selfish little boy who only cared about his own problems! Your father told you how it hurt me!*" She was getting angry at him.

Timmy's heart broke at the thought that he had hurt his mother. He had tried to be good, hadn't he? He tried to keep his fear in check.

"No, I tried to be good, mom. I tried."

"*You made me hurt so bad, so bad! I HATE YOU!!!*" She was screaming now and spit flew from her cracked lips. Her eyes were filled with hate and she was pointing her gnarled finger at him as she spoke. "*You're gonna pay, Timmy. You're gonna hurt, too. Your children will beg for mercy!*" His children? Before Timmy could process any of this she was moving.

She didn't move like a woman bedridden with bone cancer. No, she scampered like a cockroach on all fours across the floor, her long brittle nails cracking and breaking on the floor as she moved. Quicker than any human could move, Tim couldn't stop her from grabbing his legs and pulling herself up to his face, her hot breath filling his nostrils made him want to gag. He could see her eyes more clearly now and then he realized they had the same dark, hateful quality of the Bikers and the college would-be rapist.

"You're not my mother!" he shouted loud enough to startle himself. He jumped as a hand grabbed his shoulder. He swung around with his fist raised, ready to pummel whatever was attacking him.

"Tim!" it was Paulie. "Chill! I heard you talking to someone and came to check on you. You ok?"

Tim's heart was racing and he needed to sit down. He looked up to the playroom again and all was as it should be. Toys were neatly stacked in the corner and the light was off. He walked a few feet into his bedroom and sat on the corner of the bed. He looked up at Paulie with bewilderment in his eyes.

"I don't think so," he finally said. What was happening to him? He must be cracking up. Should he tell Paulie what just happened or let it go and hope that tomorrow his mind would again be strong and ready for the day? He decided to let this one slide. He needed to sort through this. "Honestly, I'm just really tired."

"Who did you scream 'you're not my mother' to, Tim?" Tim was actually hoping that was more in his head than in reality. Apparently not. Confession was good for the soul, wasn't it? Time to take one more step towards crazy town.

CHAPTER FIVE

"I saw my mom...or not my *mom,* but... something that was trying to be my mom." That didn't come out as well as he had hoped. He tried again before Paul could respond. "I was walking past this room and heard something. When I opened the door, I thought I saw my mom there and she was yelling strange things at me. I know it wasn't her, of course, but it looked like her and she said that me and my kids were going to suffer."

Paul looked with sorrow into Tim's eyes. Tim hated that look. He avoided eye contact with people at his mom's funeral... and his dad's. He hated pity. He wanted to live up to his father's charge to *be a man, fear nothing.* Paul wasn't belittling him but he could tell what he was thinking.

"Yeah, I know. Poor stressed-out Tim is losing it. His wife and kids are gone and now he thinks his dead mother is haunting him." Tim needed a drink.

"That's not what I was thinking at all, Tim. As a matter of fact, I think that maybe there's a factor that we've been ignoring here." Tim was intrigued to hear what this might be. Anything that helped him to feel less crazy was a nice change.

"Yeah? What's that?" Tim asked.

Paul was hesitant. He was only like this with one subject: religion. Paul was very respectful of Tim's opinions and never forced his views on him. There had been a few conversations that ended with Tim frustrated at Paul's apparent lack of compromise. As if there was only one way to God. That was just so narrow-minded and it bothered Tim when he heard his best friend make fanatical statements about Jesus and stuff. Was he about to get religious again?

Paul finally spoke. "I think there may be some spiritual implications here, Tim." There it was. How could he talk about religion in a time like this? Paul could sense Tim's defenses go up. "I'm just saying that we need to consider the possibilities. There have been some strange things going on today and I'm not ready to discount that there is something evil going on."

Of course, there was something evil going on. Tim's family was taken, someone set them up to get the snot beaten out of them, and now Tim's dead mother was making threats beyond the grave! Sounded pretty evil to him.

"Forgive me, man," Tim started, "I don't want to be disrespectful to you or anything but, what does any of this have to do with religion?"

"Religion? Nothing," Paul admitted.

"Nothing. Then why bring it up?" Tim was confused.

"I never said anything about religion, Tim. I said *evil*. Every time I go to share what I believe you think I'm being religious. Religion is man-made and Jesus wanted nothing to do with religion, per se." Paul was speaking with conviction and Tim could tell that he had hit a nerve with him. He didn't mean to always put his views in a box but he wasn't a very religious guy and, frankly, conversations about God made him uncomfortable.

"Sorry, man. I just think that evil is a religious thing. You know, like *God good, Devil evil*. That kind of thing."

"It's more than that, Tim, trust me. I didn't spend the last fourteen years of my life being religious. I have dedicated my life to serving God. You know me, man. You know I wouldn't just go whole hog at something unless I was convinced it was true." Paul wasn't a crowd follower, Tim would give him that. Tim knew he was sincere in his faith but so was Liz's Mormon mother and so was Ahmed Muhari, the Muslim who worked on one of his crews. That guy was super serious about his faith. Why was Paul the right one?

"I don't want to have a God argument right now, ok?" Tim had more important things to think about like his family and this progression of weirdness that was occurring.

"Dude! I'm not trying to argue God with you I'm asking you to consider the possibility that what is going on with all of this is a sort of spiritual occurrence. You saw dead kids that night at camp and now you see your dead mom? People in your past are somehow linked by the evil in their eyes?" Tim recalled his *mother's* eyes just now. "You put the pieces together and you see that this is not just a *physical* struggle."

Tim had to admit that some unexplainable events were going on. He still wasn't ready to admit that the devil was behind it. Mostly it was stress and some sicko playing games with him. He would deal with all of this in the morning.

"Ok. Listen, we'll talk about this later. I need some rest. I'm heading out early to try and see what I can find out. You going with me or what?" Tim wanted this conversation to be over for now.

Paul almost always knew when to pull back. In the fifteen years since Paul's "Jesus encounter" he had rarely ever gotten in Tim's business about anything. At first, he was kind of gung-ho about sharing his new faith with Tim all the time but he eventually got the message and backed off.

"Sure. What time?" Paul knew this was one of those times.

"Let's roll at five. That'll give us at least seven or eight hours to sleep, once we wind down." Tim watched as Paul gave a thumb's up and headed back to his son's room.

If Tim was honest, he would admit that he was a little jealous of Paul. He was a man of great conviction who was serving out a calling. Tim had no desire to be a minister or anything but he thought that Paul was lucky to be so at peace in life. Tim loved his life, or at least he loved his family. He tolerated working for his uncle. His dream would be to pursue music full time but that would never pay the bills. They already supplemented their income by having Liz teach piano lessons. That brought a whopping $60 a week in, most of the time.

But Paul was living out a dream. He felt a call to show college students how to live their faith authentically and he was doing it. He wasn't married and made less a year than Tim, but he was content. He moved down to New Orleans for three years to get his Master's of Divinity degree back in '02, right after college. Since then, he had been serving at Brunson University, their Alma Mater, as the Campus Minister of the Baptist Collegiate Ministries. Paul said that he would have gone anywhere God sent him but that he loved being able to give back to the place that gave him so much.

He was no academic slouch, either. He took his B. A in Philosophy and minor in Psychology and got his Master's in Apologetics. He said that was like philosophy but geared more towards defending the faith of Christianity. When Tim asked him what he was defending it from he simply answered, "anything that tries to make it less than the one true faith that it is." Tim left that one alone.

Tim had his B.A. in Fine Arts but he didn't graduate *Cum Laude* like Liz and Paul. He was fond of saying that he graduated *Thank the Laude*. It had always been Paul that could wax eloquent about nearly any subject. He was a gifted speaker and teacher and Tim could only assume that the students who sat under his teaching at the BCM, as they called it, meant the world to him.

Tim wasn't sure why he never liked to discuss issues of faith with him. Maybe it was because Tim felt inferior in that department and only wanted to talk about things that he knew something about. Maybe it was because he was afraid that if he listened too long Paul might convert him and his whole life would be turned upside down. Well, his whole life was upside down now, wasn't it? Maybe he would give Paul a chance to speak his mind tomorrow. He owed him that.

Tim stretched out on his bed and let his mind unwind. Surely Liz would have found some way to call him by now if she could. Was she ok? Did the police think that the person who had them was him? Were they close by or miles away? These thoughts could keep him up all night but he needed to find the switch to allow him to sleep if he was going to be on his game tomorrow. Five a.m. was not all that far away anymore.

He reached out to turn his lamp off and his mother's face flashed through his mind. No, he would sleep with the lights on tonight. Outside, clouds were rolling in and a storm was brewing. Tim usually loved sleeping through the rain but tonight it bothered him. A small flash of lightning lit up the sky a few miles off. Tim got up to close the curtains on the French doors overlooking the backyard and thick forest behind it. In a flash of lightning, he saw something behind him in the reflection on the glass. He swung around to nothing there. When he turned back to the glass, he was worried that maybe whatever he saw was on the deck and not in the room after all.

He flipped the light switch by the glass door that turned on the floodlights out back. Nothing. Near the edge of the woods at the border of the backyard he thought he saw movement but there was no way a person could have made it from the deck to the woods that fast so he assumed his mind was playing tricks on him again. Another flash of lightning and a peal of thunder.

Tonight, he would not enjoy the storm. The brooding sky matched the mood of his heart perfectly right now. There was a storm brewing, all right. And all Hell was about to break loose.

Paul couldn't give in to sleep just yet. He knew that there was something very bad going on. Any psycho can kidnap a person or commit a heinous crime. Not every bad thing was some evil spiritual assault. Man is responsible for his actions and sometimes man chooses to act in an evil manner. But this was a different kind of evil. Paul could sense in his spirit that this evil was not generated by man's wickedness alone. This was not a battle of flesh and blood, at its core. No, it involved more than that and Paul was going to begin fighting this battle with the right weapons. He closed the door to a crack and pulled his Bible out of his backpack.

Paul sat at Caleb's desk and opened the book that had literally changed his life. There was a time when Paul couldn't tell you the difference between the Old and New Testaments. He couldn't have named three of the twelve disciples if his life depended on it. He was just some backwoods Louisiana boy raised in a watered-down Catholic family. He would never have guessed that he would be a Baptist Minister one day and the thought often made him smile at God's sense of humor.

Since his conversion, he had spent the last several years of his life studying and memorizing as much scripture as he could. He meditated on it and taught from it. Paul had started to understand why Jesus had told satan when being tempted, "Man does not live on bread alone but on every word that comes from the mouth of God." Paul lived by this Word and it guided his life.

Tim may not understand that same truth yet, but Paul knew what needed to happen. He would spend the next half hour reading and praying. He wasn't sure what to pray for but he prayed for Liz and the kids' safety, for wisdom in the next step they should take, and for Tim to have his eyes opened to the spiritual battle around them. Paul borrowed from the book of 2 Kings and asked the same thing that Elijah asked for his servant. "Lord, open his eyes to see the real battle."

Paul felt like it would take a miracle for Tim to come around on these issues but wasn't that God's forte? Didn't Paul believe in a miracle-working God? To pray for something you don't expect to happen is pretty dumb, or at least faithless. Paul believed God could change Tim, but he also knew how stubborn Tim could be about such things. Regardless of Tim's stubbornness, Paul knew Jesus could change anyone who called on His name in faith.

As Paul prayed, he began to feel an urge to walk through the house. He hesitated at first but then reminded himself that prayer often required obedience if it was to change anything. It didn't make sense to him to walk through the house praying but did it have to make sense first for him to be obedient? He got up from the desk and started with the room he was in.

He then went next door to Hannah's room and prayed in it. He had to chuckle to himself because he felt like he should be slinging holy water around the room while some altar boy burned incense behind him. Oh, how Hollywood missed the mark on spiritual things. If this were a movie then midnight would be the magic time, Paul would be praying in Latin because that is obviously the magic language, and at some point, a virgin would have to be involved.

But this wasn't Hollywood and Paul knew very little Latin. And since he didn't become a Christian until college the virgin thing was out too. Paul had sown many wild oats in high school and college that he had to surrender to God. Still, that was the past, wasn't it? Paul suddenly felt ashamed of himself. He remembered so many times indulging in sin and going his own way. He was washed over with a wave of guilt.

He wasn't so different now, was he? He was only a human with needs and desires. He hadn't been with a woman in almost twenty years for goodness sake! Was he supposed to stop being a man because of his faith? What about all the pretty girls on his campus. Any one of them – what was he doing?!

Paul shook his head a bit and realized that he wasn't praying anymore but instead was being tempted by strange sidetrack fantasies. He pressed on.

He walked into the living room and began praying again that God would consecrate this place and make it holy ground. He prayed that God would open their eyes to see the next step in this crazy adventure. Crazy. Maybe Tim was crazy. He was a messed-up kid. He had lived through some rough stuff. Maybe Tim was the guilty one here. Maybe Tim had fooled everyone into thinking he was some normal guy while he was just some psycho that would kidnap his own family and not even realize it. He was seeing things and being pretty paranoid. Paul should just leave now and tell the cops that Tim is a looney. That would be – STOP IT!

What was he doing? Paul couldn't focus for one minute with all these thoughts rushing into his mind. He knew Tim didn't do this, didn't he? He was confused. So confused that he thought about packing up and heading home. This wasn't his fight. He shouldn't be here. He should go now. GO NOW!

He heard a low, guttural growl and looked over at Buckley whose hackles were raised at something. He had never heard Buck growl. He seemed scared but more than that, he seemed protective. Something was giving him a bad vibe and Paul could feel it too. More than a bad vibe, though. It was a presence. Something, or someone, was here with them in the house. It was at that moment that Paul felt the evil that Buck sensed in the room with them.

Paul stopped in his tracks. Then a still, small voice spoke through the mad rush of his mind, *"keep praying."* Paul then realized that he had been attacked in his mind by whatever hostile force was there and that it clearly didn't want him praying. But God did. Paul started bringing to mind scriptures he had memorized over the years. *"The prayer of a righteous man is powerful and effective."* James 5:16. *"We wrestle not against flesh and blood but against principalities and dark powers and evil forces."* Ephesians 6:12. *"Resist the Devil and he will flee from you."* James 4:7.

With renewed vigor and Buck by his side, Paul started his prayer crusade again. Strange and foreign thoughts would often creep in but he would bat them away like demonic gnats. He would feel unworthy and think about stopping but then would admit that he was truly unworthy and keep praying. This went on for about twenty minutes until Paul reached the playroom. This was where Tim had seen his mother tonight. Something was not right about that. It was more than just a tired mind playing tricks, there was evil here. Buck gave another low groan and bared his teeth a little.

"It's ok boy. You stay here."

Paul felt sick to his stomach as he flicked on the light. He half expected something to jump out at him from behind the door. A black cat was bound to leap from a closet any minute now. Paul prayed that whatever bad memories were in that room would go away. He wasn't praying in full voice but a soft, audible tone. When he was finishing his prayer and began to end with his normal, "In Jesus' name. Amen," something caught his eye in the hall. He could have sworn that he saw someone just pass through the doorway out of the corner of his eye. Buckley sat where he left him and was looking in the direction of what Paul thought he saw.

Though very freaked out, Paul was also emboldened by this time spent praying and went to investigate. Maybe it was just Tim heading to the kitchen for a late snack or something. But Paul knew Tim would never bypass his loyal pup. More to the point, Buck would never sit there when he had a chance to follow his Master into the kitchen. Anyway, as he stepped into the hall Tim's bedroom door was still shut. There was nothing else at the end of the hall since Tim's room was an add-on anyway. Paul began to think that he was just tired and seeing things when he heard faint laughter from his room. It was the laughter of a child.

Paul decided to forget sneaking up and peeking through the door and ran over to the room, practically jumping through the doorway. As he expected, nothing was there. Paul had saved the playroom for last on the prayer tour, except for Tim's room which he wouldn't enter tonight. He was back in Caleb's room with a renewed assurance that something evil was afoot and full assurance that this was not going to be easy. Buck made his way back to his bed by the couch. Paul sat back down at the desk and read some more from the Bible. He needed the peace it brought before trying to sleep. Who knew if sleep would come tonight after the afternoon and night he had lived through?

They would be leaving in a few hours so he needed to at least try to sleep. He finished reading and turned off the light. There was enough light from the windows to find his way into bed and prepare for sleep. The storm outside was steadily waging war on the house. The rhythm of the rain was nice but it still wasn't the peaceful rain that Paul usually loved. Those rainy nights were some of the best sleep he ever got. No, this rain seemed to be purposefully *un*peaceful. As Paul lay there, he whispered one final request of God.

"Lord, please protect us in this fight. Let Tim find You in all of this and please let him be reunited with his family soon. Remind me that this is Your fight and not mine. I'm nothing without You, Jesus. Thank You for Your love and mercy. Have Your way, Lord. And don't let the freaky stuff deter me from standing my ground in Jesus' name, amen." And with that, Paul slept.

And as he slept, the building darkness in the house turned its attention to Tim.

CHAPTER SIX

Tim lay there for about an hour and didn't do anything but breathe and blink. His hands laced behind his head and his lamp still burning softly, Tim's mind defied sleep. It was as if he refused to give in to his weariness. He didn't like to think that he was afraid to sleep. No, that would mean that he wasn't a man. Men weren't afraid to sleep in their own houses with their lamps on. But how many real men had their families abducted and saw their dead moms right before bedtime?

Tim knew that the nightmares would come tonight. He had the same dread of sleep that he had grown accustomed to for a while as a kid. Sometimes he fought it off for a day or two before he was too exhausted to resist it anymore. Then they came. His tormentors. The ones who made sure that he woke up screaming, bathed in sweat. Sometimes it was the mutilated children grabbing and pawing at him, other times it was strangers in the dark who chased him through back alleys and breathed down his neck with their sick, hot breath.

Tim was no stranger to fear. He had managed to sidestep it these past thirty-odd years by bearing down and taking it like a man. He pushed it from his mind and found ways to deal with it. The drinking, for one. He would often self-medicate even as a teenager. He beat that demon in college thanks to seeing where it could take him if he didn't stop. He also became a really tough guy. Tim proved to the guys in the alley that he was no lightweight but that was a rusty performance at best. Tim had put down guys twice his size before with one punch. And yet, when he was in the alley, he feared for his life like he never had before. He imagined the pain the punches would bring and saw himself being stomped to death in his mind's eye. Such a strange fear.

Perhaps the healthiest way he learned to deal with the fear was by diving into music. He had made music an integral part of his life as a teenager and that, more than the other things, helped him cope with life's worries and fears. Marrying a musician was the icing on the cake for Tim. In fact, since marrying Liz and starting the family Tim couldn't remember being truly afraid of anything. He was too busy being the husband and father his family deserved. There was no time for his irrational fears. He was the one sending the Boogeyman away and checking under the beds. Honestly, he rarely thought about his childhood fears while raising his own kids.

But now, tonight…he wondered how much it would take to break him. He felt so fragile right now. As he lay there listening to the rainfall on his roof and deck outside his door, he would hear low moans that made his gut tighten. It wasn't the wind, he was sure of that. He would stare at the ceiling and feel someone looking at him from the corner of the room. The closet or bathroom doors would creak open just enough to make him look but then there was nothing there. There was always nothing there. But he knew that the mind could play some nasty tricks when you were tired and stressed out. Still, *something* was there.

He told himself that's all this was. His mind was tired and he was under tremendous stress about his family. He probably felt guilty or something that he wasn't there to save them and now his mind was conjuring up the past fears to get at him. He closed his eyes tightly and rubbed his hands down his face. He was determined to beat this. As he sat up in bed and dropped his hands he was suddenly face to face with a child whose eyes had been carved out. His son.

Tim jumped up, standing on the bed in fear and surprise. This couldn't be Caleb! The boy had Caleb's face but where his once beautiful brown eyes had been were now crudely carved holes. His face was ashen white and his throat was slit. He stood there naked and castrated, not speaking.

"Oh, God. Oh, God please, no. This isn't real. Please don't let this be real!" Tim was desperately trying to will this away while looking at his son. Finally, the boy raised one hand, his finger pointing at Tim.

"*You did this,*" he gurgled. Blood trickled down the open wound on his throat as he spoke. It was a ghastly sound and Tim felt he might vomit. "You didn't save us, Daddy. *I hate you.* You're gonna hurt, Daddy. You're gonna hurt *baaaad*." The last word was drawn out and blood oozed from the eye sockets and throat as his head swiveled this way and that at herky-jerky speeds no human could manage. Then as inhumanly quick as it had started, his head froze. A playful smile twisted on his lips.

"This isn't REAL!" Tim shouted at the boy. "YOU'RE NOT REAL!"

Tim had enough. He jumped over the boy and headed out the bedroom door. As he yanked the door open there stood his little girl in the hallway. Her sweet curly hair was thickly matted with blood as a deep cut ran the length of her forehead. Deep purple patches were under each eye and she had her lip out like a child who didn't get her way.

"Why didn't you save us, Daddy? I thought you loved us. Now Mommy's next and it's *all your fault*." She scolded him with her pointed finger as a teacher might. Then she walked up to him with her arms outstretched like she expected a hug. It broke Tim's heart to run past her but he knew this wasn't his little Hannah. He *prayed* this wasn't his little Hannah.

Tim reached Paul's room and took the liberty of entering the room without knocking. He figured Paul would understand. The room was dark and peaceful, a stark contrast to what he just left. It struck him as peculiar that Paul was sound asleep. He even paused in the doorway wondering if he should actually wake him or if he should just go back to his room and hope the "children" were gone. Sensing Tim's presence in the doorway, Paul breathed in a deep, waking breath.

"You ok?" was all he asked.

Tim took a moment and decided to be honest.

"No, not really."

Paul simply rolled his feet to the ground and turned on the lamp next to the bed as he sat up. He slept on top of the covers, a habit since childhood, but had a thin Baby Yoda blanket draped over him. He cleared his throat and looked into Tim's eyes.

"Wanna talk?"

"I think I want to listen. What's your take on this whole thing again?"

And with that Paul was permitted to expound his theories without fear of offending Tim. He thanked God in his heart for having such great timing. He also prayed silently that Tim would really hear him and not just blow him off again. He seemed pretty shaken up about *something*, perhaps he was ready to hear some truth.

They went into the kitchen and Tim put on a pot of Dark Roast coffee for both of them. As the coffee pot started bubbling and hissing to life they stood with empty mugs in hand and started one of the strangest conversations they had ever had together. The clock on the coffee maker read 9:55 p.m.

"So, you think this is spiritual stuff but not religious stuff?" Tim sought clarification. "Now what's the big difference again?"

Paul felt that was a pretty fair question. Most people who weren't churchgoers struggled with understanding that difference so Paul was ready to try and give him a suitable answer. If nothing else, Paul wanted to tell Tim his convictions on the matter.

"Think of it like this: religion is like man's rules on how to get to God and Christianity is God coming down to man. Religion is a list of do's and don'ts that won't bring anyone any closer to God's *heart*. Spiritual matters aren't always religious matters because there are a lot of people that are spiritual but don't consider themselves religious." It all made sense to Paul but he could see that he was losing Tim already.

"So, Jesus wasn't interested in rules?" Tim asked with a puzzled look on his face. "Didn't God give us the rules in the first place? So, Jesus came to fix God's mistake?" Tim was trying to make sense of it all.

"No! Jesus is God. They're one and the same. God never made a mistake." Paul suddenly felt like God's P.R. man.

"Jesus is God? That's a new one for me. I thought he was God's son? I mean, Father, Son, and Holy Ghost and all that, right?" Tim honestly wanted to understand this but it was a bit out there to him.

"The Trinity, yeah. That's good. But Jesus is both the Son of God *and* God the Son. Which is the same thing but some may see it as *he's God's* son like Hercules or something when, in fact, He is God's son but is God Himself." He paused for a second. "I know it seems weird but stay with me a minute." He quietly prayed for wisdom.

"God is one God but in three *persons*: the Father, Son, and Holy *Spirit, or ghost* as some say. And that's called the Trinity. Each *person* of the Trinity is fully God but they are different *persons*. So, the Father, the Son, and the Holy Spirit are equally God. You with me?" He was hoping this basic theology lesson was hitting its mark.

"Each is God but in different forms, pretty much?"

"Well," Paul made a face, "they aren't different *forms* as much as different persons. Each is unique but all are equal. Make sense?" Tim had the look that said 'What's the difference?' but he nodded. It would have to do for now. Paul continued.

"Before time God created everything. But nothing created God. He always was and is and always will be. So, Jesus has been around from the beginning. His birth on the earth started his mission to save us but that wasn't when he came into *being*. He's eternal just as God the Father is eternal. Got it?" Paul hoped this was making an ounce of sense.

"So, Jesus is God and he is God's son at the same time. He's his own son? Sounds deep south to me." Tim only joked to lighten his mood. He knew Paul could handle it. Southern boys could poke fun at themselves now and again.

"Galilee *was* a southern town. But yeah, he left heaven, wrapped himself in flesh, and was born from a virgin woman, Mary, so he is his own son in that sense. More importantly, he lived a perfect life obeying every Law of God so that he could take our place on the cross, freeing us from sin and the Law once and for all."

"How so?" Tim didn't get the whole Law and sacrifice thing either.

"The Law, ya know, Ten Commandments and stuff, were given to man by God to show us what it meant to live a pure and moral life. The Ten Commandments were only a part of it. There were over 300 laws the Jews were required to obey to be considered right with God.

"For every broken Law, there was a punishment or a sacrifice needed for atonement. Almost every broken Law resulted in the death of some animal from doves and pigeons on up to sheep and lambs and bulls. Blood had to be shed for the sin. The animal always had to be as perfect as possible. This is mostly what the Book of Leviticus is about.

Not a real light read as far as books go but it helps put things into perspective.

"The ultimate sacrifice was the Passover lamb that had to be without blemish. This was a once-a-year sacrifice that was for the sins of the people. The Lamb had to be without defect or it wasn't good enough. Jesus was perfect, not only in a God-sense but in an earthly sense as well because he never sinned or rebelled ever. That's the only way he was fit to be our sacrificial lamb. Only his blood was powerful enough to fulfill the requirements of the Law and thereby free us from it."

Paul could talk about this all night. These truths changed his life and the words poured from his lips. He hoped it didn't sound too mechanical or manufactured. "The symbolism is that Christ was our sacrifice just like the lamb used to be for the Jewish people, but a final one. The Law was fulfilled finally, then, and no more sacrifices were needed because one perfect sacrifice was applied as payment for all sin."

"So, the Law was bad?" Tim surmised.

"Not at all. God gave us the Law, the Ten Commandments, and every little *thou shalt not* to show us how difficult it would be to earn his favor on our own. The laws were great and made sense for a nation to follow. But, He knew we'd never live up to it and wanted us to reach that conclusion too. It isn't the Law that's bad but it shows how bad we all can be." Paul wanted to explain years of theology in five minutes but knew how dangerous and difficult that could be. He tried to simplify without minimizing truth.

"The apostle Paul said that the Law made him *realize* that he wanted to sin. The argument was simple: the Law pointed out what was sin and made us aware of it. Jesus freed us from it not because it was bad but because God intended us to live in freedom from the beginning, but we messed it up." Paul thought he was on a roll.

"So then, why die on a cross? Couldn't he just have come down and said 'hey, stop sinning and believe in me' without all the muss and fuss? No more Law. Or at least give us the power to live by the Law." Tim wanted to understand and now he was asking the questions that would help him to either dismiss Paul's faith once and for all or, scary enough, embrace it as he did. "I mean, let's say for a sec that the Bible accurately describes the fall of mankind... so why should I be saddled with Adam and Eve's screw up?"

"That goes back to the penalty for sin. The Book of Romans says that everyone has sinned and that the wages of sin is death. We aren't just guilty because of Adam and Eve, we screw up all on our own. Our world is broken and so are we." Tim nodded in silent agreement on that point. "So Jesus, being God, is the only one who had the perfect ability to die in our place. The Bible even calls him the *second Adam* because sin came into the world through Adam in the garden but life came to us through the death and resurrection of Jesus, undoing the curse of Adam.

"He allowed himself to be beaten, mocked, and killed on a cross to show that he loved us and that our sins were nailed up there with him. He was the final sacrifice that the Law would demand, thus, no more Law. The cross was the popular Roman capital punishment of the day. It was painful, humiliating, and very public. It was the perfect way for God to show the world that he would do anything to prove his love for us.

"As for giving us the power to obey it, well we have the ability but that old freewill card makes it tough. We have to choose to obey it and if God took that away then we wouldn't be free at all." Paul hoped that made sense.

Tim seemed to stare at his empty coffee mug for about a minute before he spoke up again. "So, Jesus died my death?" a familiar wall seemed to be going up by the changing look on his face. "I didn't ask anyone to die for me."

"And God didn't ask us to sin and ruin a perfect Creation, but here we are."

"But surely I've done way more good in my life than bad. Doesn't that count for anything with God?" Tim was sincerely asking and not trying to justify himself or his actions.

Paul simply looked at him and remembered the joy in his heart when he first understood that he was forgiven. *Truly* forgiven. "We're dealing with perfection, not good and bad. God is holy and perfect and he can't, and won't, be in the presence of our sinfulness. He demands holiness and justice for our wrongs. Even if you had only sinned once or broken just one Law in your life Jesus said that you were guilty of breaking them all. A sinner is not measured by how many sins he has committed but by the fact that he committed even one sin.

"Think of it this way: imagine you had a perfectly white piece of paper, like spotless and perfect without any blemish at all."

"Yeah."

"It is pure and untainted right?" Paul was making a point but Tim wasn't sure where it was going.

"Sure, pure and white. So?"

"Now imagine you took the teeniest tiniest black mark and touched the paper in the bottom corner where no one would even really notice. Is it still pure?"

Tim thought he got it now. "Nope. So, I guess I'm the black spot to God?"

"Not at all, your life is the white paper and the black mark is sin. You may look good and pure but as long as there is one little blemish on your record you are no longer pure. There is no way for you to remove that dot no matter what you do or how good you try to be. If I had fifty gallons of pure water and dropped one tiny drop of poison in it, would you drink it? Of course not. God has to remove our impurity, or sin, thus removing our guilt with it."

"So how does God dying for me remove it?"

"When you become a Christian, it's not that your spot is removed but more like you become a new piece of paper, free of impurity. Or a fresh glass of water sans poison. You are made *new*." Paul liked this analogy because one of his favorite verses in the Bible was 2 Corinthians 5:17, "*Therefore if anyone is in Christ he is a new creation; the old has gone and the new has come.*"

Tim seemed to think that over a moment and said, "That seems awful generous of God, seeing as how we messed all this up in the first place."

"You could say that. But God loves us. He created us and he wants to spend eternity with us."

Paul could sense a curveball coming. He knew Tim was a guy who covered every angle. Then the issue more people struggle with than anything came out. "But anyone who doesn't become a Christian goes to hell?" And with that Paul lost his momentum because he knew where this was going.

Paul took a second and answered, "Jesus said, '*I am the Way, the Truth, and the Life; no man comes to the Father but by me.*'"

"So then, no matter how good a person is or how sincere they are in what they believe God sends them to hell if they don't believe in Jesus. Buddhists, Muslims, Mormons, even well-meaning agnostics don't stand a chance. That doesn't sound very loving to me, man." Tim truly struggled with that and Paul didn't want to give a curt Sunday School answer about it.

Paul took a deep breath and tried to be as non-confrontational as he could. "Tim, the Bible says in John 3:16 that God loves everyone and I choose to believe that. It says that Jesus came to die for us all and anyone who believes that has eternal life. If there is really a heaven then, unfortunately, there really is a hell. God doesn't *send* anyone to hell in that way. He wants everyone to be saved but he allows man free will to choose him. If man rejects Jesus as God, then they have chosen to be separated from him forever.

"The first chapter of Romans tells how creation testifies to God's existence so that no one can claim ignorance. We are without excuse. Plus, the Bible clearly explains the truth about Jesus being our only hope and missionaries have gone all over the world trying to reach as many as possible with the Gospel."

"So, what about the folks they don't reach? They go to hell because they've never heard the truth?" Tim wasn't going to settle for vague answers on the important issues.

Paul wasn't about to give vague answers. "Do you think you love people more than God does? Did you create mankind in your image? Do you think that you would be a more loving God?" His questions shocked Tim a little. "As much as you are concerned for the people who are going to hell just remember that God *is* love. He cares about every human on this earth. And not just the good people, either. God loves the rapists and murderers too. The Bible tells us that God is not *willing* that any should perish but when people reject him, they have chosen their eternity. Christianity is both the most *exclusive* system on earth because it's the *only* way. But it's also the most *inclusive* because anyone who believes is welcome.

"And as far as the pygmies in deep dark Africa," Paul had been thrown this curveball so many times that it was second nature for him to answer it, "we have to trust God on some of those issues but there have been reports of missionaries finally getting to a tribe only to find that they were already following a book very close to the Bible and that they were fully aware of God and his Son."

"How's that?" Tim was a bit intrigued.

"As I said, God loves people and he can send his Holy Spirit to people or an angel of the Lord. He could reach people through dreams or visions—"

"Hold on. Angels? Now angels are going to folks telling them to believe in Jesus?" Tim wasn't sure about this.

"Of course. Angels and demons are just as real as God. They're found all through the Bible. God used angels all the time to warn someone or protect them. Sometimes just to test them. Angels could take on human form when delivering a message. Hebrews says to show kindness to strangers because you never know when it might be an angel." Paul got the feeling that this wasn't as easy to swallow for Tim as it had been for him. It was most likely because Paul was already a believer and then began to learn about these things and Tim was just hearing about them without the benefit of being a believer first.

"You know what? Let's pause this whole salvation debate for a minute so you can go ahead and tell me your theory on what's going on here." Tim wasn't dodging the debate, he needed to mull over some of this later and get back to it.

Paul thought that was fair. He had laid a good bit of theology down on Tim and was actually kind of surprised that he hadn't dismissed him as he had done in times past when it got hard to understand. "Deal. But just remember that most people never run out of questions or objections to issues of faith. It can be a never-ending excuse to dodge the truth." Tim silently nodded in surrender and waved his hand to proceed.

Paul began to explain his thoughts on the day's events. "We just kind of hit on it. It's like this. Good and evil are always at war. What I believe to be forces of good and evil are the ones found in scripture.

It says that the devil is at work in this world and he will exploit man's evil nature to capitalize on it.

"You were traumatized as a kid and now those thoughts are coming back right when your family is missing. You are seeing things that are there one moment and then gone, right?"

Tim thought of the encounter with his kids a few minutes ago. "Yeah, and they aren't so friendly."

"Exactly. I was walking through the house praying a couple of hours ago and I could sense evil. I heard laughter and my mind was filling with thoughts that were far from godly." Paul hadn't shared that yet. "I was scared and wanted to leave at one point."

Tim was shocked and relieved to hear it. He felt comforted by the fact that even Paul had chinks in his armor. He knew Paul wasn't a prideful guy, but it took real humility to admit when you were scared. Tim had convinced himself for so long that fear was a weakness that he rarely confessed those times when it got the best of him.

"I think that we're dealing with some serious spiritual issues here. I'm not saying that this isn't also physically happening and that real people aren't involved, but I need you to be aware that whatever is messing with your mind is trying to get you to break." Paul wanted Tim to know the truth so badly but that was his choice. Tim looked down and spoke sheepishly.

"I saw my kids tonight." Tim kept his eyes on the ground awaiting Paul's response.

"Like you saw your mom?"

"Yeah. It wasn't my kids, I know, but it was real enough. Caleb looked like one of those kids from the cabin. He was all bloodied up and pointed his finger at me. They both said this was my fault and that I was going to suffer for letting it happen." Tim was shaken to the core and Paul could understand why.

"It's not your fault, you know."

"I know."

"Do you? There's nothing you could have done, Tim. You were trying to get home and it happened. It's not your fault. That wasn't your mom and those weren't your kids. Whatever is happening here is evil but we're gonna figure it out and you'll see your family again."

Tim was fighting back tears and didn't seem to be winning. They began rolling down his cheeks and onto his blue undershirt. A sob broke through and the walls crumbled. He stood there leaning on the kitchen counter and sobbed. Paul put a reassuring hand on his shoulder and let him cry. A minute later Paul spoke up as the sobs were dissipating.

"It's gonna be all right, man. We're going to find them. We'll do whatever it takes to get them back safely." Paul's words were encouraging but seemed a little empty considering their circumstances. They had nowhere to look, no clues, no leads, no real suspects. All they had was Tim's traumatic camp experience to place a familiar feeling to all of this. Paul had a strange idea.

"Hey, do you remember any of the boys' names from camp?"

Tim was wiping away the last remnant of tears. "Maybe a couple of 'em. Why?"

Paul smiled and started walking towards the computer in the dining room corner as he spoke. "You seem to be convinced that this Del kid was some junior psycho, right?

"Definitely."

"And you say that the look in his eyes was the same as the guy you saw in the alley tonight?"

"Pretty much, yeah. You still think they might be the same guy?" Tim doubted it but at this point, any leads would be great. He had regained his composure now and was walking over to Paul.

"Dunno. But if we could talk to some of the kids that were at the camp with you, then maybe we could find out more about him. Give me a name." Paul was at the computer now and had a search engine up on the internet. He would Google as much as it took to find somebody who could help.

"Umm…try Gabe Whitten. Gabriel, most likely." Tim remembered poor Gabe and the suffering he did at the hands of Del. If he had any info, he would gladly share it.

Paul typed in the name, hit enter, and waited.

CHAPTER SEVEN

"**G**ive it up, Tim. I see you plain as day walking to the front door. Now hang up and give me my flowers." Liz hung up the cordless phone and walked out to meet her flower-bearing husband. He was always calling from down the street saying he was held up in traffic or was going to be another hour or so. He said he liked surprising her. She would walk out of the house smiling when he was able to pull it off. When she called his bluff he usually just laughed and said he'd have better luck next time. She wasn't sure why he was trying so hard to fool her even after he was in the driveway but she loved that silly man of hers.

"Get the kids," was his greeting. The phone was ringing in the background.

"Well, I missed you too, fella. Is there a kiss with those flowers?" She felt a little strange but couldn't place it. He didn't offer her a kiss but instead repeated himself.

"Get the kids, we need to go. Don't worry with the phone, they'll call back."

Maybe he was taking them all out for dinner. She wanted to chide him about being so curt but figured it was part of his master plan. She walked back into the living room and yelled for the kids to come out. Buck was barking up a storm in the backyard. Tim just stood there next to the Tahoe waiting on them. She figured it was all right to let the machine get the call and just let it ring.

"Come on kids, we're going out for dinner," Liz bellowed from the doorway. Caleb and Hannah came running with smiles on their faces.

"What about leftoverpalooza?" Hannah asked. Thursday night was always leftover night. Tim jokingly referred to it as leftoverpalooza and the kids loved it.

"I guess daddy doesn't want yesterday's meatloaf or Tuesday's Salisbury steak," Liz answered with mock hurt.

"Me either!" came the brutal honesty of an eight-year-old. Caleb had chimed in with his two cents.

"I don't mind, mommy," came Hannah's tender reassurance.

"It's ok, baby. I don't mind going out. Let's go."

After throwing shoes and light coats on they were ready.

With that, they walked out the front door to see Tim already in the truck with the engine running. Liz couldn't shake a nagging paranoia about this. Tim always loved to come home and hug the kids. He almost always came right in the front door and kissed everybody at least twice before he even asked what was for dinner. Oh well, maybe he was really hungry or just in a hurry-up mood.

"Hey, babe, what's wrong with Buckley? You wanna see if he's ok?" He hadn't stopped barking and growling since he pulled up. Liz knew that it had to be something bothering him to get Buck to act that way.

"I'm sure he's fine. Let's go."

Liz cocked her head a bit and looked at him before getting in. He sure wasn't acting himself today. Normally he would fall all over himself to make sure Buck was all right. He loved that dog like a third child.

"What's the hurry, cowboy? Can't I even put my lovely flowers in water before we go?" She wasn't so comfortable with his wanting to just blow out of there so fast.

"There's no time. You can do it later. Let's go." He wasn't even looking at her when he spoke. He was just waiting impatiently for her to get in. The kids had already climbed in the back and had buckled up. They weren't so concerned with his demeanor so maybe Liz was over-reacting a little. She got in and barely shut her door before he squealed out of the driveway. She noticed Mrs. Jenkins watering the flowers on her front porch and waved politely.

"Where are we goin', daddy?" Hannah asked with bright eyes.

"Just sit back and you'll see when we get there." He was never short with the kids like that. Hannah sat back, a little deflated. Her smile faded but she looked out the window and seemed to get lost in the scenery. Caleb eyed his father warily. Tim looked up in the rearview mirror and caught his eye. "What?"

"Nothin'. You seem mad. Did we do something wrong?" Caleb had a heart of gold even if his attitude was souring lately. He was a sweet kid and never required spankings. He was the type that a stern look would draw tears. Some people said he had a guilty conscience but Liz knew that he was just tender-hearted, even if he tried to hide it by acting all crusty. He was especially sensitive to Tim. Daddy was his hero and everybody knew it.

"Just sit back."

"Babe. What's going on with you?" She wanted to figure out why she had such a knot in the pit of her stomach.

"All of you just sit back, be quiet and we'll be there soon enough."

Liz was very uncomfortable now. Red flags were going up all over the place in her mind. She recalled the phone call before Tim's arrival. He was so adamant that it wasn't him. But this was obviously her husband. How could this not be Tim? She had a strange thought. She would ask him something that only Tim would know, that way she could tell if he was some alien imposter. She was being so silly! What kind of game was she playing? This was her husband, wasn't it?

"Hey, remember when you first got this truck? Remember what you said to me on the test drive?" She was playing her little game.

Tim waited for a minute and seemed to be processing the question. She thought she had him. "I said that it completed my manly-man image." He stated it like he was on Jeopardy or something. He was right but it made Liz all the more paranoid. She decided to get her cell phone and call Tim's cell phone. If it rang then, hey, this was all just a twilight zone moment and if it didn't... then she wasn't sure what she would do.

She fumbled for her purse and realized that she had left her cell phone on the table or in the Honda. She did that all the time. If she drove then she always put it in the drink holder so she would hear it if it rang, but then she would forget to take it out and wound up missing calls all the time. Tim fussed at her about that when he had tried to reach her for something.

She looked over at her husband. It was like looking at a photograph of him. The looks were there but there wasn't the "essence of Tim" that made her feel safe and secure. In fact, she felt anything but safe and secure right now.

"Where are we going?" she asked with a firmer tone than she meant to.

He looked over at her and seemed to sense her frustration. He smiled a cocky smirk and said, "You'll see when we get there."

As he looked into her eyes, she knew then that this wasn't Tim. Tim's eyes were filled with love and warmth. This man's eyes were cold and dark. He might look like Tim but she could see beyond the mask now. A cold chill ran down her spine. Her first thought was about the children. She wouldn't do anything that might put them in danger. She would have to go along with this game for now.

Her mind snapped back to the phone call again. Tim had seemed scared that she saw him. It really wasn't him after all. Her only consolation was that Tim would be home any minute and he would find them. He might be scared and confused but she was sure that he would not stop until this little game was over.

The man posing as Tim seemed to pick up on her mood shift. Her body language sent the message that she had caught on. She stiffened and subconsciously slid closer to the door. He eyed her with little concern.

"Just enjoy the ride. This is gonna get a lot more fun pretty soon." His words were enigmatic but still scared her to death. Who was this? What was going on? She glanced back at the kids. They seemed oblivious to what was happening and she was glad for that. For all they knew, daddy was just in a bad mood.

Her mind raced with scenarios in which she and the kids could escape. She would have to wait for a stop when she could get the kids unbuckled and out before he stopped them. That seemed unlikely unless he was immobilized. What could she use to render him unconscious? She looked back and saw that the tools that normally littered the very back seat were missing. It was only then that she noticed that the interior was a different color than Tim's actual Tahoe. His had a tan interior and this was gray. It's amazing the things you don't notice when you aren't looking for them.

He leaned in close and whispered in her ear, "Try anything stupid and I'll gut your kids right in front of you. Got it?"

He smiled a sick, psychotic smile that left no room for doubt that he would gladly make good on his threat.

She was speechless with fear. She had never in her life been so afraid. Only once, in college, had she felt so helpless. She simply nodded a yes to show compliance and fought back the tears. Oh, God, please let Tim find them soon.

"Don't worry. I left little Timmy a note," he smiled.

CHAPTER EIGHT

Tim and Paul scrolled down the list of Gabriel Whitten's Google pulled up. A smattering of questionable advertisement sites had the name but no real reference to him. How did the sleazy sites always seem to get in on the search action? Anyway, there was one from a few years ago about a class of '99 2oth high school reunion listed. That put Gabe in the right age group.

"Click on that one," Tim pointed to the reunion site.

As Paul clicked the domain name, up popped an old yearbook page with senior mug shots floating across the screen. It was kind of nostalgic in a way to see the familiar hair do's and fashions of the day but Tim wasn't interested in a stroll down memory lane right now. He was looking for a face, a name, and an address. Anything that would get him some answers.

"Do you see him?" Paul asked. It was only then that Tim realized that Paul had no idea what Gabe looked like.

"Uh, no. Not yet. Hit that arrow and turn to 'W'."

Paul skipped to the last page and there was Gabe's awkward, smiling face right after some girl named Kimberly White and before some guy named Jamal Yesmit.

"There he is," Tim pointed to his face on the screen. "I'd know that face anywhere." Gabe was about seventeen in the photo but still had those kind, scared eyes that Tim remembered from years earlier at camp. Paul was already looking on the page to see how contacting someone from the class was possible. He scrolled the mouse across his picture and the name turned from black to blue, indicating it was a hyperlink to something else. He clicked it.

Tim was hopeful that they would find a current address since the reunion was back in 2019. Still, they could track him down easier if they had a good starting place and this information might be just that. The photo floated to the upper left corner of the screen and a bio popped up.

"Jackpot." Tim was chomping at the bit to talk to Gabe and this might just afford him that opportunity. It was a full page of information that was a combination of high school life and post–high school life. "Hit print and let's check it out."

Paul hit the print icon twice so they wouldn't have to share and the printer whirred to life. After they had both snatched up a copy, they made their way back to the kitchen table. Tim was scouring his page for something but they both seemed to see it at the same time.

"Got it!" they chimed in at nearly the same time. Tim ran his finger over the beginning of the last paragraph on the page as he read it aloud.

"'Gabe grew up in Georgia but moved to Metairie, Louisiana with his family at the age of thirteen. After high school, Gabe went on to attend Tulane University in New Orleans and obtained his Bachelor's in Business Management. He never married and has no children.' Where's Metairie again?" Tim asked.

"It's right next to New Orleans. Most people would just call it New Orleans but it's actually a whole other city. When I was in seminary everyone knew that you had to go to Metairie to go to a decent Wal-Mart or a good mall. It's like the 'nicer side' of New Orleans. Or at least it was before Katrina," Paul educated Tim.

"Oh, on the west side? I know what you're talking about. It wasn't quite as messed up in Hurricane Katrina, right?" New Orleans made great efforts after the hurricane, trying to recapture the greatness of the city it was before. The Superbowl victory in 2010 certainly helped and Mardi Gras happened every year, regardless of bad weather or attendance, but Paul had fond memories of the pre-Katrina New Orleans. In some ways, it was a happier place now with big pushes to bring in new blood. Anyone could buy up old, damaged properties cheap and, with enough money, turn them into renovated houses or apartments. Several pockets of the city were now posh and trendy.

"Not nearly as bad as New Orleans proper, no. It's on the other side of the levees. It had some minor storm damage but nothing like the destruction found in the Orleans and St. Bernard Parishes." Paul could tell by the look on Tim's face he wasn't completely following the whole parish thing. "Louisiana is the only state that is made up of parishes instead of counties. It's a Catholic thing. St. Bernard Parish was hit the worst. It's where the Ninth Ward is. I had some good friends there that lost everything. I mean *everything*."

Tim knew Paul lived in New Orleans for three years but never really processed that he would have known people who were so affected by Katrina. Paul had experienced the post-Katrina New Orleans early on since he had gone down a few times to see friends and old professors. He had led some college mission teams down there to do some clean-up and disaster relief a few times, as well. Tim was blown away by the stories he had heard like how long it took to repair and replace such major roads like I-10. It was proof of how devastated the town was. Ten years later entire Auto Malls in New Orleans East were still abandoned and looked like apocalyptic auto graveyards with the residue of floodwaters still mucked up to the roofs of cars. That had been a while ago now, surely there had been more done since then. Tim knew they would find out soon enough.

It struck Tim that Gabe had moved right after that summer of camp. He couldn't help but wonder if that summer had something to do with it. God knows *his* life was never the same after that summer.

"Let's call information and see if we can't find out if he's still around the area." Paul was already digging out his iPhone.

After hitting 411 Paul answered the automated question, "City and State, please" with, "New Orleans, Louisiana." After a live operator picked up and asked for the listing Paul replied, "Gabriel Whitten."

Paul mouthed to Tim, "She's connecting me" with an enthusiastic nod.

After a beat he reported, "It's just ringing. Guess nobody's home."

"But we know that's where he lives, right?" Tim looked hopeful for the first time in hours.

Paul hung up and looked at Tim. He would let him take the lead on the next move.

"We've got no cell phone number, house phone just ringing, and an address that would at least point us in the right direction." Tim was adding up the information.

"Ready for a road trip?" Tim asked with mock enthusiasm.

"If you think this guy can help then I'm up for it," came Paul's dutiful reply. "I would certainly rather get him on the phone but this may be a better face-to-face conversation anyway."

"Well, his last address was his college address in New Orleans so let's start there." A quick white pages search showed he maintained the same address from college to this day. Strange but not impossible.

Tim was running on adrenaline and Paul had a couple of hours of sleep under his belt but both were pretty awake at the moment. A quick there-and-back was the plan so they both packed light. They were aware they needed to be back by morning so they didn't cast any undue suspicion on Tim.

"Is this wise?" Tim finally asked. "I mean, I really want to find some answers and Gabe seems a likely source, but what do you think?"

"I feel the same way. And yet, there's a sense that we need to do this, ya know?" Paul replied honestly.

"Yeah, I do. I feel it in my gut, for sure. Let's do it."

Paul stood in the doorway of Tim's bedroom as he threw a change of clothes in a backpack along with his bag of toiletries. Everything a man needs for an overnighter. Paul was still packed from earlier so he just grabbed his bag and was ready to travel.

Paul was taken aback when Tim reached up on the top shelf of the walk-in closet and brought out a metal box.

"What's that you got there?" Paul asked with obvious disapproval in his voice.

"Just a little insurance man. After the way our night started, I'm not taking any chances." He removed a Glock 17 9mm and a full magazine from the box and put them in his backpack. "I'll leave the mag out if it makes you feel better."

"It's not the gun or the mag so much. Why do you have a gun?" Paul wasn't interested in a political debate on gun control or anything but didn't think Tim was in any kind of good mental space to have a gun right now.

"One of my guys gave it to me. He got sick and had to miss several days of work. He had a new baby and really couldn't afford to miss a week's pay so I paid him anyway, under the table. He was grateful and gave this to me as a 'thank you.' I've never used or needed it, until now."

"I get it. Guns can make you feel safe and in control. But are you sure that's a good idea, man? I mean, I think we can handle ourselves." Even as Paul was saying it the pain in his face and knuckles betrayed his confidence.

As if Tim knew exactly what he was thinking he said, "If we'd had this earlier then maybe things would have been a lot less violent tonight."

"Or they might have become deadly. I had to talk you out of bashing in that guy's head with a hammer, remember?" Paul was torn but wanted to trust Tim was in his right mind. He was just nervous that if Tim was in another situation like before he could do something he'd regret.

"Then you take it. I just don't know what we're dealing with and I feel better having it, ok? It's registered and legal, I promise. I'm not looking to shoot anybody, Paul." Tim was a little defensive but understood where Paul was coming from in a way. What if he'd had the gun earlier? Still. He'd feel better knowing he had it next time.

Paul was thoughtfully quiet for a minute. "Ok, let me carry it in my bag. Grab the registration papers."

It was a good compromise. Tim grabbed the papers out of the box and handed Paul the gun, the loaded magazine, and the paperwork.

As they passed the kitchen, they both saw their coffee cups sitting on the table.

"Let's take this coffee to go. I'm sure we'll need it," Tim suggested. He grabbed a couple of travel mugs out of the cupboard and transferred the cups they had been sipping on earlier. He topped them both off with hot coffee from the carafe and looked up at Paul. "Let's do this," was his charge. "Oh, wait." Tim went back to the fridge and pulled out the rest of the ham. "we'll be gone a while, Buck. You need to pee?" Paul was pretty impressed that the dog looked at the back door and gave a moan that surely meant, "no, I'm good."

It was storming pretty bad now but there was a small fenced run outside the kitchen for when Buck needed to get outside to do his business but could also get back in if he wanted to. The kitchen door had a two-way doggy door so Tim looked at Buck and said, "I've got to keep you in the kitchen, pal. Not sure when we'll be back and I can't have you trackin' mud all over the carpet or Mommy will shoot us both." Buck offered a reluctant chuff of compliance and trotted to the kitchen.

Tim moved his bed to his spot by the counter and put up the child safety gate they used to keep him in the kitchen area, not that he wouldn't stay put. It was just that thunder was a wild card for him sometimes. Like with people, fear could produce irrational reactions.

Tim opened the kitchen door to make sure the run was closed off on the other side so Buck couldn't get out and he saw the kids' bikes in the grass outside the door. Without hesitation, he ran out and made sure they were rolled under the awning so they wouldn't get wet and rusty. He came back in and grabbed a hand towel off the counter and dried his head.

Paul couldn't help but think how much Tim loved his family. If anything happened to them, he would be devastated. Tim looked up as if the same thought had occurred to him. "We've got to find them, Paul."

"We will, man. We will."

After dropping several pieces of lunchmeat in Buck's food dish they headed to the front door. Tim remembered something and held up his hand, "Hold up a sec." He grabbed the cordless phone out of the cradle and punched in a series of numbers. "I'm forwarding all house calls to my cell, just in case."

"Smart," Paul admitted.

Since Paul had managed a couple of hours sleep, he volunteered to take the first shift of driving. It would be a two-legger, at best. He said that it would be about three and a half hours to Montgomery and then not quite four more to New Orleans by way of Mobile, thanks to the weather. They could easily split it. With any luck, they would make it three and three but the last thing they needed now was police interference due to speeding. Traveling in the middle of the night might help, too. It was still only 10:50.

They chose Tim's SUV simply because they wanted the room when they found his family and because it was a comfy ride. Tim was looking forward to catching some Z's. "See you in Montgomery, man," he told Paul as they pulled out of the driveway. There were three legs on the journey to New Orleans from Atlanta. First to Montgomery, then to Mobile, and then to New Orleans. I-85 to 65 to I-10. Paul knew it well.

"Get you a few good hours, man. You need it. I'll wake you if absolutely necessary but other than that I plan on taking this time to do some thinking and praying on my own. The quiet will be good for both of us." Paul wanted desperately to return to their previous conversation but knew that now wasn't the time. He hadn't gotten a chance to tell Tim all that he was thinking about this situation.

"Just find a classic rock or oldies station and keep it low to drown out any noise, if you don't mind."

"That's cool. I wasn't going to dance around the car and pray in tongues or anything." Paul took a playful jab at Tim.

"Dude, I know. I wasn't trying to say-"

"I'm messin' with you, man. I was gonna put some music on anyway. Gosh, you are on edge aren't you?"

"You have no idea." Tim's world was crashing around him and he felt so helpless to stop it. Maybe a few hours of sleep could help his perspective. Unfortunately, he was too keyed up to sleep for almost the whole first hour. He lay there thinking and replaying the night's events in his head like some twisted movie. Somewhere before Auburn, Alabama, he dozed off.

...and I got a peaceful, easy feelin' that you won't let me down...

Tim slowly opened his eyes to daylight and realized that he had no idea where he was. He looked over and Liz was smiling at him. Liz? He tried to shake the grogginess off.

"Bout time you woke up. I promised to drive *part* of the way and you've been asleep since we left my mother's." Her voice sounded so sweet and strange.

"I was having the freakiest dream," he began. He was so groggy and confused. "You and the kids-" he whipped around and saw the kids asleep in the back: Caleb with his seat belt on and Hannah in her booster seat. He turned back to Liz.

"You ok?" She asked with eyebrows raised.

"Not sure," was his honest reply. "In my dream you and the kids were – gone. Paul was helping me look for you but, uh, strange things kept happening."

"What kind of *things*?"

"Forget it. I don't' even want to talk about it. I'm just glad you're here and the kids are safe." He was still reeling from the dream.

"Well, did you save us?" She prodded. She obviously couldn't tell how much he did *not* want to talk about this.

"No. Well, I was trying," he said reluctantly.

"Why didn't you save us?" Her sweet tone had a bit of a bite.

"I told you, it was a dumb dream and I don't want to talk about it. Let the kids sleep and I'll drive at the next stop." He was eager to drop the subject.

"Don't you love us enough to save us, Tim?" She was angry over a dream? Come on.

"Drop it, babe, it was a dream. You know I love you."

This was turning into one of those hypothetical arguments that always frustrated Tim. Why fight about what might have or could have happened? It was a dream and that's that. He was just glad it was over.

"I just think that if you really loved us, you would have tried harder. Were you scared? Why did you just let us die?!" This was too much. She was crossing the line and it started to upset him.

"Will you keep it down, the kids are asleep!" He was turning to check on them when she smiled a slight smile.

"Don't worry about them, they're dead to the world."

Tim looked back and caught his breath. He hadn't noticed before but the kids were pale. Ashen blue, even. They had dark circles under their eyes and – oh my God! Their throats were slit! Blood trickled down onto their chests, soaking into their t-shirts. Tim whipped his head back around to Liz. She was humming along to the Eagles on the radio, seemingly oblivious to what was going on. She slowly turned her head around to him, smiling her slight smile.

"You did this, Timmy. You let us die. And you and your guardian are next." As she spoke blood began to slip past her teeth and drip down her chin. She lunged for Tim.

"WHOA!" Tim jumped awake in the SUV.

Paul tried to maintain control of the vehicle but was shocked by the sudden outburst. He looked over at Tim with wide eyes.

"Dude! What the heck?" He asked.

"Bad dream. Sorry." Tim was trying to get his head around this one. They were in the Tahoe on the way to New Orleans. Ok. *Get a grip, man.*

"Must have been a doozy," Paul remarked.

"Yeah. Liz and the kids were – never mind. How long was I out?"

"About two hours." Paul was staring straight ahead but he was smiling a little. Tim wasn't sure why but it unnerved him. When he spoke again his tone gave him away. "They were what? *Dead?*"

Paul would never joke about something like this. "What do you want?" Tim asked knowingly.

"You know what I want, Timmy. What I've always wanted. I want you to cry and beg. I want you to suffer. I want you to *die.* Just like your family." The words came from Paul's mouth but they weren't Paul's words. Such *hate.* So matter-of-fact that Tim could taste the bile rising up his throat. His mouth was like battery acid. Fear and anger swam in his mind.

"Go to Hell," was all Tim could muster.

"Sure. I'll tell your folks you said 'hi'."

Paul gave a sideways glance over Tim's direction and he could see those eyes. The same eyes that had haunted him earlier tonight, in college, at camp. At that moment Tim was sure he would die in that car. As he broke his eyes away from Paul and looked forward a tree came into full view of the windshield just as it came crashing through.

Tim bolted up.

Another dream.

Paul was driving and looked over at Tim. "You ok?"

"No."

Paul waited for a beat and simply said, "Ok."

Paul knew better than to ask too many questions right now. They had only been driving for about two hours and it was becoming clear that Tim wasn't going to sleep much on this drive. They rode along in silence for about another two minutes until Paul spoke up again.

"Wanna talk about it?" He was sincere but not pushy.

"I don't trust myself to talk right now. I'm still trying to figure out what's real and what's just in my head." Tim was starting to break apart a little.

"Well, if I'm a figment of your imagination could you give me bigger biceps or a washboard stomach?" This was definitely Paul.

Tim let out a cleansing sigh and put his head in his hands. After a few seconds, he grabbed his coffee, pulled off the lid, and chugged it. Barely warm coffee was pretty easy to chug and he wanted to jolt his system a little anyway. "I'm up," he declared.

"Apparently. We should get some gas while it's cheap. Prices go up in Mississippi. Plus, we could get some more java."

"Sounds like a plan." Tim was not too quick to dream again.

Paul saw a Spectrum and pulled in. He parked at the pump and got out to fill up. He looked over at Tim sitting there. "You gonna get some coffee?" Paul wondered what the late crew would think of them with their black eyes and swollen faces. That fight seemed forever ago now.

"I'll wait 'til you're done." Tim sounded so sheepish. The guy who had nearly taken a hammer to five bikers earlier in the night didn't want to go into a gas station alone now. Paul was starting to worry about him. He knew that once they hit the road again, he would have to share more of his take about what was going on. He only hoped that Tim would listen. He silently prayed for the thousandth time that God would open his ears to hear.

CHAPTER NINE

Paul was reaching for a root beer when he noticed Tim looking through the pills at the counter. He heard him ask the cashier which one the truckers used the most. Paul considered saying something but figured even an energy drink at one in the morning was about the same thing as a caffeine pill. It wasn't like he was using drugs or anything. He let the glass door slide back into place and went up to pay for his drink and beef jerky.

"That'll be eight dollars and twenty-three cents, Sugar," the plump, elderly woman behind the counter informed Paul. Tim had ditched the hot coffee for a Monster Java. He had two vanilla-flavored ones and the No-Doze pills along with a Butterfinger and Pringles. Enough sugar and caffeine that he wouldn't sleep for a week. "You boys been getting' into trouble?" The cashier asked with a smile, obviously noticing their battle scars from earlier.

"You should see the other guys," Paul couldn't resist the cliché. He gave her a wink.

"I'm sure." She said with a chuckle. "A couple a nice lookin' fellas like you wouldn't start no trouble, I bet. And ya ain't buying no beer so it wasn't no drunken brawl, I suspect. You get mugged?" Curiosity was written all over her face.

Paul looked at Tim as if to get permission to tell the story. Tim gave a look of surrender and said, "I gotta go to the bathroom anyway."

"Doing some paperwork?" Paul teased. Tim rolled his eyes. "What?" Paul protested, "I just need to know how much time I have to tell the story." Tim made his way to the restroom.

With that, Paul looked back and set the stage for his recalling of the night's events.

"You might think we're nuts when we tell you this but it's God's honest truth."

Her face lit up at the prospect of a great story to free her from the drudgery of the graveyard shift.

Tim walked into the bathroom and nearly gasped at his reflection in the wall-length mirror. He looked rough. No doubt he would be even puffier in a few hours, especially without sleep. But he wouldn't sleep. He may never sleep again.

Right now, he had to get to the paperwork Paul had so eloquently suggested. The bathroom was surprisingly clean but he still took the third of four stalls out of habit just in case someone else came in. He always left the handicap stall available. It was late but this was a pretty popular stretch of road and anything was possible.

Tim hadn't been in the stall for a minute when his hypothetical situation became reality. The door noisily swung open and somebody walked in. Wasn't Paul, either. He could hear Paul talking in the background as the door was open for a second. Didn't matter. There was always the unspoken rule of men's room etiquette. A simple cough would notify any would-be approachers that the stall was occupied. Tim let out his obligatory cough and went back to his "paperwork."

Tim wasn't trying to pay attention to whoever came in but it struck him as strange that he hadn't heard the guy use the bathroom or wash his hands or anything. Most people don't just stand around in bathrooms they know are occupied. Tim couldn't see that side of the room from his far stall. Even when he craned his neck, he couldn't see much out of the small opening in the door jam.

Laughter. Tim heard a child's laughter. But this wasn't the kind that makes you warm inside. No, this was disturbingly out of place. Surely a kid wasn't alone in a public restroom at one in the morning.

Tim tried to fight the urge to say something when he heard it again. This time it sounded like more than one child, more like a bunch of middle school boys. He decided to end his business and get out. Just as he was about to finish, stand and pull up his pants, all went dark.

The lights went out and he was in pitch-black darkness.

"Hey! Somebody's in here!" he shouted, hoping that would cause any games to end immediately.

More laughter. And then the laughter turned to whispers. A cacophony of hushed children's voices echoed off the tile floors. Tim wanted to run from the stall but he was in kind of a precarious position. He felt helpless.

The whispers stopped. Then Tim heard footsteps coming towards his stall. He couldn't see a thing but he knew someone was right outside his stall.

"*Timmy!*"

Tim was frozen with fear. The darkness swallowed him and the voice seemed to come from everywhere at once: below, above, right behind him even. It felt like forever but Tim heard it again. This time it was like a little boy's whisper.

"*Timmy…you're gonna die.*"

As he heard the words, he also felt a hot breath on the back of his neck. There was no way a person could be in the stall with him but he felt, and could even smell, the fetid breath as the whisper lingered. Then he heard a scratching sound on the walls of his stall. Not fast but slow and deliberate. He heard the laughter again. The stall began to shudder as if someone, or several people, was trying to open the door. Then they were pounding on the stall and he felt cold hands in the dark grabbing at him. Tim had all he could take.

He grabbed his pants and bolted through the door, cutting a hard left out of the bathroom. He pulled up panting and squinting as the lights from the store stung his eyes. Paul and the woman were staring at him with their mouths opened as if he had interrupted a lively discussion. Paul closed his mouth but the cashier continued to stare in disbelief.

It was only then that Tim realized he was standing there with his pants unbuckled and barely covering his butt with sweat dripping off his face.

Paul recovered quickly. "See? He's a little on edge."

It seemed he had shared enough about the night's events to bring her up to speed on the situation. "Well, I'd be edgy too if somebody took my family! You don't worry 'bout a thing, Sugar. Pull them pants up and off ya go."

Tim swallowed and pulled his pants up. "I'm really sorry, ma'am. Whoever came in after me turned the lights off."

She stood there blinking for a moment and then Tim knew what she was about to say. "Nobody went in there, baby. You two are the only ones in here." Concern was on her face but Tim still felt like a little kid who couldn't get a grip on his imagination. He glanced at Paul for corroboration and he nodded sadly.

"It'll be okay, sweetheart. You'll find your wife and kids." Her assurance was sweet but seemed hollow right now. "Oh, hey. I was gonna tell ya'll to be careful in your car, too."

"What do you mean?" Paul asked.,

"Well, I noticed you have a Black Tahoe. Earlier this morning one was stolen right from our parking lot. Looked just like yours. I figured if that's what they want you should be careful, ya know?"

"Thanks. We will." Paul was gathering up the bags and heading for the door. Tim followed quietly. "You have a good night and be safe. God bless."

"You too, Sugar."

"Did you hear that?" Paul asked Tim as they got back into the truck.

"What?" Tim was still in a daze.

"She said that a Tahoe just like yours was stolen earlier this morning. We're only a couple of hours from your house. Could be more than a coincidence."

The cobwebs were clearing from Tim's mind. Paul could see the information sinking in. Tim just furrowed his brow and shook his head. He knew that this information wouldn't clear his name but they would still tell the police in the morning. Then it hit Tim.

"You don't think they'll freak out about me going to New Orleans, do you? The cops I mean. 'Don't leave town' is kind of clear cut."

"It's hard to say with Detective Peters. He seems like a reasonable guy but he also strikes me as a no-nonsense type. As long as we're down and back before anybody checks we should be ok. You forwarded the calls and they'll likely assume you're at work in the morning. We should be there by five-thirty or so and I don't see us spending much time there before we head back. The bigger question is what are you gonna tell your uncle about why you're not coming in to work in the morning."

"I'm not worried about that. A quick call to him to say I won't be in will be all he needs. He doesn't push for answers like dad would have." The mention of his dad made him long for one of their tit-for-tat arguments they were always getting into. But Uncle Frank was as easy-going as dad was stern. "There may be some answers in New Orleans that the police here aren't going to go looking for. We could be back by noon, right?"

Paul wasn't going to lie to the police but he also knew Tim was desperate for answers right now. Maybe they could make it back in time. Doubtful, but maybe. It was worth a shot.

"Noon would be pushing it for sure. Honestly, I think you should call in the morning and tell them the truth. We ran across a lead and headed out without thinking. If they discover you're gone it won't look good for you."

Paul made good sense. Even if you're guilty it's better to turn yourself in than be caught lying. He would call in the morning. "All right," was all he said about it. Paul was glad that he was still being sensible.

"So…what happened back there?" Paul fished.

"Oh, nothing. I was taking a dump when someone came in who didn't. They laughed. They whispered my name. Lights went out. Felt someone in the stall with me. Stall shook. Hands started grabbing at me. I was told yet again that I'm going to die. Voices were all around me. Stall shook some more. I ran out half-naked. Not much to say, really." Tim was tired of this.

"O.k. then. But you didn't *see* anything?"

"Nope. It was almost worse not seeing because I was left to imagine what was there."

"What did you imagine was there?"

"Let's just say that I'll be drinking plenty of this stuff so I won't dream and I may never use a public toilet again," he said patting the Monster Java.

Paul was about to say something but changed his mind. Tim was getting frailer by the hour, it seemed. One new scare after another was more than his system could take. He was tense, on edge, and shaky. And now he was about to put enough caffeine in his system to achieve immortality. Paul might try to diffuse his friend with some light conversation and silent prayer. Only God could handle this situation anyway.

"So, find us a station or something, man. If we're both staying up all night then we'll need the proper tunes to do it." Paul was still driving so he wanted to give Tim something to do if even for a second. Anything to take his mind off of whatever just happened.

Tim jumped at the chance to be something other than the victim for a moment.

"We need something peppy but not obnoxious. Something we can sing to if the mood hits." Tim was saying. He was a really good musician in Paul's opinion.

"You're the singer, dude. You know I'm not so musically inclined. But hey, my singing would definitely keep you awake." Paul wasn't just practicing false humility, he really couldn't sing so well. Tim had never been so brazen as to tell him this but apparently, he was self-aware enough to pick up on it.

"Yeah, but you play a mean steering wheel," Tim consoled.

Paul squinted his eyes and did his best Napoleon Dynamite, taking them back several years. "Yeah, I'm probably the best one I know at it." The two laughed and Paul thought it was good to laugh for a minute. Tim *needed* to laugh. Heck, Paul needed to laugh. This was pretty taxing on his nerves as well.

Of course, he wasn't bearing the brunt of the situation but he was definitely involved in this scenario. He was, as they say, *invested* in this situation. He was sporting cuts and bruises, he was pretty sleep-deprived, and he was traveling across three states in the middle of the night to try and track down a childhood friend with possible information about a childhood bully who may or may not be somehow involved in the kidnapping of his best friend's family. Yeah, he was a bit stretched at the moment.

On top of all of this, he was becoming more and more convinced that they were dealing with something supernatural. This was more than childhood fears coming back to roost. No, Paul was about to drop a bomb on Tim and finally share what he believed to be the truth behind all this. They had tap-danced around it all night and Paul had been so close to telling him but one thing or another kept getting in the way.

As the music began to fill the SUV Paul decided to just go ahead and be as straightforward with this as he could. Surely Tim wouldn't just cast him off after all that had happened that night. Paul again prayed that God would give him the words.

CHAPTER TEN

"So, we never finished talking in your kitchen." Paul jumped in.

"No? I thought you offered your two cents. This is some spiritual but not-religious thing, right?" Tim summed up thirty minutes of theological discussion in one sentence. That might not be a good thing but then he might just be dodging the issue as well.

"My *two cents*, as you call it, was interrupted when we started our computer search. I wasn't finished, remember?"

"My apologies. Please proceed," he said with a rolling wave of his hand.

It was now or never.

"All right. You know how we were talking about God and angels and spiritual warfare?"

"Warfare?" Tim asked with his eyebrows raised.

"Well, we didn't call it that but the fact that if God is real then the devil is real and there are angels and demons in the world?"

"Gotcha." Tim nodded.

"Well, I think that this is demonic." There, he said it.

Silence filled the cab of the SUV for several seconds. Paul wanted to go on but he needed to know that he hadn't lost Tim already.

"You know, demons."

"Yeah, I know what demonic means," Tim said with dripping sarcasm. "I'm just trying to wrap my head around it. So, you think that demons took my family, beat us up, and are trying to scare me to death?" Tim was trying to make sense of it but was not having any luck.

"Well, no, not exactly. I mean, I don't know who took your kids and I'm pretty sure that those were real people in the alley. I just know that I'm getting more and more convinced that there is a demonic force driving the situation here. I feel it." Paul was hoping Tim would jump on board with this idea but it wasn't very promising to look at his face right now.

"A demonic force? Listen, I'm not belittling your beliefs or anything but I'm not one to go for those kinds of theories. If I can touch it, it's real."

"Then how do you explain evil?" Paul shot back.

"How do I explain evil? I guess evil is bad people doing bad things."

"What's *bad*?"

"What do you mean, 'what's bad'? Bad is... not good. Hurting people. Taking advantage of them. Causing them harm for selfish gain. Stuff like that."

"How much harm? What kind of hurt?" Paul was goading him into a line of thought.

"What the heck do you think? You know what evil is!" Tim was a bit frazzled and not really in a mood for semantic debate.

"I'm just trying to get you to see that you can't just arbitrarily assign something as evil or bad. There has to be a way to determine how bad something is. Thus, there has to be something to measure it by. There has to be a standard for both good and evil."

"OK. So, what is this *standard*?" Tim was playing along now.

"God."

"God is the standard of evil?"

"That's just it. God is the standard of perfect goodness. He is perfectly good because he is *holy,* set apart. All things are measured by his standard."

"Then nothing could compare to perfection." Tim deduced.

"Exactly!" Paul was excited now.

"Why is that good news? I don't follow."

"God is the only truly good thing. All else pales in comparison. We think we're *good enough* but that's a false ideal. Nobody is good enough. When we hold ourselves up to God, we see how *not* good we truly are."

"I can see that, I guess. So how does evil come into play?"

"Evil is the absence of good." Paul had taught a Bible study up at Brunson one semester after some students were convicted of a hate crime against a homosexual student. He simply called it 'The Problem of Evil.'

"You see," he continued, "just like darkness is not really a *thing* but is only the absence of light, so evil is not really a *thing* but is the absence of good or God. Man does things that are ungodly or mean. He commits hateful acts and hurts people. We call this 'evil'. Anything that falls short of God's standard is evil but we tend to overlook the less intense sins and brand only the big ones as evil.

"Some people differ over the opinion that abortion is *evil* and yet most unchurched people and Christians alike would agree that bombing an abortion clinic is *evil*. Many people are fond of calling something evil while overlooking their own propensities to perform morally wrong actions."

"Ok, Mr. Vocabulary. I'm trying to hang with you here, but are you basically saying that everybody is evil in varying degrees?"

"*There is no one good, no not one*," Paul answered.

"I assume you're quoting the Bible when you sound all official like that."

"Yep. The Bible makes it clear that all mankind has sinned and fallen short of God's standard. We are all evil in that sense. But God still loves us and while we were yet sinners, Jesus died for us. He *makes* us good by *his* goodness. The Bible says that our righteousness, or goodness, is like a filthy rag. Our best is simply far from good enough."

"So, Christians are good but the rest of us are still dirty sinners?"

"Christians are no better than anyone else, we are just as in need of God's grace and forgiveness as anyone. But we are viewed by what Jesus did for us and not what we have tried to do on our own. Every human being is sinful. God provided a way to remove those sins by dying on a cross. True Christians live at the cross, knowing that we are not good on our own, we are made right with God by the death and resurrection of Jesus."

"True Christians. What do you mean by that?"

Paul knew this would be a little sticky but trusted that by continuing to be straightforward, God's truth would do its thing.

"Not everyone who claims to be a Christian is, in fact, a true follower of Christ. Many call themselves Christians simply because of a denominational upbringing. Some think being American is synonymous with being a Christian. But Jesus made it clear that only those who love, trust, and follow him are his true disciples."

"Jesus said that. Seems a little harsh."

"Not at all. It's actually the most loving thing he could say. He refers to it as the 'sheep and the goats.' One day he will separate those who truly follow him from those who just gave lip service to him. A real Christian is known by his love and the fruit of his life."

"So, Jesus decides who is sincerely his follower and who's a sham? And only those who really love him are Christians? And everybody else is just, what, self-deluded?"

"Sometimes. People believe what they want. But some are raised with a false sense of security, too. I find most of my students come to our ministry just because they were raised Baptist. But once they start to understand what authentic faith looks like many really trust Christ for the first time. It's really cool."

"But Jesus is still the only real way to God, according to you?"

"Of course, but not according to me. According to the Bible. Jesus is God, as we discussed earlier, so only his death would be sufficient to remove and forgive sin. Without Jesus, a person is still guilty of sin. It doesn't matter if it's a little sin or a bunch of big ones, we all sin.

"Anywho, the basic message is that Christians are people who have come to Jesus and admitted their sinfulness and accepted what Jesus did for them on the cross. Then, the perfect goodness of Jesus is applied to their tab, so to speak, and they are judged not by their own goodness but in the perfection of Jesus that now covers them."

As they passed a mile marker Paul took note that it was only another 106 miles to Mobile. He checked the gas was glad they'd stopped when they did so they would make it through Mobile with no problem and then he would push it to Louisiana. They'd be there in about an hour if Smokey didn't stop them. The rain was still a factor but it seemed to have let up a bit.

Then Tim made a statement that threw Paul for a loop. He expected some great opposition to the "only Jesus" line of thought he laid out but Tim surprised him.

"It still sounds a little too good to be true to me. We mess up, we sin, we disobey God and then he dies on the cross so we can go to Heaven? Why on earth would he do that?" Tim was trying to come around it seemed but was still not quite buying in.

"Because love isn't something that God *does*. He is love. He loves us so fiercely that he would die for us." Paul simply stated. "*Greater love has no man than to lay down his life for a friend.* Jesus wants to forgive us and love us and be with us. Most people assume that if we are such bad people then we should bust our humps trying to be good, somehow to even the score with God. Such people will work themselves to death all the while motivated by guilt, all for nothing. Salvation is a gift of God that isn't earned, it's achieved only by faith. That's grace. I know it doesn't jive with our American pragmatic thinking, but that's how the Gospel works."

"Ok, so back to the whole *evil* issue. Christians are good, everybody else is evil." Tim was doing his best not to be so difficult but he wasn't going to roll over on this issue either.

Paul took a deep breath. Then another. He looked over at Tim sitting there. Wife and kids missing. No sleep. Scared to the point of paranoia. Paul needed to be careful with him right now and not seek to "win" this debate. It was way too important to him that Tim feel loved and safe with him.

"You aren't *evil*, Tim." He finally said. "You are, by all human standards, a good and decent man. You are a caring man and a good husband and father. I think you are an excellent human being. In fact, you're one of the greatest people I know in my life." Paul meant every word of that, too.

Tim was temporarily taken aback by Paul's kind words. He then realized that he was being more obstinate than necessary with Paul. Paul was trying to explain his belief system and shed some light on his thoughts and Tim was trying to poke holes in those beliefs because they didn't make sense to him. This didn't need to be a religious debate. He softened a bit and restated himself.

"Ok. So, Christians are no longer guilty of sin but the rest of us are? When God says 'game over' then Christians go to Heaven and everybody else to Hell, right? That is basically what you're saying isn't it?"

Paul calculated his words. "Basically, yeah. Anyone who rejects Jesus on earth is choosing Hell. But please understand that God doesn't want people to go to Hell any more than you do. Even more so because we are his creation and He loves even the ones we don't. Jesus died for everybody, not just the pretty people. But that doesn't make Christians any better than anyone else. We are all guilty of sin, those who trust Christ are just forgiven of it."

Then Tim logged his greatest protest against Christianity. He honestly hoped Paul had a good explanation for this one.

"And this means that all other faiths of the world are wrong. Millions of people are misled and duped into thinking their religion is ok, but it's Jesus or nothing. That's so narrow, dude." Tim was looking at Paul with desperation to understand.

"There have been different religions and gods since the beginning. The First Commandment is that we shall have no other gods but *the* God. The devil has been seeking his spotlight forever and that's why there are so many false religions in the world. Tons of faiths seem nice and sweet and good on the surface but really are ploys of the devil. Scripture says that satan comes as an angel of light, but is actually the father of lies. Both Joseph Smith and Mohammed were visited by "angels" who taught them the *real* truth of Christianity. That's how this whole demon/angel thing works."

"Nice segue," Tim mocked a little. "So, Muslims and Mormons are following a demonic religion. That'll go over nicely with Liz's mom." As he had previously mentioned, Tim's mother-in-law was a Mormon, but not the most devout one. She would drink caffeine and swear and stuff. She went to church on occasion but Liz's dad was a military man who didn't subscribe to religion much. "Seriously, though. You're saying all other religions are *demonic?*" Tim still had a hard time with this.

"I'm saying that there is One true God. Jesus Christ is that God and any other gospel is a false one that is a satanic tool to get people away from the Truth. The Bible is the Word of God and cannot be changed, added to, subtracted from, or given a companion to. I know this sounds narrow, and it is in a way, but as I said in your kitchen, there is one way, one truth, one life and that's Jesus."

Paul knew where this line of thought came from, as he also wrestled with such clearly drawn lines of faith sometimes.

"You are looking at your friends who are of different faiths and thinking they are good folks. I'm sure they are. But remember, good isn't the goal here. Being faithful to their specific religion isn't the goal. If there is one way then that applies to everyone. I found that way in college, or rather it found me."

"You mean God found you?" Tim was intrigued by the statement. "What does that mean?"

As if on cue the radio began to fill the car with the sounds of the Doobie Brothers' *Jesus Is Just Alright With Me*. Both Tim and Paul chuckled at the melodic irony. It was good that they could laugh right now. Paul continued, a little more light-hearted.

"It means, as I said earlier, that God is always at work in the world trying to get our attention and get us to his truth. The Holy Spirit is constantly at work in people's hearts leading them to himself. But the devil is hard at work getting people distracted and comfortable where they are. When I look back at my childhood, now I can see God at work. It's cool. As a teenager and college student, I was oblivious to God but when I look back through the eyes of my faith, I can see God at work so many times. Calling me, protecting me, wooing me. It's all quite awesome, really."

Tim was almost jealous of Paul's faith again. He seemed so at peace with it. So comfortable in his skin. So sure of his declarations that Jesus was the only way. Maybe he was. Maybe Christians were too full of themselves and just didn't want to share the playing field. Either way, Paulie was a good guy and a great friend and he was the most authentic Christian Tim ever knew.

"Ok. So, the other religions are the devil's schemes to manipulate mankind. Jesus is the only true God and the only way to Heaven. God forgives the sins of those who believe and trust Jesus. What does that have to do with my situation?" Tim asked with no malice in his words.

Paul was impressed with Tim's summation of their conversation so far.

"Everything, I think," Paul said with utter conviction.

"Explain," Tim requested.

"Stay with me, man. This might get wacky again," Paul warned. Tim sort of smiled and waved his hand again to continue. "I have no idea the reason, but it seems to me that you are under a spiritual attack of sorts."

"The devil is out to get me?" Tim asked jokingly.

"Pretty much." Paul was dead serious. He gave his statement a second to hang in the air before continuing. "Scripture says that satan roams around like a lion seeking whom he can devour. It says he only seeks to steal, kill, and destroy. Sounds crazy but I think what you're going through is demonic. And again, I don't know who has your family or what's going on but, from what you describe you're going through the past eight hours I would say that something evil is at work in your thoughts and is possibly behind the physical attacks as well."

"How is that possible? Aren't angels and demons and stuff spirits? How can a demon take my wife or punch me in the face?" Tim couldn't believe he was entertaining these thoughts but he was at least curious as to how all this might work.

"Well, you're half right. Demons are spirits but they can both take bodily form and take over a person's body at times, according to the Bible."

"You're talking demonic possession? Tell me you aren't serious." Tim was incredulous. "This isn't some B-rated horror movie, man, this is my life!"

"I know this is your life but I'm telling you that the Bible not only says that it happens but has several recorded instances of demonic possession as well as people talking to demons and angels." Paul was calm but insistent. "If it was real then, it's real now."

Tim looked at Paul for what seemed like an hour and finally spoke again. "So, what happened in the Bible when this demonic possession stuff happened?"

Paul was a little surprised that Tim opened up to that line of questioning and jumped at a chance to share. "The most abundant records are in the Gospels, you know Matthew, Mark, Luke, and John. They all tell of the life, death, and resurrection of Jesus. There were many times that Jesus traveled to desolate places where he had a showdown with a demoniac, sometimes in a town that had several of them."

"But come on. Surely these were people suffering from some undiagnosed disease or some form of schizophrenia. You can't say that they were possessed by a demon."

"The Bible was pretty clear in its delineation between a person who had a disease and a demoniac. Luke was a physician and knew well about diseases like epilepsy and more mental issues like psychoses. He even said that Jesus went around healing the sick *and* driving out demons. Plus, when the possessed person saw Jesus, they always cried out and said things like, 'Son of Man what do you want with us.' Jesus would tell them to hush and come out. And they did."

"Interesting," was all Tim could muster.

"Jesus wasn't the only one in the Bible to do this either. He empowered his followers to do it. He sent out seventy-two of his followers once and they reported the casting out of demons in his name. Another Scripture says the other disciples were able to perform this miracle in his name, too. My favorite demonic encounter in Scripture happened when a group of brothers tried to cast out a demon in Jesus' name but they weren't even his followers."

"How's that? They weren't Christians but used Jesus' name to cast out demons?" Tim was intrigued.

"They tried to. They were sons of a Jewish priest named Sceva. They apparently thought it was cool the way the disciples were going around casting out demons so they went to a demoniac's house and said 'in the name of Jesus, who Paul preaches, come out!' It wasn't pretty."

"What happened?"

"The Bible says, in Acts 19, that the demon answered them, 'Jesus we know and we've heard of Paul, but who are you?' and then beat the snot out of 'em." They shared a chuckle at that. "They ran out in the street naked and bruised. You don't go around misusing Jesus' name."

"Guess not." Tim mulled over the story a moment. "So, anyone who is a Christian can tell a demon what to do?" He was curious as to how it worked.

"Uh, that's an interesting way to put it. Jesus has all power and authority so in his name Christians can do whatever he wants them to. He told his followers that they would perform many signs and miracles in his name. He even said that his followers would perform more miraculous things than he did. Demons must submit to Jesus since he's God. When we use his name and authority, we get the same red-carpet treatment."

Tim had a strange look on his face. "So, if there is a demon attacking my mind, as you say, then you can tell it to go back to hell and leave me alone?"

Paul often wondered to himself what he would do face to face with a demoniac and always saw himself victorious in battle. He would stand with his chest puffed out for all the other demons to see and proclaim himself the mighty demon slayer. That fantasy didn't feel quite so likely after the events they'd been through this night. Still, he would use the authority Christ had given him to battle if necessary and he would do whatever it took to protect his friend.

"I'll do whatever I can. If this is something demonic then I am certain that God will provide us the tools we need to beat it. But there is one thing that concerns me."

"I know, I'm not a believer therefore I don't have any authority, right?" Tim was a bright guy. He liked to feign ignorance in discussions about religion or politics but the truth was that he could hold his own intellectually with just about anyone. Paul was always impressed with his grasp on deep issues.

"Nail on the head, my friend. It's just that I want you to be able to deal with this but right now you simply can't."

"Well, that's why I'm lucky I have you. I'll let you do the spiritual stuff and I'll concentrate on finding my family. Somebody has them and that somebody is going to be very sorry when I find him."

"I'm not sure that's how all this is going to go down but I'm in your corner, I promise you that."

Tim and Paulie didn't try to be brave for one another. They both readily admitted their lack of confidence in the situation but Paul saw beyond the *"what was"* to what *"could be."* Tim was still pretty understandably focused on the immediate reality. Within a few more hours they would be in New Orleans and what waited there was more than either was currently ready for.

PART TWO

"For our struggle is not against flesh and blood, but against the rulers, against the authorities, against the powers of this dark world, and against the spiritual forces of evil in the heavenly realms."

EPHESIANS *6:12*

CHAPTER ELEVEN

The next couple of hours went by with relative ease. The rain began to lighten and they were able to pick up some speed. Neither said anything but it was as if they were being ushered into the city. It wasn't the most comforting feeling that someone, or something, was waiting on their arrival.

They both agreed that it was probably best for Paul to drive. He was a trooper about it. By this time both were dead tired but knew sleep wasn't an option just yet. Not only would they have to try to contact Gabe at four-thirty in the morning because of the one-hour time difference, but then they would have to hightail it back for Tim not to seem suspicious for leaving town.

They only hoped that Gabe would be able to shed some light on their otherwise pitch-black situation. Tim hoped that he wouldn't come off as some psych ward escapee or something. At this point, he felt like one so it wouldn't be that big of a shock. Paul began to slow down and put his blinker on as they approached a BP gas station.

"Seems like we just stopped for gas. You don't think we could make it there?" Tim recalled their last pit stop. They were coming into Slidell, the town just opposite Lake Pontchartrain which you cross to get into New Orleans.

"Uh, we're already below a quarter of a tank and gas is crazy expensive across the lake. This is probably our last fill-up until the return trip." Paulie understood Tim's hesitance, but gas wasn't going to put itself in the tank either. "I know these exits pretty well and this is probably the last one unless we go through New Orleans into Metairie. I'm not sure where all we're going but to be safe, we need to go ahead and fill up now."

"But hasn't it been a few years since you were here? I heard it's really bounced back." That was true, but Tim was still stalling.

The Big Easy lights weren't quite as bright at this hour but still caused the sky above the lake to turn a brilliant purple. Streaks of pale-yellow office lights pushed their way through from the downtown high rises. The sun would start to rise in about an hour or so and then the sky would be a majestic site over the water. With any luck, they would be on their way home by then.

"Look at that sky," Paul was trying to lighten Tim's tension.

"Nice," was all Tim could muster.

"Nice? A popsicle is nice. Coming in under bogey is nice. An early morning sky is God's signature on a new day. It's his way of letting us know we have at least one more chance to live for him before he pulls the plug on this world. *Nice.*" Paul was playfully indignant.

"Sorry. It's lovely. Spectacular. Awe-inspiring. I think I'll write a poem and plant a tree."

"Do I detect some sarcasm over there? Maybe a little bite in your tone, sir?"

"Nah, I'm *never* sarcastic."

It was a quote from a skit done by an old eighties comedy team. They used to quote so many movies and stand-up comics in college that people begged them to find new hobbies. Tim's mood was lifting, at least a little.

"Well listen, this BP has a full coffee bar and a pretty nice selection of dried beef jerkies so we're stopping. Stay in the car if you want and I'll get us the goods."

"I'll come in. All that liquid caffeine has worked itself to my bladder so I'd better empty and refill. Wouldn't hurt to get some water so my kidneys don't shut down on me." Tim was trying.

"Alrighty then. I'll join you at the urinals and we can stand in awkward silence together."

"Sounds like a plan."

As the Tahoe pulled up to the pump Tim noticed that it was a truck stop rest area as well. A few big rigs were in the back parking lot, no doubt housing some sleepy drivers. That meant that they would carry the good stuff here. Tim was plotting his next caffeine purchase before they killed the engine. He told himself that he needed to be awake for what might happen but he also knew that he was nervous. It made him sick to his stomach that while his family was missing, he was too afraid to go to the bathroom by himself. What had become of him in these last few hours that he couldn't get over these irrational fears of his? But it was these outlandish hallucinations that were shaking his resolve to the core. He could hear Del's mocking voice in his head. *"Timid Timmy's afwaid of da boogeyman."*

Tim dragged himself out of the car and walked into the store. The familiar sound of the cowbell tied to the door jangled and Tim waited for the usual *"mornin'"* greeting but he was instead greeted with eerie silence. He looked up and noticed that no one was in the store with him. Not even the clerk. The place didn't feel much like a popular truck stop. It felt cold and deserted. There were several ceiling lights burned out and there was a fluorescent light flickering in the middle of the store casting sporadic shadows on everything. Tim had a strange feeling that he was a mental patient of old waiting for his shock therapy to begin.

Something scampered across the floor. Tim only caught it out of the corner of his eye but noted that it was either the biggest rat he'd ever seen or some kind of wild beaver was loose in the store. He was craning his neck to see if he could see where it ran off to and heard another scamper behind him. He wheeled back in time to see a creature with yellow-orange teeth and a long, hairy rat tail.

Nutria, as they're called in New Orleans, are a cross between a beaver and a rat and are supposed to be strict vegetarians. Tim had heard Paul talk about them but they were supposed to live in the waterways and canals and only come out on land to move from water to water. It was a disgusting-looking creature with dark beady eyes and sharp claws used to dig for vegetation.

Tim was in a stare-off with this one when he heard another set of scampering claws on the concrete floor. Then another. And another. Before he could look around and count how many were there, the first one he saw lunged at him. So much for being strict vegetarians. It caught his shin just below the knee and Tim went down hard. These little beasts weighed a good fourteen pounds, easy. It happened too quickly for him to process but he at least knew he didn't want to be on the ground with these things.

He put his hand down to push up and one sunk its teeth in his wrist. Blood sprayed out like a busted garden hose. Tim wailed in pain and shock and yanked his arm away. He shot up to his feet without planting his other hand but it was almost pointless. The floor was changing from a concrete grey to a nutria dirty brown by the second. There had to be dozens of the putrid rats swarming around. How did they even get in?

Tim tried to run for the door and was greeted with a flying beaver-rat coming from a Budweiser display case. It nearly caught him square in the face but, luckily he tripped over one on the floor and it missed. But now he was back on the ground with them. A ground that was now almost completely covered with huge, brown rats.

Tim could feel teeth ripping into his legs and arms but tried to get up anyway. He covered his face because he had no doubt that one was bent on eating his eyes right out of his head at that very moment. He was convinced that his jugular was about to be torn open any second.

One was trying to push its head up his pant leg but was too big to fit. It clamped down on his calf. He was sure he would die in here, eaten by vegetarian beaver-rats. Finally, he summoned enough strength to hurdle himself to the door on his knees and grabbed the cowbell-clad handle. He had to push past a huge nutria, hissing and clawing at his eyes just to get the door open but then he tumbled out screaming for Paul.

Paul came running over to Tim lying on the ground in the middle of the doorway. The clerk behind the counter had a bewildered look on his face and Paul could only assume that Tim had suffered another attack of some sort. Tim was kicking his feet at nothing and Paul reached his hand down to help him up. Tim slowly realized the situation. He stayed there on his knees for a second, embarrassed and unsure of anything. Finally, he took Paul's hand and rose to his feet.

No blood. No beaver-rats. Just the awkward stare of a bewildered stranger, once again.

"Hey, don't let it get you. Your mind is fragile right now. You know whatever it was is gone, right?" Paul tried to comfort him.

Tim stood there holding his wrist. He examined it and found no bite marks from yellow-toothed rats. It was just in his mind, apparently, again. He began to question his ability to be of any help to his family in this state and almost began to weep. But his love for them was far stronger than his self-pity and he regained his composure quickly.

"Yeah. I know. But it was the most real feeling I've ever had. The pain and fear were real even if the rats weren't."

"Rats? Man, that's a real mind job."

"Huge, brown rats with glow-in-the-dark teeth."

"Nutria? You were attacked by nutria?" Paul asked with wonder.

"Apparently not. But yeah. Hundreds of 'em. All over the floor biting and clawing at me from head to toe. Not fun." Tim could still feel the sting in his shin from the first bite. His calf ached a dull pain as if it had actually been bitten into.

"You know they're vegetarians, right?"

"Not in my psycho world. I was dinner tonight." Tim could see the absurdity but the mind can make something seem so real that it doesn't have to make sense.

"Fair enough. Still have to pee?"

"Thank God yes. I'm just glad that I didn't leave the night clerk a present on the floor."

Tim didn't want to go back in and face the clerk after what must have appeared to be him having a psychotic breakdown. But the truth was that he was honestly too tired and frayed to care right now what others thought of him. Ever the vigilant friend, Paul walked in ahead of Tim and whispered loudly to the clerk behind the counter, "He's crazy. Don't look at him. Deathly afraid of Twinkies. Freaks him out." Tim tried not to smile despite himself as the clerk tried to make sense of his outburst and Paul's revelation.

A few minutes later the tank was full, their bladders were empty, and they hit the road for what they hoped would be a light-shedding conversation with Gabe Whitten.

CHAPTER TWELVE

As they made their way across Lake Pontchartrain, Paul was amazed to see how much had been done on it since his last visit in 2012. Like many others in various parts of the country, he didn't fully grasp the widespread, long-term damage to New Orleans because he didn't live there anymore. Some things around here took ten or more years to rebuild, but they were looking good now.

They zipped down I-10 into New Orleans east and Tim was impressed at how clean it looked. He expected abandoned car lots and flooded out houses for no other reason than it was still 2005 in his mind. Whole shopping complexes would be deserted. Entire car lots would be empty. But, other than a few empty houses and apartment complexes, everything seemed pretty normal.

Paul was pretty quiet taking it all in and Tim honored that with his silence. For the second time Tim was struck with the realization that Paul once lived here and, for that matter, thousands of others used to live here up until that late August day.

"Used to buy my running shoes there," Paul said as he pointed to what used to be a decent-sized Mall. "Malls over here in the East weren't nearly as crowded as in Metairie or Kenner. Prices were pretty good too." His nostalgic tone was laced with a hint of... longing. He must miss this town.

"You ever think about coming back here?" Tim knew Paul loved it here, but once he graduated he followed 'the call' back to Georgia. Paul was a single man and a free spirit and it wouldn't shock Tim at all if here were to announce one day that he was moving to some exotic location to do some dangerous missionary work or something. Paul would follow his God anywhere, it seemed. Tim was once again jealous of such a strong relationship with God. His was peripheral at best.

"If I felt like God was telling me to, I'd be back in a flash."

"So, how's that work, exactly?" Tim inquired.

"How's what work?" Paul didn't quite follow the question.

"The whole 'if God tells me' thing. I mean, is there a burning bush or does He shoot you an e-mail? How do you know when God is talking to you?"

"Ah. Well, how do you know that I'm talking to you?" Paul asked quizzically.

"This isn't one of those Grasshopper moments, is it? When I take the pebble from your hand and leave no prints on the sand, only then I'm ready?"

"Uh, no. Simple question, simple answer. How do you know when it's me that's talking to you and not some telemarketer?"

"You're right here with me."

"Fair enough. But what if you couldn't see me. How would you know it was really me?" Paul pressed further.

"I know your voice, for one."

"Exactly." Paul let that sink in for a minute and continued. "Scripture says that the sheep know their Shepherd's voice. Jesus is our Shepherd and when we truly know Him and listen to Him, then we hear Him."

"So, you pray and God talks to you? You hear voices? I guess I'm not the only crazy one." He said with a smirk.

"Yes and no. I mean, the Bible is full of times when God spoke in an audible voice. He often spoke through things like a burning bush or a donkey just to get His point across. Jesus appeared several times after His resurrection and even after he ascended back to Heaven and I believe that He still speaks to us today." It sounded so simple it made sense. "What I do *not* believe is that all these people claiming God told them to kill their kids or steal money or whatever lame thing a televangelist says is from God. God will never contradict Himself and His word is how we can gauge what we think He's saying.

"In other words, I fully believe that God can, and does, speak to me as His child but I also know that I have to be discerning and test that against Scripture to make sure it's really from Him."

"Who else would it be from?" Tim asked a little confused.

"Well, it might be my own thoughts trickling in." He paused for a moment considering their current situation. "It might be demonic."

Tim seemed to mull over what he was saying. Before tonight that statement might have brought some ridicule from Tim but he was more open to the possibility at this point. It was still hard to swallow.

"How can a demon talk to you?"

"Like we were talking about earlier, demons can torment, tempt, and even possess people. Talking to them is just setting the stage. Satan tempted Jesus in the wilderness, why wouldn't he be able to do the same with us? The devil is a liar and his chief weapons are deceit and fear. He might even try to sound like God, which is why you need to know the difference."

"But you've said before that the devil doesn't have power other than what God allows, right? So how can he get in our heads like that?"

"I see it like throwing stones at a window. Satan can only plant seeds of sin. The Book of James tells us clearly that it is the evil within us that causes us to sin. Not the devil, not God, but us. Satan just helps it out by tossing sinful doubts our way or by tossing proverbial rocks at our window. We choose to open the window and listen."

Tim chewed on that for a minute.

"So then, if you don't know the Bible and aren't much of a pray-er you won't know the difference in who's talking to you?" It was more of a statement than a question but Paul answered anyway.

"Pretty much. And the devil is clever, too. He knows how to sound like the good guy when he's actually out to destroy you. Scripture says he comes as an Angel of Light. For those without the Holy Spirit of God, it is almost impossible to tell a difference sometimes."

"That kinda sucks."

"Yeah, it does. But God has given us everything we need to know the difference and to have authority over him. We aren't subject to the will of any demon in hell, thanks to Jesus. We have the same authority over them that Jesus did, in His name."

"What about those Sceva guys? They used His name and got the stuffing kicked out of them."

"True, but what was the difference?" Paul was acting as a teacher now, goading Tim into answering his own argument.

"They weren't actually followers of Jesus and just tried to throw His name around." He said nodding.

"Very good." He said it like he was speaking to a child who gave the right answer. He laid it on thick for Tim. Tim shot him a look. Switching to an ancient Chinese accent Paul continued, "You are nearly ready to take the pebble from my hand, Grasshoppa."

The two rode for a moment in silence taking in the pre-sunrise form of New Orleans. It was so dark in some places you could barely make out the forms of buildings and only a smattering of lights illuminated patches of others.

As they crested the hill of a bridge Paul pointed to his right. "There's the seminary." It was like a beacon of hope in a dark city. It was clean and lit up like a Christmas tree. It almost looked out of place in the darkness. "You'd never know that whole campus was pretty much underwater seventeen years ago."

"That's wild. It looks like nothing happened to it." Tim was impressed.

"Oh, it had some serious damage. The whole back of campus took years to rebuild. They had to tear down everything and rebuild it all. The campus is an old Pecan Grove so it's slightly slanted back. The front of campus had some water damage up to a few feet while third-floor apartments were flooded in the back. I used to live on Lipsey Street. It was the Staff Housing at the time and I was working as a grader and with the Campus Police so I got to live there. It pretty much cut the campus in half. Everything past that street got totaled."

As Paul made his way to exit Tim felt very uneasy. He wanted to say something but felt awkward because he couldn't describe it. Paul noticed but didn't say anything. They pulled around what used to be a Winn Dixie but was now a Wal-Mart Supercenter and turned left onto Gentilly Boulevard. The campus was barely offering life at this hour, but the city was slowly waking up.

"What are we doing here? We need to get to Gabe as fast as possible." Tim wasn't counting on any detours.

"Just a quick stop. I think an old professor of mine might be able to help us out here."

Paul pulled up to the security guard at the front gate. Before Katrina, the campus police force was made up of two types of positions: security guard and Policeman. The security guards wore tan shirts with the campus security logo and carried a Monadnock Friction Baton, flashlight, and a radio. The Campus Police were commissioned officers through the NOPD and wore blue police uniforms and carried loaded .38s with hollow-point bullets, cuffs, Batons, and radios.

For a good while post-Katrina there was just the Campus Police that wore all black, carried shotguns and .38's, and were a good bit more hardcore than the average student. Many of these men were on the campus while Katrina hit and stayed there, stranded for three days after. Ultimately, they followed a backhoe out of the city with loaded shotguns drawn for safety, though mostly just to deter any criminal interference. But now the seminary had gotten back to a state of normalcy and a young officer manned with a clipboard sat in the security check-in booth at the front entry gate.

Paul didn't recognize the young man, but it had been a while since he had been on campus for any length of time. He looked pensive but wasn't rude.

"Can I help you?" he asked.

"Hi, I'm Paul Thibodeaux. I graduated here a few years back. And by 'few' I mean sixteen years ago. I need to speak with Dr. Taylor, please."

The young student\officer wasn't quite sure what to make of them. "It's kind of early, isn't it?" he said sheepishly. He took his radio off his hip and held down his transmission button. "160 to Base, we have a 107 here wanting to talk to Dr. Taylor."

"This early? You'd better call Cappie on this one" was the response.

There was once a fatal flaw of the New Orleans Baptist Theological Seminary Campus Police Force. You had commissioned officers with the power to arrest and use firearms who reported to some bleary-eyed student who worked at the Providence Guest House. The dispatch for the campus police was the campus hotel. Talk about limited jurisdiction.

But post-Katrina there was an actual police station that handled security needs more "in-house." Paul was glad to see that change.

After hearing the exchange Paul spoke up with some calm authority.

"I'm not a 107. I'm a former student. If you call Captain John Wilkes or Lieutenant Brad Dikes and tell them that former officer Paul Thibodeaux is here then this will all work out much quicker." Paul smiled a polite but firm smile.

The young officer was taken back by Paul's knowledge of the Campus Police hierarchy and his claim to have been a part of it. "You were an officer?" he managed.

"Yup. Pre-Katrina. I got out of this place a year after the big one hit but I really need to see Dr. Taylor now, if possible. It is a bit of an emergency. I promise you he won't mind being bothered at this hour." Paul looked at his watch. Almost five. "He's up now anyway. He always does his morning Bible study at 4:30."

"No offense but you two look like you've been in a bar fight or something. I wouldn't normally put my neck on the line like this but since you guys seem to know Dr. Taylor pretty well, I'll call him."

Just as the young officer was about to return to his guard post to get the directory, a figure approached them from the library area. He was an unassuming figure but he walked with purpose. As he came closer Paul smiled widely.

"Mr. Thibodeaux."

"Dr. Taylor."

Tim sat there wondering what in the world was going on and, apparently, so was the officer.

CHAPTER THIRTEEN

"I thought you might be coming here." Dr. Taylor had a gentle voice but something about it resonated with strength. He had the slightest accent but obviously, he had spent much of his time in the states. It was South African if Tim's ear could be trusted.

"Figured I'd save you some trouble and meet you at the gate. G'Morning, Mr. Li," he said looking at the young officer.

"Morning, Dr. Taylor," Stephen Li responded.

Tim wasn't sure what was going on here and he wasn't sure they had time for a class reunion. Dr. Cornelius Taylor, a.k.a. Neil, a.k.a. Dr. Taylor, looked at Tim with wisdom and seasoned compassion. "You must be the young man who needs help." He said with a fatherly tone. He was only older by about fifteen years but he still came across as a father figure.

Tim looked over at Paul. "When did you talk with him?"

"I didn't," Paul answered with a smile.

Now Tim was really confused.

"I had originally planned on going straight out to Tulane Campus but in Slidell, I began to feel like this pit stop was a necessary one for us. I didn't want to bother you with the 'how' factor so I just popped in. This won't take long, I promise. But I think that Dr. Taylor can be useful for us." He looked up at his old friend and mentor. "Can we go to your office and talk?"

"Of course." With that, he patted Stephen on the shoulder and pointed to his office not fifty feet away on the left. Dodd Hall was the first building on campus and there were a few parking spots along the road to its right. They were all empty this time of morning so Paul pulled the Tahoe up to the side of the building and they got out.

There is twenty-four-hour security on campus and many professors keep strange hours, so there is no alarm system in Dodd. Dr. Taylor used his key to open the side double glass door and locked it behind them. His office was the second on the right. It had a smaller office in front where a secretary would take calls, grade papers, and file things for him, and then it opened into a modest-sized office lined with hundreds of books and had one mahogany desk in the middle. There was a single banker's lamp that he pulled the string on that provided ample light to fill the room. They all sat.

"Tell me about your family, Mr..." he looked to Tim for a name.

"Tim. Tim McDaniel." Part of Tim wanted to get up and leave, go straight to Gabe's house, and find the answers that might save his family. But another part of him already trusted this man and wanted to hear what he had to say. Tim took a deep breath and filled him in on the abduction and the events of the last 12 hours or so.

It sounded concocted and fanciful coming out of his mouth. Like folklore or a campfire story. But when he was finished recounting the whole tale Dr. Taylor looked at him with misty eyes.

"I'm so sorry, son." His sincere compassion made Tim want to break down and cry but there was no time for that now. Dr. Taylor ran his hand through his moppy brown hair and sat up straight.

"I bet you're wondering what's behind all of this, aren't you?" he asked like a man about to reveal a magic trick you just couldn't figure out.

"Paul says it's spiritual. *Demonic* was the word. I'm not a religious person, per se, but that is making more sense, I guess. Not to be rude but what can you do to help us?"

Dr. Taylor looked at Paul, then at Tim. He was a rather calm person but his eyes began to dance as he spoke. "I believe that you are on the verge of a cataclysmic spiritual battle. God has shown me my role in this and I have accepted it."

Tim had no idea what to say.

Paul spoke up, almost defending the doctor's claim.

"This guy has been a missionary all over the world. He was raised in South Africa as the son of a missionary couple. He's seen some wild stuff. You talk about hearing God, this guy has a hotline to Heaven like few I've ever known."

Tim had the look of a man who wanted to believe but couldn't get over the craziness of it all. He slowly shook his head until he looked up and asked sheepishly, "So what is your role in all this, then?"

Instead of answering the question directly, he began to share another wild-eyed bit of information. "About a week ago I had a dream. It was the kind you wake from and instantly know it was from the Lord. You were in it." He was excited, it seemed, but he remained calm. Tim lifted his eyebrows in shock that a man he'd never met would dream of him.

"You were standing by a small lake. It was storming outside and debris was flying everywhere. You were rather frightened but determined. A man stood before you laughing, but not an ordinary man. It was you, too." As he said that, Tim's heart almost stopped. "The one of you who was laughing pointed to the water and there was the body of a small boy floating in it. He looked up to you for help. As you jumped in and tried to swim to him and pull him out there suddenly were several young boys in the water with you and the others grabbed you and started pulling you out deeper. They were hellish in appearance but it wasn't their appearance that frightened you, it was that you couldn't get to the other boy. It was *your* boy, I believe.

"You tried to grab hold of the shore but there was nothing to grab as you were already too far out. You tried to fight them off but couldn't. As you fought to free yourself a young girl, who looked to be your daughter, stood off to the side of the shore crying. You tried desperately to reach her but she was too far away. A woman stood on the porch of an old cabin screaming your name. There was a darkness behind her that was coming out onto the porch all around her. You fought harder but the storm raged, the small hands grabbed at your hands and feet, the little girl cried, the little boy was giving up hope and the woman screamed as the darkness wrapped around her.

"As the darkness enveloped the woman the small hands managed to bring you into the water. It appeared the battle was lost. The storm raged, filling the sky with lightning. Hope was slipping away."

At the point of the story where you would expect him to be somber and gentle, he nearly stood as he leaned forward, grinning broadly now.

"But then," he said expectantly, "a great hand from Heaven reached down to you in the water. The storm continued, the darkness swirled and the other *you* laughed with mockery, but the hand reached down to you still. It was a strong hand. It was a mighty hand. It was the hand that would lead you to victory." He said the last part in almost a whisper.

"What happened then?" Tim asked nervously.

"I woke up," he answered flatly, his smile still in place.

Tim sat in stunned silence for a minute. He looked at Paul, then back at Dr. Taylor. He finally spoke, but his tone was bitter now.

"You woke up. Great."

"Don't miss the connotation here, Tim," the doctor was saying. "This is a wonderful opportunity."

"An opportunity for what?" Tim almost shouted coming off his chair. "My family is in danger, I'm apparently in some kind of a losing battle but because some big hand reaches down from heaven, I'm supposed to see the silver lining? Please pardon my lack of insight but kindly explain this opportunity to me."

Dr. Taylor was not offended, nor was he taken back by Tim's lack of understanding. He simply stood, put his hands together like a child about to say a prayer, and said, "All you must do is take the hand."

"That was a waste of time," Tim mumbled as they pulled back onto the main road.

"I don't think it was, man. I think you'll find that Dr. Taylor has a ton of wisdom and experience with this kind of thing." Paul was sympathetic to their time constraints but he knew this was no waste of time. "Besides, how would you explain his dream except that God wanted us to talk with him? And don't feed me any coincidence mumbo jumbo. We both know better than that."

"I can't explain it and I'm not going to try. But it doesn't feel very helpful right now. And what kind of experience does he have to help me? Which part of his life is so like mine? The part where his family is stalked and kidnapped? Or maybe when he was tormented by insane visions? Or the part where he went through months of therapy as a child because of some deranged prank? I'm sorry but I fail to see his credentials in this particular matter. He was a missionary, great. How exactly does that make him an expert here?"

Tim wasn't really like this, Paul knew that. He was dog-tired, stressed to the limit, and scared out of his mind about losing his family. Factor in the freaky visions and you have every reason to be a little testy. But Paul understood a facet of this situation that Tim still refused to fully accept.

"First of all, he's a very godly man who only wants to help." Paul wasn't trying to shame Tim, just stating a fact. "Second, he served as a missionary in Africa, China, India, and Thailand. He has seen his share of spiritual warfare and demonic activity. He was raised in St. Lucia, a coastal town outside of Swaziland. He was seeing demonic activity daily.

"You said I was your go-to guy on the spiritual stuff and he's my go-to guy on spiritual stuff. There was no phone call here, Tim. I knew to come to him and God sent him to the gate to meet us. That in itself should give you some sense of purpose here. Not to mention that he saw a hand of *victory*! That's good, huh?"

Paul was taking some back roads to Gabe's house because he wasn't getting back on I-10. At this time of the morning, it was still plenty dark but the early morning sun was revealing brightly colored houses everywhere.

"I hope it's good because right now I feel anything but victorious."

. They weaved through back roads in silence for a few minutes until instinctively Tim pulled out the printed page with Gabe's address on it.

"He went to Tulane, right?" Paul asked.

"Uh, yeah. I guess this is his old college address but maybe someone can get us a more current one."

"Well, if he went to Tulane, he was either pretty smart, pretty wealthy, or pretty lucky. Or a nice combination of the three. Chances are good that he had a house off-campus and might even still live there."

Tim hoped so. As the sun began to paint parts of the sky a lighter purple the realization of how much trouble he could get in dawned on him anew.

"You think Detective Peters is going to bust us?"

"Bust us? We're not selling Crystal Meth here, man."

"You know what I mean. I could get put in a bad situation if this proves to be a wild goose chase. I need to call my uncle and tell him that I won't be in until after lunch and that if anyone comes looking for me to call my cell." The last thing they needed was to come all this way for nothing.

Paul knew this and prayed fervently that this wasn't a wild goose chase for Tim's sake and the sake of his family. However you looked at it, time seemed to be a precious commodity that they were a little short on right now. Paul didn't want to alarm Tim but he was starting to get a not-so-great feeling about this encounter. Apparently, Tim picked up on it.

"What aren't you telling me?" Tim asked.

"Nothing," Paul answered unconvincingly.

Tim stared at him for a moment as if maybe his thoughts would pour from his head like a teleprompter or something. He let it go and looked at the page in his hand.

"His place is on Freret Street," he said with the typical French pronunciation.

"Down here most people say it with the hard 't'. He must have had some money to have a house on Freret." Paul remarked.

Tim had no idea where they were but after a couple of turns, he looked up and they were on Freret. After conferring on the street numbers Paul pulled up into a large, two-story antebellum home. There were hundreds like it in this area, but either none were too damaged on this side of town, or money to fix them was no object. There were no lights on but they had come too far to worry about waking someone up.

"Ready?" Paul asked. He was still pensive but Tim chalked it up to the weirdness of the night.

Tim took a deep breath, exhaled in a puff, and said, "Yep."

CHAPTER FOURTEEN

L iz didn't know how long she lay there in the dark, gagged, blindfolded, and hogtied. At some point in the Tahoe, she had closed her eyes for a moment and was overcome with fatigue that wouldn't allow her to open them again until now. She had no idea where she was or where her children were. Or how they had gotten to wherever it was they were. This made her struggle against her restraints to the point that she could feel the blood trickle down her arms and legs.

Strangely, she wasn't so much concerned with where they were but why were they there? She tried to scream but it was a muffled nothing of a sound. She couldn't stand up and the absolute darkness made it impossible to get a bearing on the room she was in. She strained her ears to hear but only heard the faint ticks of her own body and her ragged breath.

If she could work the blindfold off, she might be able to find a way out of this but blind, bound, and gagged she was helpless. She flexed her facial muscles and raised her eyebrows but the blindfold was there to stay. She could easily tell that it was just as useless to try and push the gag from her mouth by the tightness she could feel with her tongue.

It was a strange feeling to be so limited in the use of her five senses. She felt like she could just as well be in a cardboard box on Broadway in New York and never know it. Aside from the earthy smell of wood, she could have been back in the womb for all she knew. Her mind flooded with questions she couldn't answer.

Where were her children? What had the faux Tim done with them? Who was he? If she had no idea where she was how could her Tim ever find them? This seemed to be a hopeless situation but she was a fighter. And strangely, a voice from somewhere deep inside the darkness with her encouraged her, gave her hope. She felt the desolation and despair but this voice seemed to keep them on the periphery. She was not swallowed by them. She could tell herself that Tim would find them. She knew it. She had to know it. Because if she didn't know it then all was lost.

But there was another voice in the darkness. A strange, evil voice that she faintly recognized. Was it only in her mind or did she really hear it? It pounded its message relentlessly through her mind and heart. It kept repeating its macabre mantra over and over and over until she almost believed it was a simple statement of fact... *"you're gonna die."*

CHAPTER FIFTEEN

Tim and Paul stepped up onto the front porch of the beautiful, albeit run-down, two-story antebellum home. It was a faded gray and it didn't take long to see that it lacked a woman's touch. The old couch on the porch surrounded by beer bottles and cigarette butts was the first clue. Paul gave three quick raps on the door.

The guy who eventually opened the door was bleary-eyed and was not accustomed to waking at 5:30 in the morning very often, if ever.

"Yeah?" was his greeting.

"Hi, uh, we're looking for Gabe Whitten. This was his last address that I could find." Tim looked around the man into the house hopefully. "Is he here?"

"You know Gabe?"

Thank God.

"Yeah, well, a long time ago. We need to speak with him. It's an emergency." Tim's desperation didn't seem to give any aid to the rousing of the man at the door.

"Ain't here. Hasn't been for a couple years. Used to crash here between binges but now he lives down at some shelter or somethin'. Downtown."

Binges? Shelter? This certainly didn't sound like Gabe but it had been an awfully long time.

The three of them stood there for a few seconds and the sleepy man picked up on the fact that these guys weren't leaving without some more information. He peered up warily through dirty brown hair that hadn't been washed in a couple of days.

"The name's Trey. I've been friends with Gabe since high school. When did you say you knew him?" he asked probingly.

Tim understood that he and Paul might look a little suspicious showing up so early looking for Gabe. He wanted Trey to be as helpful as he could so he was honest with him.

"We went to camp together in sixth grade. Camp Muscogee. I only knew him that one summer but something happened at that camp that I think Gabe might be able to help me put some pieces together that would help me find my missing family. I know it's nuts but I don't have time to tell you everything right now."

"You Tim?" Trey asked with an eyebrow raised.

Shocked but not too freaked out Tim looked at Paul and answered, "Yeah." He wasn't sure why but he stuck his hand out. "Tim McDaniel."

Trey took his hand with what seemed like pity and awe.

"Gabe mentioned you a few times over the years. More recently it was all he could think about, it seemed."

"Why more recently? I haven't spoken to him in almost thirty years."

"I don't know, man. Gabe was kinda troubled, ya know? He was cool for a while but just a few years ago it cranked up big time."

Paul decided to join the conversation.

"How do you mean, troubled?"

Trey looked him over and decided he was trustworthy. He tipped his head over to the couch and pulled the door shut behind him as if he didn't want to disturb the other inhabitants who were occupying couches and mattresses on the floor in the dining room. He plopped down and offered a seat to Tim and Paul. Paul grabbed the wicker chair and Tim stood. Trey took in a deep breath and blew it out fast.

"Well, he and I hooked up freshman year in high school. We both went to Jefferson in Metairie. I was a sophomore his senior year. Neither of us was really into anything so we just kinda hung out. Not much for the extra-curricular, if ya know what I mean." He patted his pockets then hopped up off the couch with his finger up. He stepped through the door and came back a second later with a pack of Marlboros and a Zippo knock-off.

He lit the white stick and took a big drag. Blowing the smoke out the side of his mouth he continued.

"He was kinda jacked-up from your camp deal. He went to a counselor and stuff once a week, that I know of. He had bad nightmares and saw stuff sometimes."

Tim and Paul looked at each other again and Tim asked the million-dollar question. "Saw stuff like what?"

Trey scratched his long goatee mulling over what exactly he should say. He rolled his eyes as if to surrender to the truth and leaned in close to Paul and Tim.

"Dude said he saw demons."

He sat back and took another big drag as if to let the word sink in. He must have expected to hear some sort of objection to that because when he didn't hear one and he saw the look on Tim's face, he raised his eyebrows again and said intuitively, "Guess he ain't the only one."

"What happened after that? He obviously went to college and stuff." Tim was looking for any sign that there was hope for him in this conversation.

"Well, yeah. He and I discovered the healing power of weed in high school and the demons seemed to go away. His nightmares pretty much stopped and he lived a pretty normal life 'til a few years after graduating from Tulane."

Paul prodded. "Then what?"

"His folks were pretty well off so we knew from his graduation we were gonna go to Tulane, live together and party like rock stars. He knocked out a couple years of school until I joined him and then we were on track still livin' that dream right up until a few years ago.

"We had this awesome place," he said sweeping his hands around displaying the porch, "that's like a minute from campus. We both went the business school route so we could have plenty of social time. We took our sweet time getting out of here, like 7 or 8 years or so for a B.S. And to top it all off we had this buddy who could score us all kinds of goodies, cheap."

Tim hated to think of his innocent friend from camp doing drugs and *partying like a rock star* but to be honest, he had self-medicated for the longest time as well. Drunk, stoned, wasted... it was all just a form of escape, wasn't it?

"But then," his tone changed and Tim noticed Paul's brow was furrowed as Trey spoke. "Then those religious whackos tried to *convert* him or whatever."

Tim couldn't miss the disgust in his voice and assumed some blood-drinking cult had assaulted his friend.

"Which religious whackos, exactly?" Paul was the one to seek clarification, though Tim was curious.

"*Baptists.*" He spat out the word. "Those freaks from the BCM up the street there. He started hanging out with them after one of our buddies ODed."

Paul didn't seem to react at all, at least from what Tim could see out of the corner of his eye. He knew Paul wouldn't jeopardize getting some more information from Trey by getting all offended or anything.

"You mean the Baptist Collegiate Ministries people?" Paul asked calmly.

"Yeah, you heard of 'em?" Trey still had a face that looked he took a bite of something sour.

Tim hoped this wouldn't take a wrong turn here but he trusted Paul.

"Yeah. Most of 'em seem like decent folks to me. You know, for Baptists." He added for effect.

"If you say so. Bunch of hypocrites and do-gooders if you ask me. They messed up our plans, big time."

"How so?" Tim asked this time.

"Well, like I said earlier, we had this buddy who scored us good stuff pretty cheap. We had already long since graduated but this house is ours, well Gabe's but still, and we were about to be cut in on a slice of the action. But then our boy Toby did a little too much Heroin one night and we found him dead in the bathroom upstairs. Gabe didn't take it so well. He went to one of those midnight pancake thingies up at the BCM and wound up talking to some dude all night about Jesus and drugs and stuff. Then he quit. Cold Turkey. He didn't want to take 'em or sell 'em. Ruined everything."

It was hard for Tim or Paul to not look at this self-absorbed, drugged-out, middle-class white kid turned burned-out parasite with pity and disgust, but they knew not to bite the hand that could feed them more useful information too quickly. Tim took a cleansing breath and seemed to be searching for the perfect question when Trey started back in.

"He wasn't like *saved* or anything." He did jazz hands when he said the word *saved* for emphasis. "We talked about it and he wasn't so sure about the whole religion thing but he liked the folks up there for whatever reason and hung out with them... a lot. Even though we hadn't been students for like ten years. They still hung out with him and invited him to stuff. They were in my house, man." Paul was surprised that he didn't spit after saying that.

"And you said he got worse after that?" Paul was steering him back on course.

"Not at first but yeah. Way worse. For years he had been fine but then once he gave up the weed for religious nuts, he started having nightmares again. One night, a few years back, he woke up screaming your name." He pointed at Tim as he spoke.

That was kind of a shock. Tim was a little anxious to find Gabe but wanted to know what strange connection he shared with him after so many years.

"*My* name? Why *me*?" Tim asked.

"The whole camp thing, I guess. He said you were, like, attacked... or something and some kid was behind it."

"Did he ever mention a kid named Del?"

"Oh yeah. That's the kid. But towards the end, you know after his breakdown, he said crazy things. Things like Del was the '*demon king*' and junk like that. I thought he was just some mean kid from your camp but Gabe started acting like he was being *tormented* by him or something. Bizarre stuff."

"His breakdown?" Paul got him back on task as he looked at Tim.

Trey shook his head like he had forgotten to add some details. "Yeah, my bad. A couple years ago he snapped. The brain is fragile, ya know?" he said tapping his head. "He had been talking to himself and stuff for a few weeks and had finally stopped going around that BCM, thank God." Paul almost laughed at the irony of such a statement but figured the irony would be lost in the moment and remained quiet.

Trey started a new cigarette and continued. "Then it was getting weird around here because, at first, he still wouldn't participate in our *recreational* drug use but he still looked wasted all the time. Never slept anymore and pretty much stopped eating. Gabe was always kind of a solid guy, ya know? He had that round face and maybe ten extra pounds all the time but towards the end there I hardly recognized him. He looked like a crack-head or something. He fits in fine at that shelter downtown. Those guys creep me out, man. Always twitchin' and talkin' to themselves." This was the second reference to the shelter he made. Tim would definitely find this shelter next but for now, he wanted to hear about Gabe's spiral into darkness.

"Then he all of a sudden starts doing massive amounts of stuff. I thought he must be trying to *OD*. And he did junk he had never tried before too, man. I was a little shocked, to be honest."

"You never tried to stop him?"

"Hey, man. I'm no killjoy. He's a big boy. He can make his own decisions. I'm his friend and all but I don't get into people's business."

Paul knew his type. He used Gabe for fun and connections but as soon as Gabe showed interest in getting clean or took addiction too far, he was a burden. A fair-weather friend was the easiest and most accurate description Paul could think of.

"I asked him once why he was so *cuckoo for cocoa puffs* all of a sudden but he just shot me a look that was all sad and scared and so..."

He trailed off like he forgot the word he wanted to say. Tim and Paul waited uncomfortably for about ten seconds until Paul patiently helped him out.

"So...," he waved his hand in the typical 'go on' manner.

After thinking for another few seconds, he finally chose his word and looked up with a resolute face. There was a moment when Tim was about to burst, wishing he would hurry up and finish his thought but then he nearly whispered the word that struck fear even deeper into Tim's heart. "Defeated."

CHAPTER SIXTEEN

After getting what Trey *thought* was the name of the shelter downtown, Paul and Tim were quick to get on to their search for Gabe. The French Quarter was only ten minutes from the campus so they hopped in the Tahoe and headed out down St. Charles.

"You think you should call Detective Peters now?" Paul asked.

"Let's find Gabe first. If he goes all 'by the book' on us then we'll have to head out and I want to make this trip worth it. I'll need to call Liz's mom, too." Tim sounded distant and he was lost in thought.

"What are you thinking?" Paul wondered aloud.

Tim rubbed his day's growth of stubble and sighed. He took in a deep breath and was about to say something but then he just exhaled and started the process again.

"What?" Paul goaded.

After a few moments of contemplative silence, Tim answered his question with a question.

"Am I like that to you?"

"Like what?" Paul asked with his brow furrowed. Then an incredulous smile crossed his lips. "Like Trey? Are you serious?!"

"I mean, do I act like that?" Tim wondered.

"Dude! He makes Shaggy seem like an intellectual. He's a user and a parasite. Don't get me wrong. I know God loves him and could change his heart and life given the chance, but as he currently is… pathetic and completely self-absorbed."

"I don't mean the drug use. I know I'm clean and he's a drag away from using up his last few brain cells. I mean his mentality. Did I make you feel like a freak when you found religion?"

"First of all, I didn't –

Tim interrupted before he could answer.

"I know, I know. You didn't find *religion*, you found Jesus. Or He found you. I mean did I act like you joined a cult and lost your mind? Do I make you feel like that now?"

Tim was quite distressed by this possibility. He had never thought about how he made Paul feel when he stone-walled him or constantly played *devil's advocate* in their conversations.

"I mean, you gave me a hard time when I was a little overzealous to share my new faith but I think I was a little obnoxious without meaning to be. But no, you weren't ever like that. You were, and are, a true friend and I never doubted that." Paul was sincere but it didn't make Tim feel absolved from his guilt.

"I'm sorry man. I never meant to belittle you or make you feel awkward around me." Tim's contrition was touching but seemed out of place in the present situation.

"It's all good man. Seriously. Don't sweat it. You were kind of a punk from time to time but it was more good-natured ribbing than you making me feel like a religious nut or anything." What was meant to be consolation was just fuel on Tim's self-loathing fire.

"But man, you've always been there for me and you're the most genuine Christian I've ever met. You take what you believe to heart and there's not a hypocritical bone in your body. Sometimes I envy your assurance." Tim had never affirmed Paul like this for anything, especially his faith.

"Well sign me up for Sainthood!" Paul drawled out with a big smile.

Tim got the point. Paul didn't want apologies and he didn't need to be told what a great guy he was. He was Tim's best friend. End of story. But at least Paul now knew for sure that Tim respected his beliefs and that made him feel a little better.

"Yeah, well, let's not go that far." Tim was reeling his emotions back in.

After a minute Paul decided to let Tim off the hook of awkwardness that he seemed to be dangling from.

"What brought all that on, man?"

"It's just that Gabe was a good kid. Sweet and sensitive. Innocent even. That Trey guy makes it sound like they did all this together but I have the feeling that he used Gabe a lot more than a friend ever would. Gabe needed a friend and Trey was willing to fill the slot as long as the party continued. When Gabe was desperate and reached out to some people who might be able to actually help him, Trey turned on him and made him feel like a loser. Now he's in some shelter with no friends and this parasite sponging off of his family's money. He gets to live in that house using it for all kinds of illegal, immoral, and stupid stuff. It just made me super thankful for you and I'm sorry if I ever made you feel weird about your decisions."

"Fair enough." Paul's understated appreciation of the moment was the perfect exit to the male bonding moment. But Paul was never one for graceful exits. "Should we hug and sing '*You Got a Friend In Me*' now?"

"I take it all back," Tim said dryly.

"Too late. I've got it all recorded for future use. Now," Paul switched gears, "this shelter must be new cause I've never heard of it."

"It can't be that new if Gabe's been there for a couple of years," Tim answered.

"Well, at least post-Katrina 'new' then because I used to know the shelters and rehab clinics around here pretty well. Granted, it's been a few years but still. It's gonna be kinda tough to get in to see him this early." It was barely 5:45 in the morning.

The French Quarter was dark and ominous this time of morning. They pulled onto Decatur and followed it down almost to the French Market before turning left onto Toulouse then right again onto Dauphine. Tim was struck with the eerie feeling that this town was swallowing them. He shuddered the thought away hoping Paul didn't pick up on his shift in body language.

"Yeah. Driving through here in the dark was never very pleasant." was Paul's subtle indication that he did, indeed, pick up on Tim's shift.

They pulled up to a shelter that doubled as a church locked on either side by typical French Quarter shops. Paul was shocked to realize that this was, in fact, a church when he was a student here. It was a tiny church attended by mostly homeless and transient people in the French Quarter.

"I remember I visited this place once before with another student when doing a research paper for a class. Back then there was no solid leadership here and worship was more of a glorified AA meeting, but now it seems to be doing fairly well. Got an 'A' on the paper, by the way." Paul commented with a slight smile.

Pastor Bobby Zelewski was painted on the door in red and new artwork adorned the walls of the dilapidated building as well. The name was somewhat familiar to Paul but he couldn't place it. The name of the church was painted in a brilliant mix of typical Mardi Gras purple and gold: Church of the Lost Sheep. New name as well. He liked it. Paul could see from the street that there was an apartment located on the second floor. Chances were good they also housed the residents of the shelter in a separate room on that level. He was pretty sure the old pastor had left with Katrina so he wasn't sure where this guy had come from, but hopefully, that apartment was his or at least one of the associate pastors who could help them.

Most rehab clinics in New Orleans were live-in only as there had to be daily tests to monitor the use of any substances. People could come and go during the day at some but the residents were usually told that they were to report back by a certain time and then remain on the premises.

There was a phone number painted under the Pastor's name and Tim and Paul decided to call it.

On the fourth ring, a tired but pleasant-sounding voice answered.

"What can I do ya for dis blessed mornin'?" came the thick New Orleans accent which was like a seamless combination of Southern drawl, Boston vowels, and Cajun-French ooh-la-la all sown into one beautiful garment.

"So sorry to bother you at this hour but we need to talk to one of your residents. A Gabriel Whitten." Paul was handling the talking since he was more familiar with the way of the people here. And because right now Tim's people skills were a cross between *brash* and *call the cops on this guy*.

"Wanna talk to Gabe, huh? Mind if I ask what about?" still pleasant but with a hint of concern in his voice.

"It's a little strange. I'm afraid we might need to explain it in person, if you don't mind." Paul was hopeful that he would come down and meet them but wasn't sure that he would if the roles were reversed.

"Strange, huh? Well, I saw plenty of dat in my life." He sounded like he was moving through rooms on the phone. As Paul waited for a few seconds thinking the pastor would give him an answer and maybe come down a face appeared from behind the curtain on the door. A man on a cell phone eyed them once and opened up.

As he hung up his phone, he put out his hand to Paul and said, "Pastor Bobby Zelewski. You can call me Pastor Z. Everybody does."

Paul raised his eyebrows in recognition as he put his phone away.

"Z! I knew that name sounded familiar."

Tim stood there in ignorance as he was not privy to the conversation that had transpired over the phone but he was at least hopeful that they would gain entrance to talk to Gabe now. Paul seemed to remember that Tim was out of the loop and tried to explain the connection as he figured out some details that he was missing as well.

"Z was in a shelter I used to volunteer at when I was down here getting my degree. It shut down after Katrina and I lost contact with almost everybody who was there." Turning to Z he asked, "What happened, man? Where did you go? When did you start this?"

Smiling at the reconnection to an old buddy he answered each question in order.

"Well, I was in my last month of treatment when Katrina showed up uninvited so I had to haul tail outta here and go crash with some friends in Baton Rouge. Almost lost it then. They was a bad crowd but I had nowhere else to go. I almost started using again when the Lord shook me outta my bed one night with a vision."

Tim almost rolled his eyes at the talk of more visions and dreams. What was with these folks? Didn't they know that we lived in the 21st century and stuff like this didn't just happen anymore? Thinking about the last twelve hours Tim's knee-jerk response seemed inappropriate now. Strange things were happening but was he ready to buy into all this? The Pastor continued.

"He told me, 'Z, get yo butt back to Nawlins and get yo junk together. I'm gonna make you a preacher!' Now I was just like Moses and started arguing about how I can't be no preacher cause I can't preach good and I'm just an addict and all that, but the Lord wouldn't hear none of it. He just told me to trust Him and that His power would be perfect in my weakness. Can't argue with that cause as much weakness as I got, I know His strength must be crackin'!

"So, I made my way back and started this prayer meeting with some other folks in the area and we started trying to meet the needs of the other homeless and addicted folks offering them a better life in Jesus. I called Brad, who used to run my old shelter, and asked him to pray for me and help me with the details of how I can get folks better connected. Whoo, boy! He sent me a whole heap of materials and books and such cause he was sure I was the guy to carry on the ministry they had here, though the Lord had moved him and his family down to Miami to start some shelters that way.

"So long story short, this church was born about thirteen years ago and it doubles as a shelter and recovery program. I even got yo seminary up da road there to send me some students to help with the music and stuff. They some great folks, too. We meet on Friday nights and have a good time singing and studyin' the Word then again on Sunday mornin' to do it all over again." With a reflective pause, he finished with, "God is good, brother."

Paul was grinning from ear to ear about this news. "That just shows how out of touch I am with stuff down here. I've kept up with a few folks and even come down a couple times right after Katrina to help out with stuff but I had no idea you were even here."

A little afraid of offending the Pastor Tim spoke up. "So, can we see Gabe?"

Paul was a little ashamed of himself for getting off task, even if the news of this ministry was great to him. His best friend's family was still missing and he needed to focus.

"I'm sorry, Z. This is Tim McDaniel. His family was abducted from their home yesterday and we have reason to believe that Gabe might have some insights into what's going on."

Z took Tim's hand with sad eyes and shook it in both of his. Though they bore into Tim's soul he didn't resent the pity. He felt a kinship with this man for some reason and knew intrinsically that any trial he had faced in this life that Z could match him scar for scar. This man was weathered and tested by life and he was a shining example of the grace Tim had heard Paul talk about so often.

"I hate to tell you dis, but he didn't show up for dinner last night or tonight and didn't check-in after dark. My heart was heavy tonight cause that means he's out of this round of the program. If he wants to continue, he has to start all over again. He was doin' good, too." He sounded genuinely saddened by Gabe's absence. "About two days ago he started gettin' real anxious and paranoid and I was sure he was usin' again. But he tested negative. He was clean but actin' like he was strung out. I wasn't sure what he was doin,' but then I didn't see him at all yesterday or today and, like I said, is still AWOL tonight."

This revelation hit Tim hard. He looked at Paul who wore a similar scowl on his face.

"You don't think-"

"I don't know what to think." Paul interrupted.

"But it makes sense, time-wise. He could have left here yesterday and been able to steal that Tahoe in Auburn."

"Whoa, now. You thinkin' Gabriel took yo family? I doubt that very much." Z interjected.

Tim was building up steam now. "If he's a junkie then maybe his mind snapped. And Trey said he would talk about me from time to time. Maybe he snapped and decided to take my family. Maybe he somehow blamed me for his tough life after camp."

Paul stood there wanting to tell Tim he was just jumping to conclusions but the more he thought about it the more he was unable to tell Tim that he was off base. He looked at Z as if asking for some reason not to follow this logical path.

"Look," Z continued, "I have been workin' with Gabriel for a couple years now and if there's one thing I know it's that he wouldn't hurt nobody. He's a confused, lost soul that needs Jesus in the worst way but he hasn't jumped them hurdles of fear and doubt just yet. He's hanging on to somethin' that won't let him accept that forgiveness but I can't figure out what yet."

"So, you're saying that because he won't become a Christian he wouldn't hurt my family? I'm sorry but with everything you folks have said about Jesus, seems maybe that's why he's capable, ya know?" Tim didn't want to believe that Gabe would or could do something like this but facts were pouring in and they were all telling the same story so far.

"Listen," Z started again, "I know that would make some sense to you but trust me. Gabe is a tender soul and he so wants to do good. He's just scared."

"So am I," Tim said solemnly. "I'm scared for my family and, no offense, but I don't trust anyone right now except me and Paul. Drugs can do a lot to change a person. And so can fear. If Gabe is not involved in this then he at least knows something. Either way, do you know how to get in touch with him or his family?"

"Got no family that I know of. His folks either died or went outta the picture with him years ago leaving nothin' but money for him. He used to live over near Tulane but said he couldn't be around that stuff no more. Only other place I know to tell you is down by the bridge." He was pained to reveal that Gabe might be living under the bridge with the worst users and abusers the town had to offer.

Paul knew the bridge well. During the day and into the evening it was a gathering place for the worst of the down-and-outs; those who either didn't know about or didn't want a shelter and some of the transients passing through New Orleans knew to go there for a place to crash or a fix. After dark, it was none too friendly but at this hour in the morning, most would either still be asleep or cops would have begun ushering them off to different areas of the city.

Downtown New Orleans is such a place of extravagance and waste that the average homeless person could find leftovers and meals so readily that the shelters were a last resort. Only the users who were too high to take care of themselves and desperately needed another fix resorted to violence and extreme theft. Though a city of great fun and worldly pleasure, it was nonetheless a dirty city that sold sex and alcohol twenty-four hours a day. Renowned thoroughfares like Bourbon Street were all glitz and glam on television but in reality, were raunchy venues of prostitution and seedy living. Even locals who loved New Orleans and wouldn't live anywhere else, hurricanes or not, would admit that the French Quarter is not the most family-oriented location after dark.

It was time to hit the ugly side of town.

CHAPTER SEVENTEEN

Even at 6:00 a.m. Tim could see about a dozen figures milling about in the shadows. Sunrise was imminent and there was a pinkish tint to the bruised sky. As they parked in a Loading/Unloading Zone Only spot Paul took a moment to school Tim on some homeless etiquette.

"Dude, these are some desperate people so please don't tick anybody off. They have so little to lose that consequences aren't as important to them as they are to us." Even as Paul said it, he registered that at this point they probably weren't as important to Tim as they had been even twenty-four hours ago.

"Fine, you do the talking. But if I see Gabe, I don't guarantee silence."

The two climbed out of the Tahoe and started toward the Wall. That was the place many street people gathered. Some for safety in numbers, but some to perfect the day's scam that awaited. As they approached several started towards them with no fear. It was as if the confrontation was expected.

"Whatchu want?" came the gruff question from a tall, middle-aged black man with about three teeth in his mouth.

"We are trying to find a friend. Name's Gabe. White guy in his late thirties. Seen him?" Paul was as *to the point* as he could be and the man was equally terse.

"Nope," was his reply.

As Paul and Tim started to veer away from him and angle towards the others, he spoke up again.

"You needs to go. Only trouble here for you." He stood at least 6'3" and was lanky from what Tim guessed to be drug use. Still, he had an intimidating presence. Tim wasn't easily intimidated.

"We'll go when we find him." Tim was trying to end the conversation but apparently, this was a challenge to the older man. He stood straight and came at them lightning-quick.

"Look around you, Snowflake. This ain't a place for you. You best be goin'... now." His tone was rough and firm but not necessarily threatening. Tim could tell that maybe this guy was trying to look out for them to an extent. He tried to reassure him of their intentions.

"We're just looking for Gabe and we're gone. Promise. No trouble."

Toothless looked them over then backed off as a few of the others approached. In a few seconds, Tim and Paul were practically surrounded by about ten drunk, stoned, or emotionally disturbed people because they looked and acted pretty strange. Some sniffed the air and others growled in low, guttural sounds.

Most were black men but there was a white guy, not Gabe, and a Hispanic woman. They all had vacant eyes and Tim couldn't shake the feeling that these people were more like zombies than people.

"This normal?" Tim asked quietly of Paul.

"Not exactly but let's see where this goes." Paul wasn't gonna tuck tail and run either. "Anyone here know Gabe? White guy stays at the shelter on Dauphine?" Nobody answered but one of the guys grew agitated and started moaning louder.

Tim wanted to get answers and this wasn't getting them so he started to gently push past the small crowd. Paul was a little more political in his approach.

"If you see him, please tell him Tim McDaniel needs to talk with him and to call Z." As Paul began to follow Tim's lead and make a hole in the mini-mob, someone drew their attention about thirty feet away. The group dispersed quickly without fanfare. The whole moment was surreal.

Tim craned his neck to see who, or what, had drawn their attention so quickly. He could make out a lone figure leaned up against a light pole. He wasn't looking their way but Tim could tell he was the reason for the exodus.

"Gabe." Tim knew it instinctively. Paul seemed to trust this claim as they both started toward him. Within a few feet, he spoke up.

"I didn't do it, Tim. I promise."

"Didn't do what, Gabe?" Tim asked evenly, like talking to a child.

"I didn't have anything to do with it! I'd never hurt your family, I promise!"

Tim and Paul glanced at each other. Tim couldn't help but state the obvious.

"Then how do you know anything about it, Gabe? Maybe you didn't do it but you know something. Please tell us, Gabe. Where are they?" Tim was trying to calmly coax information from him but Gabe wasn't playing along.

"He told me he was gonna do it and told me I had to help but I said 'No!' I swear I didn't have anything to do with it!" Gabe was on the verge of tears.

Gabe was not just thin, he was downright skinny from drug use and hard living. It was only his kind, scared eyes that proved to Tim that this was the same Gabe he knew many years ago.

"Who told you? Help us out here, Gabe." Paul tried to get somewhere as well.

"You know who!" he snapped.

Tim didn't want to say it for fear it was true. "Del?" It was more a statement than a question but Gabe still answered.

"Yeah, man. I don't know who, or what, he is but he's really got it out for you. Has for years. Tim, you gotta be careful. He's not what you think."

CHAPTER EIGHTEEN

"What do you mean, he's not what I think?" Tim was confused by the statement and was more than a little eager to hear Gabe's explanation.

Gabe licked his lips and screwed up his face as if he were a little reluctant to share his thoughts. Finally, he took a breath and began.

"He's —," was all he got out. Without warning, one of the members of the odd little group that they thought had dispersed leaped a good eight feet and tackled Gabe to the ground. Hard. It was the Hispanic woman.

"Shut your mouth!" she was screaming. "Say nothing, you pathetic coward! You useless waste!" She was only about five feet and four inches, maybe 120 pounds soaking wet, and yet she had brought Gabe down with ease and was now kneeling on his chest like an oversized cat.

"Hey! Get off of him!" Tim went to grab her but she hopped off and ran. Tim and Paul were bewildered at this turn of events but the confusion was short-lived as it was soon replaced with fear. The crowd was back and more agitated than ever. They were circling around them.

Gabe shot up to his feet, obviously hurt by the tackle but not incapacitated. With the wall to their backs and the small mob of *unstables* starting to block their only exit, they made a choice to run. It wasn't a group decision brought to fruition through a discussion but a natural, almost intuitive decision made by each of them all at once.

They bolted together through a gap in the closing circle. Tim couldn't help but notice that this group of homeless people was like nothing he'd ever seen before. They weren't the standoffish, humbled folks asking for help. They certainly weren't the type to play an

135

instrument or dance a jig for money. No, these were the real down-and-outs. Most likely lost everything, including hope, through drug use and mental illness.

And with this crowd, it was as if they had all escaped from the same maximum-security mental ward that morning. Some were drooling, some growling. Most were agitated and angry but they all had malice in their eyes. A few of the larger men had their chins down and were simply fixated at them with dark, hollow eyes.

Tim couldn't help but think of them as zombies again. But that was ridiculous.

As they made their way to the Tahoe the crowd pivoted towards them and turned from a slow-moving team to a motivated mob. They picked up the pace of their pursuit and were upon them before they could get the doors open.

Paul was momentarily caught off guard and the small Hispanic woman that had attacked Gabe appeared on the roof of the Tahoe. Had she already been there or did she jump up there?

"Stop the guardian!" she hissed to the crowd with a slight Hispanic accent.

Before Tim had time to ponder what she meant by that, one of the larger men inhumanly catapulted himself the last ten feet separating them and slammed Paul into the rear driver's side door. He crumpled to the ground like a rag doll leaving a man-sized dent in the door. The large man picked Paul up over his head and threw him over the hood. Like a pack of hungry dogs, they began to advance.

Tim hoped with all his heart that this was another one of his hallucinations. This couldn't be real. He was scared to death, but not for his own life or sanity. He knew this crowd was about to tear Paul to pieces. Gabe stood there with his face in his hands cowering like a child.

"No!" Tim instinctively ran over to Paul and threw himself on top of him to protect him. If he could get Paul to his feet maybe they stood a chance. He hefted him up to his feet and draped one of his arms over his shoulder. He looked over to Gabe and shouted, "This way!"

They started for the street behind where they parked. The Tahoe now separated them from the crowd and they hurried down and cut right into an alley that connected a restaurant with a boutique.

They turned left at the end of that alley and found themselves in another alley that dead-ended after about fifty feet. Their only hope was to force one of the doors to a building open and try to hide out or barricade the door.

Gabe had taken Paul's other arm over his shoulder to help Tim carry his still dead weight. Hopefully, he would wake up soon. They traveled in silence for a moment, neither knowing what to say about what was happening. But Tim had to ask his question one more time.

"What were you saying a minute ago about Del not being what I think? What does that mean, Gabe? Shoot straight with me here."

The crowd closed the alley with a human wall. If they couldn't find a way out right away, they were toast. Several of them had a low, guttural growl, and others were speaking incoherently as if in an unknown language. As one they began to advance.

Gabe let go of Paul and adopted his cowering posture again, this time squatting on the sidewalk like a little kid. Tim laid Paul gently down and stood sentinel in front of him.

"What do you want? Who are you people? What did we do to you?" Tim was shouting at them hoping to get some answers before it was too late. The thought of coming this far only to fail was a terrible, gnawing pain. The Hispanic woman stood in the middle and seemed to be the leader of this crew, which was strange in itself. She was angry, violent. She had a face that was once lovely, before the drugs and hard living. But then she changed. Her demeanor, her face, even her smile just... changed.

"You know what we want, Timmy." It was still her yet it was somebody else. "We want you to suffer. To know fear in its purest form. To fail and ultimately, to die."

There was no way this could be happening. *No way*. Even her voice was different, lower, and without a trace of an accent. And now her eyes. Those eyes.

"Del?" Tim somehow managed to embrace the crazy possibility. But there was no way this was possible!

"Well, well. Looky who's starting to catch on." She stood there, cocky and proud. Her face beamed with delight like a schoolyard bully who just knocked down a weaker child.

Tim's face must have been pretty easy to read. Confusion, anger, fear. Trying desperately to make sense of this.

"What's wrong, Timmy? Don't you miss your old pal? We left things on such...uncertain terms."

"Listen. I don't know how you're doing this. And I don't know why you hate me so much. I—"

"You want to know why I hate you?!" She was livid. Her eyes burned with anger. "I despise you for *so* many reasons, Timmy. I hate you most because you think you're so strong when you're so weak." Then the anger turned to arrogance. "But I'll show you how weak you are. I'm going to break you. I want to break that proud, brave spirit of yours. And then I'm gonna break your will. And then, I'm gonna break your wife's neck right in front of you."

Tim's heart quickened. There was not a trace of doubt in Tim's mind that Del was capable of doing exactly what he said. "Please." he practically whimpered the word. "Please, I'm sorry. You win. I'm broken. I'm scared. I'm at your mercy. Just, please. Please give my family back."

Instead of being moved by this confession, the woman who was also Del seemed to feed off of it. She inhaled deeply as if she was being empowered by his fear and weakness.

"Not yet." She savored the moment like she could taste it and wanted it to last forever. She closed her eyes and smiled that sick, joyless smile. She opened them and looked Tim in the eye. "Not just yet. You can slip much further than this. There's more fear in you. Just wait until you see them. You'll see them and be completely powerless against me because you are so... brave. But not for long."

As she spoke the others were at bay but her eyes drifted to Paul then to Gabe. But at that moment Tim could feel that a torrent was about to be unleashed on them. He knew Paul was about to be ripped apart in front of him. He could already see in his mind's eye Gabe being pummeled to death while he was helpless to stop it. His heart was racing and there was no plan he could come up with to stop what was about to start any second now.

Pointing to Gabe she announced, "This one's useless to us now. Help him understand why he *should* have helped us. And kill the guardian before he wakes."

He threw Gabe to the ground with Paul and covered their bodies with his. Before he was securely over them the inevitable happened. The other nine were unleashed upon them.

The crowd tried to pry Tim off but he had a death grip on Paul's chest, nearly crushing Gabe in between them.

This was far worse than the bikers earlier that night had been. These weren't just angry men, this crowd was insane with rage. So many hands grabbed at them, trying to rip Paul and Gabe away from him. As two of the men yanked hard, he felt Paul's arm snap and saw it bend at an unnatural angle above the elbow. The only consolation was that Paul was still knocked unconscious from when the large man had slammed him into the truck. How strong were these guys to break a man's humerus?

Gabe looked up at him as, ultimately, he was dragged out from under Tim. As he was being pulled away, he mouthed the words, "I'm so sorry," to Tim. But as hopeless as this situation seemed in that moment salvation came for Gabe and Paul in the strangest of forms.

Suddenly Pastor Z was standing at the entrance to the alley holding a Bible in one hand and what looked like a mini baseball bat in the other. He was yelling at the crowd.

"Ya'll get away from him in Jesus' name! Go on, git! Move back now!" He was swinging the bat in the air to make the point that he would use it if necessary. But the crowd stopped so suddenly that a thick silence filled the early morning air. Everyone stood and flanked the woman again, now their backs to the wall as Z walked past them to where Tim, Gabe, and Paul were.

They were tense and ready to pounce but stood steadily. Tim couldn't understand why they obeyed Z but was glad regardless. Surely they weren't scared of his L'il Louisville Slugger. Still, another few seconds, and Gabe would be dead, and most likely Paul too.

Though the crowd was angry and restless, the woman simply smiled again and said, "Soon, Timmy. We'll finish this game very soon."

"How?! When? What do I have to do?" Tim was desperate to know what was expected of him.

"We'll finish this—"

And then Tim's mind was blown even worse than before. As if well-rehearsed, four of the others spoke the rest of the message with the same tone and inflection, in perfect conversational rhythm, one by one.

The white guy. "Where."

The tall black man on the far left. "We."

The short, stocky man on the right. "First."

The man closest to Tim. "Began."

And then every last one of them crumpled to the ground like puppets cut from their strings.

CHAPTER NINETEEN

L iz had worn her wrists raw moving them back and forth to loosen her restraints to no avail. Her mouth was dry from biting and slobbering on her gag. But that had paid off because she was finally able to push it out of her mouth with her tongue and move it to her chin by flexing her lower jaw over and over. She dared not cry out yet for fear that she would only draw the attention of her captor and she would be silenced before she could accomplish anything else.

For all she knew she was being watched right now. But she had to try.

She gave up on freeing her hands and instead focused her energy on sliding them over her butt and forcing her feet through her arms to bring her hands in front of her. The problem with this plan was that her feet were bound as well and she wasn't sure she could get both feet through without dislocating her shoulder.

It had been hours that she lay in the dark. She didn't know where she was, where her children were, or where her husband was. A dislocated shoulder was worth finding at least one answer.

She bowed her shoulders back and pushed down as hard as she could. The oh-so-slight loosening that moving her wrists achieved allowed her hands to part just slightly enough to get her palms on either butt cheek. She shoved down again and brought her knees up and was ecstatic that her hands went down to her upper thighs without too much pain.

This was the hard part. She slid her hands down to her feet and rolled over to her back. She pulled her knees up as far as she could. She pulled one of her shoes off while sliding her bound hands over her heels,

141

but it only helped. With the guttural cry of a desperate mother, she shoved her hands down one more time while forcing her feet through.

Freedom!

She immediately pulled the blindfold down and was prepared to be blinded by light but it was still rather dark. Only the soft glow of a small candle lit the room. She realized it must have been night by now. The ride had been a couple of hours and she must have been lying in the dark trying to get free for at least an hour, not to mention that she had no idea how long she had been unconscious. It could be the middle of the night for all she knew but it didn't matter much since there were no windows.

She was in what appeared to be a rustic basement with dirt floors and wide plank boards for a ceiling. There was a musty odor but also the faint smell of something else. Fish? Three walls were simply cut into the earth and the fourth had a wooden staircase that surely led to the surface. She had to get to those stairs. She needed to be sure she was alone first.

As her eyes scanned her surroundings she jumped with fright as she noticed a man sitting in a chair in the dark corner. But as she steeled herself for his response to her escape-in-progress, she saw that he was bound to the chair and gagged as she had been. His head was hanging as if he were asleep. Large plastic tie straps bound his wrists to the ample wooden armrests and equally thick straps held each ankle to a leg of the chair.

How peculiar that his eyes were uncovered but his mouth was gagged. She hadn't heard him the whole time she had been awake. She had strained her ears for any sign of life or help and heard nothing. How had he been here this whole time and said nothing? Was he dead?

Just as the thought began to tickle the back of her neck with fear, she noticed his chest moving slightly with ragged breath. He was alive.

So why was he so quiet? Had he been unconscious this whole time? Since the only light was from the candle, it was difficult to make out any of his features as it did little to cast the shadows from the corners. As she moved slightly closer to him, she was slow, deliberate. Almost cat-like in her approach. From just a few feet away she realized she was holding her breath. What was she afraid of? Waking him up? He was bound to the chair, it's not like he could hurt her.

Still, she didn't want to draw unwanted attention so she knelt down four feet from his chair and hunched over to get a better look at his face. Her breath caught.

This was the Other Tim. It didn't look nearly as much like his doppelgänger as he had before, but this was definitely him. He had a similar haircut and soul patch but he was a good twenty pounds thinner than before. And his face looked more Hispanic now. She couldn't see his eyes but there was no doubt this had been the man who abducted them.

A barrage of questions flew through her mind. Who had tied this man up? Did that mean there was another person involved in this? Did they have her kids? Why did this man look so different now? It had only been mere hours since she was so sure this was her husband that she willingly loaded the kids and herself up to ride off with him. Maybe she could get answers from him. Had he been double-crossed by the other person or something?

When she remembered how he had looked at her and how he had spoken so casually about "gutting" her kids in front of her, she knew she could never trust this man. Still, he might have some helpful information she could get out of him. She looked around the room for something, anything that could be used as a weapon.

There was nothing. Dirt and shadows. She considered her options: see if she could wake him up and get answers out of him, or see if she could get upstairs and find a weapon there. This guy was out of it and she wanted to get out of here. Option two seemed more logical. As she was about to move towards the steps movement caught her eye.

A deep inhalation made her jump but then she realized the man must have woken up. She turned towards him expecting to see him trying to adjust his eyes or fidget against his restraints. Just as she was about to try to speak to him, she saw his eyes, and her words caught, hung up in her throat.

He was staring right at her with the same unflinching glare in his eye he had in the truck. It was an even, full stare and it unsettled her. She was glad he was restrained.

As if he could read her thoughts he glanced down at his wrists and flexed them up and out of the thick plastic ties as if they had been made of grass. He pulled the gag out of his mouth but remained sitting.

Had this been a trick? Was he not unconscious this whole time? Why the show of the fake restraints? Then he spoke.

"Well, well. Looks like we've got a feisty one. I tied those things pretty hard and yet here you are about to just walk out of here. Guess I underestimated your resolve."

"Who are you? What do you want? Where are my—"

"SHUT UP!" he spat. "All you need to know right now is that the time is coming very shortly for you all to play your part in my plan. Your knight in shining armor will be coming soon and then we'll finish this."

"Tim is coming here?" She was almost relieved but the way he said it took the joy out of the thought. What did he have planned?

"You just stay put. That door's locked," he jerked his head towards the only exit, "and there's no way you're gonna get out of here until I'm ready for you to be, so you might as well sit down and get comfy."

She wanted to test that but as soon as she moved an inch towards the door, he snapped the restraints off of his legs as easily as he had his wrists. He was standing in front of her before she could advance. He was even more emaciated in the light. And he was shorter than before. How could she possibly have thought this was her husband? His eyes were uncomfortably familiar though.

"I can see you're a little confused." He had a mirthless grin on his face. "Let me really blow your mind."

As he stood there his face and body began to change. She could hear the skin stretching and his clothes began to fill out. He grew a couple of inches and his face transformed until it was, again, the image of her husband in front of her.

She had no words. A crippling fear filled her. Her question was no longer *who* was this but now *what* was this? She stood unblinking as he made his way back to the chair.

"I've got some unfinished business to take care of so you stay put. I don't care if you try the door and there's nobody to hear you screaming so have at it. Tim's not gonna kick open the door and pull me off of you this time." He winked at her and then she instantly knew where she had seen those eyes before. There was no way this was the same guy from that night. Something she couldn't wrap her head around was going on here.

As he sat down, he was quickly transformed back into the smaller, weaker man. He grabbed four thick ties from a bag on the floor. First, he cinched his legs back to the legs of the chair. Next, he placed a tie strap around the arm of the chair where his right wrist would go and held it in place with his knee. Then he cinched down his left wrist. Finally, he bent over and used his teeth to cinch down his right wrist.

Watching him restrain himself was surreal. At least she had one question answered. This man was clearly behind this and was capable of much more than she would have thought possible.

"I'll leave the gag off this time in case you two want to chat. I suspect he'll be pretty out of it for a while though."

Was he referring to himself in the third person? She was not as much confused as she was afraid of the implication.

Liz stood there for a moment wanting to say something but at a loss for the words. After a moment, a phrase came into her mind. She thought it was an absurd thing to say in a time like this but she felt compelled to say it. It didn't come across as childish or insincere when it came out of her mouth.

"I'm not afraid of you."

It had much more of an effect on him than she would have thought possible. He looked like she had just spit in his face. His eyes burned with anger and hate. His jawed tightened as he clenched his teeth. He tried to play the mirthful grin across his lips but it lacked the confident arrogance it had earlier. After a moment he relaxed his jaw muscles and spoke evenly.

"Oh, sure you are. I think you're terrified of what I'm gonna do to you, your husband, and your sweet little babies. I think you're trying to look brave but you're just a scared little girl locked in a room with a killer." He bore into her with those eyes. "Just like you were a scared little girl locked in a room with a would-be rapist. Maybe we'll finish what we started before we're through here as well."

But something had come over Liz. She couldn't explain it. For no good reason at all, she had… hope. She didn't *know* that everything would be fine, but she would not give herself over to fear and abandon all hope. It was more than just a feeling though; it was more like a conviction.

"I don't know who, or what, you are. I don't know why you're doing this. But I know my husband will stop at *nothing* to save us. He'd forge his way through Hell itself to get to his family." She had faith in her words, even if she didn't have any great reason to. But his dark and enigmatic response drained some of her optimism.

"Oh, I *know* he will. In fact, he's already halfway there."

CHAPTER TWENTY

Pastor Z moved quickly over to Tim. He was very cautious moving past the piles of people that were a seething, violent mob only five seconds ago. He helped Tim up, made sure Gabe was ok and winced when he saw Paul's arm.

Pointing to Paul's arm he commented, "Dat's gonna leave a mark." His casual assessment was little relief to Tim. Twice they had called Paul his *guardian* and now he was bruised and broken. But at least he was still out cold and not fully aware of the pain. They needed to get him medical attention, and fast.

"Gabe, you ok?" Z was not too much older than them, maybe his late forties or early fifties from what Tim could tell. But he still had a tender and fatherly tone.

Gabe didn't look him in the eye. He only nodded and muttered a barely perceptible, "Yeah." It sounded like he was ashamed.

Tim was still in too much shock at what had just transpired to grill Gabe at the moment, although he still wanted some answers. But Paul needed help first.

"Help me get him into the Tahoe," Tim was saying even as Z and Gabe were moving to help. It was only then that Tim saw the extent of Gabe's injuries. He was bleeding from his face and neck from scratch marks and he was holding his wrist as if it had been injured or, possibly broken. Had that happened when the woman first attacked him or when the mob was ripping him out from under him?

It was at that moment that Tim more fully understood that Gabe was not to blame for this. He knew in his heart that Gabe hadn't betrayed him and now he almost gave his life trying to get a final word to Tim about Del.

"You ok, man? For real?" Tim genuinely inquired of his old friend.

Gabe just humbly shook his head and muttered, "I'm fine." But he didn't look fine. He looked done. Tim was worried about him.

"You did good, man. I believe you. I know you had nothing to do with this and that Del, whatever he is, is behind it." Recalling the fact that "Del" referred to Gabe as *useless,* Tim made a sobering observation. "He would've killed you, man."

"He *will* kill me," Gabe admitted with certainty in his voice. "It's just a matter of time now. I wouldn't surrender myself to him and he's done toying with me." What a strange way to put it, Tim thought. Sure, Gabe wouldn't be a part of his plan but to say he wouldn't "surrender" to him sounded so primitive and, well, melodramatic.

Tim grappled with the events that just played out in front of him. Maybe not so melodramatic after all. He still couldn't wrap his head around how the Hispanic woman was Del. Or maybe just that Del spoke through her somehow. Or whatever that whole freaky thing with them all talking in Del's voice in sequential order was. But there was no mistaking Del's hateful eyes and menacing tone, regardless of the face that accompanied it. Same as at camp long ago, the eyes of the rapist in college, in the biker in the alley tonight. Impossible.

But as much as Tim would love the answers to this riddle, now was not the time to press Gabe for more info. He was physically and emotionally beat up at the moment. Not to mention he was probably right, Del would kill him if he had the chance. This weighed on Tim's conscience for some reason, as if he alone were to blame for Del's homicidal tendencies.

But another part of him knew better. Del was on his warpath and Gabe was another piece of collateral damage. And now, so was Paul.

They arrived at the Tahoe and Z was opening the back door to lay him in. Tim didn't see any other car parked near them and asked, "Did you walk here?"

"More like jogged." He was hefting Paul's feet in one side and then hustled over to the other side to help pull him through as he spoke. "I had a bad feelin' in my spirit when you two left. Figured if I was jus' over reactin' then you might gimme a ride back. But apparently, I was hearin' da Lord correctly. Grabbed my little 'convincer' here and my

Bible and came to see what the fuss was all about." Tim had no trouble seeing Z "convince" somebody if the need arose. He may be a pastor, but it didn't take a genius to see that he had lived through hell and was a no-nonsense kinda guy.

"I'll ride in the back with Paul," he was saying to Z, "and Gabe, you take shotgun. Z, I need you to get us to the nearest hospital quick." Both complied readily. "Keys are still in the ignition."

Z jumped in the driver's seat as Tim ran over to the rear passenger's side door. He lifted Paul's legs and placed them in his lap. Gabe sullenly, but dutifully, climbed in the front seat and buckled up. As Z cranked the engine and started to back up, the tall black man from before approached. Tim had nicknamed him "Toothless" in his mind. Tim was afraid there would be more trouble at first but, he had forewarned them. Z rolled down the window to talk with him.

"Hey, Claude. You know what all dat was about?" Z clearly knew the man so maybe he could shed some light on what just went down.

Claude looked with pity and frustration in the back seat. He shook his head with an *I-told-you-so* look on his face. When he spoke, the gruff and intimidating tone was gone.

"I tried to warn 'em, Z. Them fools back there are the worst kind of trouble. Most of dat crew be into the occult and voodoo and such. They're just an open channel for the devil and his demons." Tim was listening but only half understood what he was talking about. Was he being serious or were those some kind of cajun euphemisms for druggies?

"Ok, Claude. Stay clear. We needs to get this fella to the doc. See you in church tonight?"

"Yeah. I'll be there." Turning to Tim he said, "Besta luck wit yo friend, Snowflake." Then he turned his eyes to Gabe. "I told you there was trouble brewin', Gabe. You needs to quit yo procrastinatin' and git yo heart right. You ain't no help to nobody right now." And with that, he turned and walked off.

His enigmatic charge to Gabe made Tim want to ask what that was all about but his mind had other fish to fry at the moment.

"Dat's Claude LaGasse. He been comin' to the shelter for years now. He has a good heart but he's still pretty rough around the edges. Crack don't let go too easy, even when Jesus is pullin' you. He fought for years and finally overcame that demon." There was that word again. Tim decided to go ahead and ask this time.

"Is that what he was talking about when he said those guys in the alley were an open channel for demons and stuff? Is that code for drugs?"

Z laughed a hoarse, throaty laugh. "Code? We ain't the CIA, son. Generally, demons means demons. But fightin' your demons can also mean somethin' that trips you up and keeps you down. Either way, it's from Hell."

Tim sought to clarify, "So those folks fought the 'demon' of drugs? Or were they possessed by actual demons?"

"Yes." He said to Tim's dismay. "Sure, drugs can be a gateway to the spiritual world but them folks are into voodoo and such. That's bad mojo and opens a person up to the devil real quick. That's like invitin' him in. Most folks don't look at it like dat but it's the truth." But he pronounced it *troof.*

"So, we're back to actual demons again." Tim shook his head and closed his eyes. "Paul was telling me about all the 'demons and angels' stuff earlier. I'm not sure I believe in all of that, to be honest."

Z laughed again, a quick chortle. "After what you jus' saw you can still say that? I don't know what else it's gonna take to convince you then."

Tim dropped it. He wasn't sure what that was in the alley and he didn't have the energy to figure it out right now. He could feel Paul waking up.

"He's waking up. How close are we?"

After turning on his blinker and making a quick left Z reported, "About three minutes to the E.R."

To Paul, Tim whispered, "Hang in there, buddy. We're gonna get you fixed up. I'm so sorry I dragged you into this, man."

To Tim's shock, Paul replied, "What happened? I feel like I got run over or something. I can't move my arm." He was in shock so the pain wasn't as extreme yet. His mind and body were dealing with the trauma. He was on his back with his broken right arm wedged between his body and the seat so it wouldn't move on the ride.

"Try not to move. Your arm is broken. We're almost at the hospital." Tim was glad he didn't wake up screaming or something, but he hated seeing him out of it like this, too. His eyes were glazed over and he kept lifting his head off of the seat and looking around.

After another minute Z announced, "We here." He pulled right up to the doors of the E.R. and parked. He ran in and got somebody with a wheelchair and was on his way out by the time Tim was out and had gone around to Paul's door. With the help of a male nurse, they got Paul in the chair as Tim was trying to explain what happened.

"We were jumped by some crackheads downtown and he was thrown into the side of my car and then they broke his arm." It sounded fishy even to Tim.

The nurse cared more about getting Paul in than hearing a satisfactory explanation at the moment. He was polite but dismissive, focused.

As soon as they were in the E.R. the nurse was barking out requests and codes. Tim tried to walk with Paul but was asked to stay in the waiting room until they came out of X-ray. He was about to insist but then thought better of it. He wouldn't be any help at the moment. They needed to check the extent of the damage and see if surgery would be necessary. Tim hadn't even considered that Paul might require surgery.

He felt helpless again. It was one thing to struggle with your own fear and weakness but to watch your best friend suffer because he was helping you was another kind of helplessness altogether. This sucked.

Tim took advantage of the moment and sat down by Gabe. After taking one look at his face and neck he hopped right back up and went to the front desk.

"Ma'am, my friend here needs to be checked out as well." He pointed over to Gabe and when the lady at the counter looked and saw the blood and scratches she was less "all business" and more "what the heck?" She looked back at Tim with wary eyes.

"Do I need to call the police, son? What happened to you all?" By her accent, Tim was sure this was not a New Orleans-born-and-bred gal. She had a strong southern drawl; maybe south Alabama was his guess. He did NOT want the police involved at this point. His mind raced to keep her from seeing the need to call them.

"No, ma'am. There's no need for the police. We were in the wrong place at the wrong time and some drugged-out homeless guys jumped us for no good reason. We got away but the cops probably couldn't do anything about it and there's no way we could identify them anyway 'cause it was too dark."

That rolled out way too fast to sound convincing.

"Whatever, honey. That's your call. Your friend might need some stitches. Bring him back and you can start the paperwork." Tim couldn't believe she bought it. Well, maybe she didn't buy it, but at least the cops weren't coming. In a town as busy and famous as New Orleans, the cops probably had their hands full anyway. At least that's what Tim hoped.

He motioned to Gabe to come on back. He looked pretty reluctant but came anyway. Tim was glad when Z came with him.

"I'll be back there in a sec. Z will be with you, man."

The nurse buzzed him back and Tim started trying to fill out the entry papers. He realized that he had no idea what to put for some of the information. He didn't want any record of his name here in case it came back to bite him so he tried to put Gabe's info on everything. But, of course, he didn't know Gabe's current address, telephone number, date of birth, or any other vital information required. He made it up.

Surely other people got medical attention without having all this info handy.

He handed the clipboard back to the nurse and walked over to the door. She looked like she wasn't going to for a second but then she buzzed him in. Tim was glad he didn't have to make a scene or anything.

He saw Gabe sitting on the edge of a gurney getting what he assumed was some kind of antiseptic wiped on his wounds. He was wincing at some of the touches but other than that looked absolutely sullen. Tim walked over to him.

"What's the verdict?" He asked the nurse attending his wounds.

"Nothing's broken but some of these scratches are deep. You say a bunch of homeless people did this?" Her question was somewhat rhetorical as she just kept cleaning the wounds when no one answered. Accepting the fact that she would get no answer she moved on. "I don't think he'll need stitches, though I recommend we dab some dermal glue on some of these deep ones. That'll help them seal up quicker."

When Gabe remained silent Tim spoke for him. "Sounds good." He wanted to see Paul now that he knew Gabe was ok. "Where did they take my other friend? I think they were taking him to get an x-ray?"

She gave him a sideways glance. I guess she had seen and heard it all too because she just motioned towards the door over her left shoulder and said, "When he gets back from x-ray they'll put him in room three. You can wait there."

Z, who had been awkwardly silent this whole time, finally spoke up. "I'll get a taxi and take Gabe home." Tim didn't know what to say.

"I, uh. I don't know how to thank you both. I'm so sorry about all this." Gabe kept his head down but Z put his hand on Tim's shoulder and smiled.

"Son, we are not your problem. It is *ok* for you to go. Me and Gabe will be fine." He looked at Gabe as he said this. "I assure you dat fella ain't gonna come near us. And if he do? I'll give him a what for again, haha." Tim wanted to trust that Z could take care of them again, but what if he didn't? The nurse walked away for a moment and, sensing Tim's struggle, Gabe spoke.

"Listen, Tim. You gotta find your family. He's for real got them and you have to get there. Whatever happens to me you have to try and stop him from hurting them." He knew what he had to say and worked up the courage to say it.

"Tim, Del isn't just some sick person out to get you. He wasn't just some twisted kid at camp and he isn't just some psycho that popped up after almost thirty years to mess with you. He's..." Gabe was resigning himself to what was about to come out of his mouth. There was no one to pounce on him to shut him up this time. Finally, he just let it out.

"He's a demon."

CHAPTER TWENTY-ONE

Paul lay on the x-ray table and his mind was swimming. He silently prayed for lucidity, a clear mind. He wanted to think straight about what was going down. He had concluded something that he knew Tim was going to have a hard time accepting. When he saw that lady jump on Gabe and then again when the guy flew through the air and slammed him against the Tahoe it all finally made sense.

These weren't just people with mental disorders or just down-and-outs hopped up on LSD. No, this was definitely of the spiritual variety and Tim was gonna need to listen to what he told him if there was any hope of defeating this enemy.

Paul was slipping out of consciousness again. *No! Stay awake*, he told himself. *I have to warn Tim. He has to know how to fight!*

But it was too late. Paul was out. And the most vivid, heart-wrenching nightmares he'd ever had began to torment his comatose mind. Paul knew this was an attack from the Enemy and prayed, even in his subconscious mind, for Divine help.

Tim waited in room three and pondered what Z had told him after Gabe's solemn declaration. "You don't believe him, huh?" Well, no, he thought. And yes. But mostly... no. How could he wrap his head around something like that? Z had been straight up with him.

"Whether you believe it or not doesn't make something true. It can still be true without your little stamp of approval. I know it sounds strange to you but consider the facts, son."

Tim's mind was reeling with facts.

Fact: someone who looked enough like him to fool his wife had kidnapped his family.

Fact: he had been having horribly vivid encounters and waking nightmares ever since.

Fact: this Del had been able to show up in various forms over the years, especially lately.

Fact: those people who jumped them tonight were not a typical crowd of homeless people, for sure.

And fact: deep down Tim had always known there was something evil about that kid, Del.

But fact: this stuff wasn't real. Not really. Demons and angels toying with mankind? Come on! He had to be losing it to buy into a theory where demons were manipulating people, possessing them and whatnot just to, what? Mess with him? There simply had to be a better answer to all of this.

When Paul was awake, he'd talk with him about it. He was afraid he already knew where Paul would land on this particular topic but wanted to hear him say it. It would help him to figure out where he stood just to hear Paul explain his take on it. Unfortunately, it could be hours before Paul was able to talk and Tim was terrified that Detective Peters would start trying to find him soon.

There was no way they were going to let Paul go any time soon with his injuries but maybe he could stay with a friend in New Orleans or something. That Dr. Taylor guy might let him crash for a few nights until Paul could find a ride back.

Come on, Tim. You can't leave your best friend behind.

Tim decided to go find Paul and maybe, just maybe, be able to get out of here sooner rather than later. He had given them trumped-up names and addresses so maybe they could sneak out. He headed for the hallway behind the E.R. and looked for a sign on the wall indicating which way the x-ray area would be. He saw a wall plaque that, among other things, said "X-Ray, 3rd Floor."

He rounded the corner to the elevator and hit the "up" call button. As it dinged open, he stepped in and hit the button for the third floor. Deep in thought, he was unaware of what was happening around him.

Instead of going up, the elevator took him down. As the doors slid open Tim walked out, oblivious to his new surroundings. Only after he noticed how much darker it was did he stop and look up from his thoughts.

He wasn't on the third floor.

The elevator doors had already shut behind him and started heading back up. He saw two walls of square metal doors stacked on top of each other. Each had a large metal handle. Six gurneys were filling the middle of the room, each with a white sheet covering a lumpy silhouette.

He was in the morgue. That wasn't even possible. You couldn't just take the elevator into the main room of a morgue like this. You had to sign in and there were always people to escort you into the morgue. He had definitely hit the "3" on the elevator and morgues were always down.

Just as he was realizing what this meant there was a moan from one of the sheets. Not a 1950's ghost moan, either. This was a truly unnerving sound. Tim immediately turned around and hit the elevator call button. It didn't light up.

He put his back against the elevator doors and watched in panicked horror as each of the six sheets began to move. There was only a door to the left that led to a dark hallway and experience told him that wasn't the best option. He would ride this one out right here. If this was anything like the others, he knew it wasn't real and only had to keep his wits about him until it was over. Unless it was like the alley. This might be bad.

As the first body sat up the sheet fell from the face of his father. The large scar from the autopsy ran down his chest. He remembered seeing him in a room just like this to identify the body. His dad had died of a massive heart attack in his office almost fifteen years ago. His face was bloated and bloodless now.

"Timothy," he spat the name with disdain and disgust, "you worthless little maggot. First, you drive your mom to an early grave and now you're gonna get your family killed. You stupid, selfish boy."

As he spoke the sheet next to him came off to reveal the body of his wife, Liz. He almost forgot that this was another horrible vision and ran to her, but he didn't. He stayed there fighting back tears and the urge to vomit at the sight of her bruised and naked body. It was as if she was beaten to death. Or worse.

As she lay there, her head turned to him. She had tears in her eyes but no sadness, only hate. Her abdomen was torn open and her arms and legs were sliced up. She opened her mouth to speak but Tim had all he could endure of these attacks.

"NO! Shut up! None of this is real! *You aren't real!* I will find you, so help me God. So help me GOD!"

As he was yelling two other sheets slipped off and Tim saw his two children as before. Their bodies were also bruised and beaten. The next sheet to come off shocked Tim as it revealed the body of Paul. Paul's arm was broken and his ribs were cracked. But he also had a broken neck. He sat up, looked at Tim with a twisted face, and said, "This is how I'm going to wind up, thanks to you."

Finally, when he was done cowering to fear and refused to meltdown this time, the last sheet fell and revealed… him. He saw himself dead on the table. He looked like he had drowned because he was wet and was a bluish color.

Tim again gritted his teeth against the fear and bile rising within him and said, "I'll find you, so help me God."

His dead self sat up and smugly claimed in a voice not like his own, "God can't help you, Tim. We'll finish this where we started it. Time is running out for your little family, Timmy. Better hurry."

All six rose from the table and started towards him. He wasn't sure how real this was and how much was just in his mind. He tried hitting the call button on the elevator again and again. Just before they reached him the doors slid open and he fell backward into the open, empty elevator. They were about to follow him in when the doors slid closed.

Tim lay there for a moment, purposely keeping his eyes open as he regained his bearings. As the doors slid open, he cautiously stood and exited, keeping one hand on the elevator doors just in case he needed to re-enter again quickly. But all seemed normal and he could see a large "3" on the wall in front of him indicating which floor he was on now. Time to find Paul and get the heck out of here. He knew exactly where to go now.

CHAPTER TWENTY-TWO

When Tim found him, Paul sat on the edge of a doctor's table bed with his right arm in a cast up covering his shoulder. It was attached to another cast around his ribs by a plaster rod, essentially keeping his arm up at a nearly right angle to his body and immobilizing it. He looked pretty wrung out from the night.

"Hey, man." Tim greeted him sheepishly.

"Bro," Paul replied, not trying to hide his weariness. Tim appreciated his lack of effort to appear chipper. Their friendship had never been forced before and it was a welcome reminder that they could still be brutally honest with each other, even after a night like they just had.

"Yeah." That was all Tim needed to say about that.

Changing gears, Tim sat down on the stool across from Paul's table and put his hands on his knees.

"You always do that when you want to broach an unpleasant subject with me." Paul declared.

"What?" Tim asked, confused.

"You sit down and put your hands on your knees and lean in like you're about to say something I don't want to hear. You've done it forever." Tim hadn't even realized this tick, but apparently, it was true because he was about to delve into unpleasant waters.

"Do I?" he said, unconvincingly. "Well then," he dove in. "What in the frig is going on, man? Please help me make sense of all this."

Paul slowly nodded his head, understanding the precarious nature of this topic. The drugs they had given him for the pain were kicking in and he wasn't very confident in his ability to make a lot of sense right now. Thankfully Tim picked up on this and changed his approach.

"Wait. I'm sorry, man. You're in no shape to talk right now. You need some rest."

"Doc says that they want me to stay the night to make sure there isn't any internal bleeding."

This news was a blow to Tim's heart and mind. He hadn't considered the extent of Paul's injuries. Internal bleeding? Oh man, this was bad.

"Dude, what can I do for you?" Tim wanted to comfort his friend but he also secretly cursed himself for wanting to hit the road as soon as possible. Apparently, and unfortunately, without Paul. This wasn't how he saw this going down but he didn't want to make Paul feel bad about needing to stay either.

Paul was always so intuitive with Tim. "I know it sucks I can't leave with you but you need to get back man. I'll be fine. I've got plenty of contacts down here that will help me out. You're not abandoning me or anything like that. Go get your family."

"Thanks, man." After a beat, he dropped his big news. "I think I know where they are."

Paul perked up at this, despite the narcotics in his system. "Really? Where?"

"The camp. Camp Muscogee over near Albany."

Paul was more familiar with Georgia than he was when he moved there as a teenager so he knew the area pretty well. Most folks would assume Albany was pronounced like the city in New York, ALL-bunny. But in southwest Georgia, it was pronounced by locals as all-Binny.

The camp was actually twenty miles west of Albany but that was the closest city so it was easier to say that's where it was. The good news is it was only a six-hour drive taking I-10 almost the entire way. Before you got to Tallahassee the last hour was up a country highway. Tim was sure he could make it in less than five hours if traffic wasn't bad.

"What makes you so sure?" Paul inquired.

"Let's just say that while you were out, Del paid me another visit and dropped the hint." He raised his eyebrows for effect and continued. "And again, just now in the morgue."

"The morgue? What were you doing in the morgue? Is everybody ok?" Paul was concerned about this possible turn of events.

"No, no," Tim reassured him. "Another one of my... *episodes,* I guess. But it was real enough and now I'm sure that's where this is going down."

"Del visited you? Like for real or in your head?" Tim wasn't offended at the way Paul asked this. It was the only way to ask it.

Tim answered, "For real. In the alley after you were out. The Hispanic lady just...became...Del." This sounded so lame and unbelievable out loud.

And unfortunately, Paul was getting woozy fast. A nurse came in and looked disapprovingly at Tim. She parked a wheelchair in front of Paul and helped him in it as she scolded him.

"This is no time or place for visitors, young man. This is an x-ray room, not a private place to chat." Her tone was terse but not mean. Tim was glad Paul would be in good hands.

He followed them to Paul's room and despite the nurse's efforts to simply shoo him away, he was able to convince her to let him stay with Paul for just a few more minutes. Paul had something he needed to tell him. After the nurse got him comfortably positioned in his bed, he looked at Tim.

"Listen, Tim." He was starting to sound a little drunk, slurring from the pain meds but he persevered. "You need to understand something here." He licked his lips and closed his eyes for a second until he opened them and said, "Demons." He nodded his head for a full five seconds and repeated himself. "Demons." And then he was out.

"Paul. Wake up, man. What about them? Come on, man." Tim could tell the meds had taken full effect and he was checked out. He was already sleeping with his jaw hanging open. He was about to resign himself to the fact that he would get no help, no answers when a familiar voice said, "I can tell you what you need to know, my friend."

Dr. Taylor stood in the doorway. Tim was shocked and impressed at this man.

"Did God tell you to come here?" Tim asked. Based on what happened on the campus earlier, he assumed this was another case of holy appointment. This guy had a direct line to God Tim didn't understand but was glad for.

"This time, Pastor Zelewski called me. And the nice nurse down the hall told me which room he was in. But the Lord works in the natural as easily as the supernatural." He replied coyly with a smile. So much for a "holy appointment," Tim thought.

He didn't know whether to laugh or be angry. But he was desperate for answers and this guy claimed to have them so he wasn't going to be belligerent with him over something like this. He was still a little frustrated at the whole *dream* thing from his office earlier though.

"Ok. So, tell me." Tim was far blunter than he had intended, but Dr. Taylor was unfazed by this and his smile never wavered. He began.

"Demons are especially fond of destroying human life. The thief comes but to steal, kill, and destroy. This is referring to satan, of course, but his fellow fallen angels will be about the same goals. The surest way to destroy a life is to ultimately possess it. Demons can and do possess individuals who have sufficiently opened themselves up to their malevolent influence. This has always been true. Both the Old and New Testaments tell of individuals that were under the power and authority of a demon or demons."

He seemed to check Tim's response before continuing. Sensing no abject dismissal of these claims, he proceeded to explain his perspective to Tim.

"Once there was a man who had *thousands* of demons living inside of him. They had driven him mad and he lived in a cave by a graveyard. When Jesus confronted them and asked their name the spirits inside the man replied, '*Legion, for we are many.*' This is a military term that can mean a thousand or more."

"What did Jesus do? How did he defeat them?" Tim was eager to devise a similar plan.

"He told them to leave." His plain and simple statement brought all the anger back into Tim.

"Yeah, well I don't think that's very helpful again, Doc. Do you believe that story, about the guys with all the demons in him?"

"I most certainly do." He said calmly but certainly.

"OK. Great. First, you have a dream that I'm drowning but God reaches his hand down to me and all I have to do is *take the hand*, and now your advice is I simply tell the demon *to leave*?"

161

Dr. Taylor was unhampered by Tim's frustration. He calmly corrected him.

"No, dear boy. I'm not suggesting that *you* tell him to leave. *You* have no authority to make such a demand, at present."

Tim looked at him, trying to figure out just why Paul liked him so much. "I don't have the authority? What does that mean? Because I'm not Jesus I can't do squat? Or is this like the whole sons of Sceva thing?"

"Exactly! My, you are astute." Dr. Taylor commended him. "Such commands cannot be made outside of a relationship, Tim. Authority comes from relationship." Tim thought he understood what he was getting at.

"So, Jesus can just tell demons to leave, and Christians can, but I'm outta luck because I don't have a relationship with Jesus? And I can't just find the guy that has my family and deal with him because he's likely under the control of this demon? Great." He was deflated.

"My boy, this is not an unrepairable situation. As in the dream, you have a choice in this. You can attempt to fight a spiritual war with physical weapons, or you can change your arsenal." Dr. Taylor was insistent without being pushy, matter-of-fact without arrogance. Tim could see now what Paul saw in him. There was no mistaking the concern for Tim in his voice.

"I really appreciate what you're trying to say but it just doesn't work like that with me. I can't make myself believe something that doesn't click."

With sadness and understanding in his eyes, Dr. Taylor looked at Tim and said, "That's truer than you know. All faith is a gift. Jesus claimed that when He was lifted up on the cross He would draw all men to Himself. This means that there isn't a person on earth that Christ isn't trying to bring into the right relationship with Himself right now. Including you. So, no, you can't make yourself believe. But you can lean more on faith than mere understanding.

"You see, most people are the type to say 'I'll believe it when I see it' or 'prove it.' But faith says that when you believe, only then will you truly see things for what and how they are. Faith is the bridge to reason, not the other way around."

Tim had the impression that he was having a conversation with a modern-day Yoda and stifled a dry laugh at the thought. "I'll chew on that," Tim promised.

"Please do. And know that all authority in heaven and earth is given to those who truly know and love Christ. But that power is not available to those who simply want to *do religious things.* The seventh chapter of the book of Matthew reminds us there are those who do miraculous things, even in the name of Jesus, that are not truly His. They will cry 'Lord, Lord' but He will reply 'Depart from me, I never knew you.' It is all about the relationship, not the religious fervor that you show."

This made sense to Tim because he was the kind of guy who assumed goodness or religious zeal was what earned you points for heaven. That foundation of thought was starting to crumble in light of the last fifteen hours.

"Any rubber meets the road advice for me? I'm about to head out to face this guy, or demon, or whatever he is." Tim wanted any help he could get.

"Actually, yes. But first, has Paul ever told you why I find your friendship so interesting and fantastic?"

Tim was stunned by this question. First off, it hadn't struck him that he would have been any topic of conversation outside of his sphere of family and friends. But then again, he spoke about Paul all the time, so it wasn't all that strange to think about. But why would this guy find it at all *interesting* or *fantastic?*

"Um, no."

"I know you aren't yet a believer and you haven't read much of scripture, but you understand who the Apostle Paul was, correct?" He asked.

"I do now. Paul," he said pointing to his sleeping friend on the bed, "quoted him earlier tonight."

"Yes. Well, the Apostle Paul had a young friend that he loved dearly named Timothy. He called him his 'son in the faith.' Two of the letters Paul wrote to Timothy are in the New Testament."

Tim didn't know that. How weird. Dr. Taylor continued with his advice.

"In 1 Timothy 6:12, he tells Timothy to 'Fight the good fight of the faith.' One cannot fight the good fight of the faith without faith. My advice to you is this: find your faith and fight the good fight, Timothy."

This didn't sound like rubber meets the road but that's probably the most straightforward thing he had heard him say yet. Dr. Taylor wasn't finished though.

"And the devil is a liar. The only way to fight a lie is with the truth. Be cautious not to believe what your mind is telling you. He will surely twist the truth and use it against you. This spirit of fear wants to make you think he is fear itself. But he is not. I will be praying for you and your family. Praying God's protection on them. I will place my shield of faith over you, your wife, and your children until you are equipped with your very own."

Tim shook his hand, thanked him, and stepped over to Paul. He shocked himself by bending over and kissing the top of his head. "I hope to see you again, my friend."

With a somber resolution, Tim walked out of the hospital and to the Tahoe. What he didn't know was that all of this, and his own life, was coming to an end in the next ten hours.

PART THREE

"For God has not given us a spirit of fear, but of power, and love, and a sound mind."

2 Timothy 1:7

CHAPTER TWENTY-THREE

The morning sun was already warm. 7:24 a.m. They never bothered to switch to Central Standard Time so it was still only 6:24 in New Orleans. It had only been fourteen hours since that awful phone call to Liz that started all this. Tim had decided not to even bother to take Paul's bag up to him and just hit the road. He was bone tired and running on pure will. He'd have to hustle but he could maybe be there by 1:00 or 1:30. One way or another, this would be over sometime today, he could feel it.

The sky above was patched with clouds but it was balmy. As he cranked the truck he thought of Gabe, Z, Dr. Taylor, Paul. All of these men had helped him tonight. All of these men knew what kind of messed up stuff was going on right now and they were on his side. This didn't necessarily put too much wind in his sails but it was a glimmer of hope in a dark situation.

As Tim drove towards I-10 he tried to pull up Camp Muscogee on his GPS but it didn't exist anymore. He knew it was this side of Albany but couldn't remember the name of the town it was in. Generally a very safe driver and never one to text or play with his phone while driving, Tim made an exception and googled the old camp on his phone at a red light.

It provided not only the name of the town, Barnesville, but also had a few interesting articles about the murders from the '70s and the short-lived camp from Tim's day. One, in particular, caught his eye as the light changed granting him the left turn onto the highway he needed. Since traffic was light, he took advantage of the long shoulder ramp and opened the article titled, "*Sheriff Graham to Step Down After Camp Incident.*"

He had a feature on his phone that he used when driving that read texts and emails to him. He slid two fingers down the screen and the automated voice began to read the article to him so he could have both eyes on the road.

Sheriff Luke Graham has informed the residents of Dougherty County that in light of recent events at Camp Muscogee he will be resigning after serving twelve years as sheriff. A camp for boys ages eleven to fourteen has only been open for two years following the donation of the property from the Clement family to the Agape Baptist Church. The church has been without a Pastor for three years since Pastor Steven Larkey stepped down one year into the Camp's construction. The church building sits on the northern edge of the church's new property that once served as a popular fishing and hunting area. The property has largely gone unused since the bodies of fourteen young boys were found in the bordering property of the lake in the summer of 1978.

The boys went missing from their homes over a period of two months. They ranged in age from twelve to fourteen years. Local police and the Sheriff's department launched a full-scale investigation and searched for the killer, but no arrests were ever made in the case. Locals were shocked to learn that the boys' bodies had been dumped in the lake, no other details about the case were released to the public.

Sheriff Graham lost a younger brother, Scott, in the case and claims it was this incident that persuaded him to enter law enforcement after graduating college six years later. The opening of the camp was supposed to lift the dark cloud hanging over the town, the property, and the Graham family until another young boy, whose name was not released, was attacked on the property and found in a near-comatose state at the site of the fourteen-year-old murders this past summer. The boy's father, an Atlanta Construction Contractor, demanded the camp be shut down under threat of a lawsuit. It has been four months since the incident at the camp and the doors have been closed and the property is up for sale.

The news of Sheriff Graham's resignation shocked the community as it was disclosed at a press conference last night. Sheriff Graham was quoted as saying, "I deeply regret that any other child had to suffer like this in our town. I believe that I am fighting the wrong war. I have been wrestling against the wrong enemy and I intend to change tactics. I have appreciated the support and commitment of the good people of Dougherty County as Sheriff, but I will be taking the position of Pastor at Agape Baptist Church starting immediately. I may not be able to bring the perpetrators of these heinous crimes to justice and avenge their families but I can fight back the darkness behind crimes like these, one soul at a time."

Agape Baptist Church has seen a steady decline in attendance over the past three years since the construction and opening of the camp and members have cited the camp's closing, as well as the loss of their former pastor, as a financial loss as well. Nearly $200,000 had been raised to turn the property into a camp and the closing at the start of the third year made any return on the investment nearly impossible.

Locals have rallied behind Sheriff Graham's announcement and the election of a new Sheriff will begin next month in November. Until then Deputy Lance Baker will assume the title and duties of Sheriff.

Dougherty Gazette A.P.
22, October 1992

Tim knew this was about him. Obviously, he was the young boy found comatose nearly thirty years ago but to hear an article written about it made it seem like it was someone else entirely. And to think that this Sheriff quit his job and became a Pastor over it. Man, that was a reality check. He wasn't the only one affected by those events.

The thought of finding this Sheriff-turned-Pastor sounded like it might be a good idea. Not only was he aware of the criminal activity that surrounded events like these, but as a Pastor, he would surely be sensitive to whatever spiritual stuff was going on. Tim still wasn't a hundred percent on what, exactly, that was but he knew he needed someone with a working knowledge of spiritual things that also knew how to use a gun on his side.

He didn't even know if this guy was still alive, much less in the area or not, but he was hoping it wouldn't be too hard to find him. He hit 4-1-1 on his phone and when the automated voice asked, "City and state, please," he enunciated, "Barnesville, Georgia." When the actual human picked up and asked, "What listing in Barnesville?" He dutifully replied, "Luke Graham."

He was taken aback when she said, "I have two Luke Grahams in Barnesville."

"Um, maybe Reverend Luke Graham?" he tried. Kind of a small town to have two Luke Grahams. Tim deduced it was a relative with the same namesake. His father or an uncle perhaps.

"Thank you, one moment."

He drew in a quick breath when it began to ring. He forgot that with cellphones it was an automatic connection these days. Gone were the old landline days when you were given the number or address of the person you wanted and had to hang up and dial the number yourself. Technology was great but sometimes he greatly disliked the way the world was going where everything was intuitively done for you. Tim was a *do-it-yourself* guy in an *autocorrect* world.

Oh well. He hoped he didn't scare this guy off or sound like a raving lunatic. On the third ring, a gruff but kind sounding voice picked up and said, "Hello?"

"Is this Sheriff — I mean, Rev. Graham?" Not off to a great start.

"Yes, this is Pastor Graham." The slight correction came off as a humble request meant to lose the more official "reverend" for the more approachable "pastor." He liked this guy already.

"I'm not sure how exactly to start this conversation so I'm just going to jump in there, ok?" Tim hoped a former sheriff would appreciate the direct approach.

"Ok," he replied with an intrigued tone.

"My name is Tim McDaniel. I was the little boy they found in the woods at Camp Muscogee thirty years ago."

"My Lord. I always wondered what happened to you after that summer. How are you, son?" His tone was fatherly and genuine. He had no trouble recalling that summer, not that Tim thought he would. "I've prayed for you often."

That last part caught Tim off guard. A total stranger prayed for him? He felt appreciative but awkward.

"Um, thank you. Actually, I'm on my way to Barnesville right now via New Orleans and I was hoping to maybe meet up with you. I'm in a bit of a situation and I'd like your help if you're up for it."

"Of course. That'll be around 1:30 or so?" He was a quick thinker. "Would you care to have lunch at my house?" This guy was the real deal. Opening his home to a guy who might be a whacko wasn't something Tim would do, but then he wasn't a sheriff turned pastor.

"I appreciate the offer, but I am in a pretty bad time crunch. The purpose of my visit is a little…" he wasn't sure how to put this, "precarious."

"I see. That's no problem. Well, I live in the parsonage next to the church so it would be no trouble to have you here if you're planning on going to the camp, but I'll leave that up to your discretion." He didn't sound offended at all. "You'll find I'm pretty open to precarious situations so I look forward to the conversation."

"It's only fair to let you know that this is a potentially criminal situation and also a strangely spiritual one at the same time. I'm not sure how else to put it."

"Well, those are two areas I'm fairly familiar with. I should probably ask you… are you in trouble? Legally, I mean? I don't want to scare you off but harboring a criminal is not the best idea either."

"Not really." That wasn't as reassuring as he'd hoped. "I mean, I'm not running from the law but I was told not to leave town. Which I did anyway. So, there's that."

"I see." He was a cool character. Nothing rattled him so far. "Well, I very much want to help you, but you can understand how I might need to know a little bit about this upfront. If you wouldn't mind."

"Of course. I'm sorry. I know this is coming off a lot sketchier than I intended." Tim took a breath and gave the Cliff Notes version of the last fifteen hours.

"My wife and two children were abducted from our home yesterday evening. I was on my way home from work when I called my wife.

While I was on the phone with her, she thought I pulled in the driveway and hung up. But it wasn't me. Whoever it was looked enough like me to fool them, and my neighbor told the police that I picked them up.

"I'm trying to find them but I'm kind of the only suspect as far as the police are concerned right now. And ever since then I've been having some very… strange encounters that I can't explain. My best friend, who is also a Pastor on a college campus, has been helping me but he was jumped tonight by a crazed homeless person and is in the hospital, so I'm on my own again. This is sounding way out there, I know. I hope to make more sense in person. But I have reason to believe that my family might be being held at the camp and that this is somehow related to my experience there years ago."

"I see." Those must be his favorite two words. But this wasn't the *I see* of a skeptic and didn't sound at all patronizing. It was methodical and conveyed much more than the flippancy those two words could denote. "Would you mind if I placed a call in to the detective working your case? Perhaps some professional courtesy might keep you out of trouble so we can talk without fear of you being arrested."

This guy was too good to be true.

"Uh, sure. If you think that's a good idea. It's Detective Peters of the Alpharetta Police Department. I don't have his number on me and I can't remember his first name."

"That's ok, I can find it. I'll see you at 1:30, Lord willing."

Tim wasn't nervous that this guy was gonna pull a fast one on him or anything. He could feel the genuine concern this Pastor had for him and decided to simply trust him. This was new for Tim as he didn't trust people very easily.

"Great. Thanks so much. I'll see you soon then."

Tim wondered what he was going to tell Detective Peters. Whatever he told him would sound far better coming from Pastor Graham than it would from him. He wasn't terribly sure how jurisdiction worked in cases like this but he also wondered if Detective Peters might be at the house when he arrived. Honestly, that would be ok as long as they followed the trail and tried to find his family.

Tim needed to concentrate and get there. Without Paul to keep him focused he was nervous that another "episode" could further undo him. For the first time in, well, almost thirty years Tim lifted a quick prayer for help. It was a little half-hearted but if there was a God and He could be of assistance then Tim would cover his bases.

And with that Tim put the pedal down to make some time. He made a mental note to call the hospital later to check on Paul. He chided himself for not offering proper goodbyes to Gabe or Z but he was in a terrible hurry to get on the road.

The dark, rainy morning continued to hold an ominous expectation. He was desperate to save his family. This might be the longest five hour drive of his life.

CHAPTER TWENTY-FOUR

Fighting fatigue that was bone-deep, Tim scanned the radio for a station that provided upbeat music. Although he normally wasn't a Talk Radio kind of guy, he found himself stopping on a station that was interviewing a serial killer. Morbid curiosity got the best of him.

After a few minutes, he had gathered that this guy had run along the same lines as Ted Bundy or Jeffrey Dahmer. After years of engrossing himself in pornography, he eventually killed a girlfriend during sex. This led to luring young men and women with sex or drugs and killing them after sometimes doing unspeakable acts to their bodies. And now he was in prison telling his macabre story.

Why was he listening to this? He was about to change the station when the interviewer asked a question that stopped him in his tracks.

"You claim you've become a Christian while in prison, correct?"

"Yes, that's correct." He asserted.

Tim was thinking to himself, *well of course he did he wants to get out of jail* when the man followed up his reply with another statement.

"I deserve to be here. What I've done is wrong. Awful. And, honestly, this is the reaping of what I've sown. I don't expect to change anyone's opinion of me and I'm certainly not trying to gain sympathy. I don't deserve to have any of the families of my victims think better of me and I know that. But I also know that, for whatever reason, Jesus has forgiven me. Even me." His voice almost broke on the last two words.

The interviewer pushed a little. "How can you say, for all the world to hear, that Jesus forgives you after what you've done?" A dramatic pause. "Why would God forgive you?" It wasn't a venomous attack but more of a setup question.

"That's a great question. What I've come to understand is that forgiveness is for anyone who wants it. It isn't based on merit or the person's record. Honestly, I don't think I deserve forgiveness, but I sure want it. Jesus forgives based on His record, not mine. I resisted it for months, even in here. I deserve Hell, nobody would argue that. But forgiveness is a gift and nobody deserves a gift, right?"

Tim noticed how childlike and humble this vicious serial killer sounded. As if the interviewer could read his mind, the next thought Tim was forming was asked.

"So, what changed for you? How do you go from murderer to believer? From serial killer sinner to saint?"

Tim was very interested in his answer. He had always wondered about "jailhouse religion" and such. These *scum-of-the-earth* types were always finding Jesus in prison. His answer was more relevant than Tim would have thought possible.

"I was in darkness. In fact, according to the Bible, I *was* darkness. My mind was broken and I was under the most demonic strongholds you can imagine. I know many people will find this ridiculous," he seemed to steel himself for his next statement, "but I was possessed by demons.

"I could hear them in my head, urging me to kill, to torture. The pop-psychology culture would have called me schizophrenic and moved on. But I know better. That's not an accurate diagnosis for me. But I gave in to them so often that when I tried to resist, I thought my mind and body were going to be ripped into pieces. I could never think straight anymore.

"After I was arrested it was as if they knew they couldn't use me anymore and many of them just... left me. I could think more clearly again, but it was too late. A fellow inmate gave me a Bible and I read it. I read how Jesus cast out demons in His name and I wanted them out of me. Once I truly believed Jesus would forgive me and that he alone had the authority over any demonic power I told them to leave in the name of Jesus. And they did. So, Jesus saved me then and there.

"No more voices, no more darkness. And I know He forgives me, even though what I did was my choice and it was terrible. I'm the villain, not the victim. But Jesus died for the villains, too. When I confessed my sin and was truly sorry... *repentant*, he simply forgave me and washed me clean. I don't know how else to explain it."

Tim swallowed. He had never thought of it in terms like that. Prisoners no longer being "useful" to the powers of darkness that goaded them into violent and murderous action. There had to be a least a few that were genuine. He remembered hearing something similar about Dahmer just weeks before he was killed in prison. Was it so hard to think that even serial killers could find redemption?

Tim didn't know how he felt about it. But if this guy wasn't trying to use this newfound faith as a platform to be released then maybe there was some validity to his testimony. Maybe it was a bigger scam, he had no idea. He had always assumed and even hoped, that guys like this burned in the hottest part of Hell for their crimes. But what if they went to heaven?

The very prospect made him question God's judgment. All this evil in the world had to be brought to justice somehow. Even as he thought it Paul's voice was in his mind saying something like "Jesus' death was the justice we all deserved so that we get grace and mercy instead of justice." Even when he wasn't in the car with him, he was part of the conversation. Tim chuckled at the thought of how much his friend had impacted his thinking.

As Tim was reaching for the scan dial to find some music a voice spoke to him from the speakers.

"He isn't forgiven of anything. He'll be roasting in Hell along with all the others like him. There is no grace, Timmy. Or justice. God doesn't care. Jesus died for nothing, just a confused Jew. And there's no hope for you either. Or your doomed family. Your kids are already dead and gutted, now I'm just having fun with your pretty wife again. And you're not here to stop me this time." His sick laughter filled the Tahoe.

Tim was caught off guard with this but then calmed himself and tried to turn off the radio. It wouldn't cut off.

"You think it's that easy to get rid of me? I'll let you enjoy some music to my ears. Here are the screams of your children, for your listening pleasure."

And with that Tim heard the tortured screams of his little Hannah and Caleb. They were crying and yelling for him to save them, to make it stop. It was a full minute that he listened, powerless to help. He slammed the radio dials, click the volume off, to no avail. Tim felt warm tears streaming down his cheeks. *Oh God*, what if this is real? He heard Dr. Taylor's reassuring words come back to him. "The devil is a liar..."

He pushed the power button again and it all ended. He rode in silence for many miles. Tim wasn't sure he could take much more of this. Each new torment brought him to a more fragile state. And now he was alone. He wasn't ready for this. His family was going to die because of him. They were probably already dead! *They were dead and he was next!*

Stop it! Stop thinking that way. Tim had to shut down the voice in his head.

And with a new and better understanding, Tim could appreciate what the former serial killer was talking about. We all have voices in our heads from time to time. Cartoons and goofy movies made them the little devil and little angel on our shoulders. One leads us to the good and proper course of action while the other tempts us to the fun and frivolous life. It was all too common.

Some would call it our conscience. That little voice inside us that guides our way. Well, this voice was definitely not his conscience and he knew it wasn't the little angel on his shoulder filling his mind with that morbid filth. Maybe the devil does talk to people. Maybe God does too.

Tim pondered this chain of thought for a good hour or more until he realized he was almost halfway there. He had been driving about ten or twelve over the speed limit, hoping to avoid being noticed by any law enforcement so he was making great time.

About 400 miles to go averaging eighty miles per hour. At this rate, he'd be to Pastor Graham's a little after noon.

CHAPTER TWENTY-FIVE

"Detective Peters?"

"Yes, this is Sean Peters. Who is this?"

"I'm Pastor Luke Graham. I was the sheriff in Dougherty County for twelve years and retired to Pastor a local church back in '92."

"What can I do for you, Pastor?" Detective Peter's tone was respectful and light.

"I spoke with a mutual acquaintance today. A Tim McDaniel?" He let the name drop to see what Peters made of it.

"Oh?" He was playing it cool. Pastor Graham was forced to reveal his hand first.

"Yes. He called me not long ago. I was the Sheriff when Tim was a young boy at a camp in our town. He was, for lack of a better word, traumatized by an event that happened that summer here."

Silence on the other end only revealed that he was going to have to spill the beans before they were going to reach any solid ground. He would have done the exact same thing in Peters' position so he didn't begrudge him at all. He exhaled and laid it all out for him.

"I know that Tim McDaniel's family was taken and that he is the only suspect at this time. However, he believes that whoever has his family might have them at the campgrounds here." Another pause. "And he's on his way now. I asked him if I could call you since you specifically told him not to leave town and he trusted that would be the best option."

That was a risky move but Luke knew better than to be coy or elusive with a detective. If he was worth his salt, he'd smell BS a mile off and this whole thing would implode before any help could come for Tim McDaniel or his family.

"And you think he's telling the truth?" Detective Peters questioned with neither malice nor skepticism.

"I tend to think so, yes. Based on the history of this area and his story lining up with the events he endured nearly thirty years ago, I am inclined to believe him. Or I at least believe that he believes it. Either way, I wanted to bring you in on this as you're working the case. It's more than professional courtesy, I felt obligated to call you." Pastor Graham knew that last part sounded flighty but he never withheld the truth, if at all possible.

"I see," replied Detective Peters. Now that he was on the receiving end of the *"I see"* Pastor Graham could see why it put everyone on edge so easily. But he still believed detective Peters was not being elusive or purposely enigmatic.

Pastor Graham sat in slightly uncomfortable silence for a moment. He wanted to give Detective Peters a chance to respond in his own words, his own way. After an awkward silence, Detective Peters spoke.

"Pastor, I want to level with you. I am a man of faith. I've been a believer for about eight years now and I've seen some strange stuff in my life. Both on the job and in my own life. I'm not sure what, exactly, we're dealing with here concerning Tim McDaniel but I think there is something bigger than just the law of man at work. I've felt it since I met the man. I don't know what truth is to be discovered in your town but I'm on my way. I'll come alone."

Pastor Graham almost sighed in relief but instead, he simply said, "I look forward to it. I hope to the Lord we can help this young man and his family."

"As do I, Pastor."

Luke Graham gave Sean Peters his address. It was more than a retired sheriff giving an active detective an address, it was almost like two old friends reuniting under unpleasant circumstances.

"I'd like to fill you in on our town's history before you come so you can have the full story from me." Pastor Graham decided.

"Ok. Fill me in."

Pastor Graham took him back to the summer of 1978, complete with the horrific details of the murders that were never released. He confessed that one of the fourteen victims had been his younger brother and how that made him vow to fight crime. He also included his own salvation experience in college that challenged his worldview and made him more sensitive to the events that were currently unfolding.

It was when he recounted the events of the summer of 1992 involving Tim McDaniel that the hairs on Detective Peters neck stood up. This young boy, new to the area, was one of the campers in the third year of the new camp. His descriptions of the fourteen boys and the man he claimed had grabbed him were an exact match to the information the Sheriff's department had on file of the murders fourteen years earlier.

Some of the locals knew a little about the murders and people talked, of course. The description of the suspect in the case was released, but never proved helpful as he was never found. Still, some of the details of the boys were never released to anyone but family so there was no way Tim could have known many of the things he said he saw that night.

The description of the other boy, Del, also proved to be a strange facet of the case as no child under that name was registered to camp that summer, despite the insistence of several of the other boys of seeing and talking with him. Many even insisted he stayed in their bunkhouse but the Camp Counselor denied his existence as well.

Tim's family had effectively shut down the camp after the event and Tim was protected from the media and any legal ramifications, but that was the event that made Sheriff Graham transform into Pastor Graham. The evil forces he believed to be behind the murders long ago were at work again and he meant to fight them.

Detective Peters listened attentively, even jotting some notes here and there. This certainly shed some light on their current case. At least as far as what made Tim McDaniel tick. This guy knew fear. Peters knew what evil was capable of and he knew that it would take more than bullets to stop this specific brand of bad guy. From what he could tell from the police station earlier last night, McDaniel believed that there was someone capable of impersonating him and Detective Peters that was trying to taunt him into action. Well, he was on his way to the camp so he guessed it had worked.

Pastor Graham said Tim was on his way from New Orleans. What had he unearthed there, he wondered? After they hung up, Peters let Calloway know he would be gone for the afternoon and headed out. This was going to be interesting, for sure. He prayed for wisdom and protection, for all involved.

CHAPTER TWENTY-SIX

Tim opted to drive in silence for a while longer. Even though they filled up outside of New Orleans, he was going to have to stop for gas again soon. He loved the room and horsepower his Tahoe afforded but the gas mileage was nothing to brag about. In a world of hybrids and gas sippers everywhere, he drove a tank that gulped gas by the gallon.

Strangely, his lack of sleep was no longer weighing him down with fatigue anymore. That last encounter via the radio had him plenty awake. When his thoughts drifted to the dark, hopelessness of his situation he tried to steer them back to his conversations with Paul, Dr. Taylor, and Z. Honestly, those were as frustrating to him as they were reassuring. But they gave him food for thought.

There wasn't as much traffic on the interstate as he would have thought so he was able to keep a steady pace in the fast lane. Up ahead he noticed a hitchhiker. A man with a cardboard sign and a backpack slung over one shoulder. Given the nature of his trip, there was no way he was going to stop to give anyone a ride but curiosity caused him to read the man's sign.

He assumed this guy was some kind of jokester or something because he didn't get what his sign was saying. It simply read *headed to Hell* with a smiley face at the bottom.

He was smiling as Tim drove past. Tim just shook his head as he passed him. People are weird.

As he drove a few more miles down the road he was lost in thought again as he noticed another hitchhiker ahead with another sign. He knew he hadn't paid super close attention but he was struck with the notion that this was the same guy. Cardboard sign and backpack slung over the shoulder. But that wasn't possible. Must be a busy stretch of road.

This sign was equally enigmatic. As he drove past, he noticed the man had a similar smile plastered to his face. As Tim read the sign, he would have just shaken his head again if this wasn't so *déjà vu* and all. This time the sign read *pain awaits you* with another smiley face. Was this some freaky planned-out thing like a flash mob or something? Were there folks up and down the roads with weird signs trying to gain attention for some group or new product?

He didn't think that's what this was, honestly. He had that sick feeling in his gut again.

It was barely two miles before he saw another guy with a sign up ahead. Not another guy. The same guy. He was sure this time. Same clothes, bag, even holding the same sign with new words.

This time the mystery was stripped away. The sign read *Camp Muscogee or Bust* and had the smiley face at the bottom. There was no way on earth Tim was stopping but he had the feeling that he wasn't expected to. This was intended to be more of a tormenting thing, he decided.

He tried not to look as he passed but he couldn't help himself. Only now did he look into the smiling face of the man. Those eyes. How did he not notice before? Such a smug smile, too.

It was close to three miles before he saw him again. He made up his mind to ignore him. But just as he flew by his eyes flicked to read the sign. This one was more to the point and read *better hurry, Liz needs her hero.* But the smiley face had a bullet hole in the head with red Sharpie blood coming out of it.

This went on for the next 50 miles. Every two or three miles the same hitchhiker holding a sign with some ominous, macabre, or vile message and some form of a brutalized smiley face at the bottom. He only saw a few as he forced himself to drive past most of them. The last one caught his eye and his breath. The sign read *too late, they're dead* with no smiley face.

It bothered him when he realized that a couple of miles down the road there was no more hitchhiker, no more signs. What had he missed? Maybe he should have read them all. No, this was a twisted game and there were no rules that made any sense. This was designed to mess with his head. It worked.

He decided after another ten miles with no roadside messengers that he would go ahead and get gas. Secretly, he hoped for another visitation of sorts to at least confirm that he was still on the right trail. He was told to go to the camp and he was going as quickly as he could. He still couldn't shake off that last sign though.

The Citgo gas station was not large, but it also wasn't so tiny as to not have all the energy drinks and restroom facilities he needed. He started to fill his 32-gallon tank up at $3.28 a gallon but reached the $75 automatic cut-off most pay-at-the-pumps had these days. He hadn't realized he was that low on fuel.

He went in to make a quick bathroom break. Remembering what had happened the night before motivated his brevity. He also needed a knock-off five-hour energy deal. Any of the vitamin B and caffeine combos would be fine. As he came out and was putting his Dasani water and Hacker energy shot on the counter, he noticed the television in the corner behind the counter. The sound was low but he could hear it ok. His face filled the screen.

"Timothy McDaniel is believed to have murdered his family and is on the run from state officials. Last identified in an Auburn, Alabama gas station last night, he is believed to be headed to Albany, Ga by way of I-10 from New Orleans today. He is considered armed and dangerous and if you have any information on his whereabouts, please contact Detective Sean Peters of the Alpharetta Police Department."

What the —? Apparently, that *good feeling* about Pastor Luke Graham was wrong. What a lying scumbag! Tim was not happy. And he was scared. The guy ringing him up hadn't paid any attention to the news flash so Tim played it cool. He paid cash for his items, now convinced they would be searching his debit card. But wait! He just filled his tank on the card. He had to get out of here, quick.

He still couldn't believe that he was betrayed by that lying preacher. *Once a sheriff, always a sheriff* he thought. Well, he still had to get to the camp but now there were surely going to be roadblocks and maybe a SWAT team waiting on him. What was he going to do?

His mind raced. He was only about an hour out. It was 10:55 and he knew he could be at the camp by noon. They'd be looking for his Tahoe. Maybe he should steal another car. What if he could find an off-road dirt bike? That would get him into the woods a lot easier than his truck. And maybe he could sneak past any checkpoints.

Part of him wanted to call that piece-of-work preacher back and throw him off the trail. Make it sound like he had another bit of news of where his family was being held and say he wasn't coming there anymore. That might help. He wanted to give him a piece of his mind but that wouldn't help anything right now.

Why had the report said he murdered his family? Did the police know something? Oh, God. Did they already find his family and now they think he killed them?

Tim's knees buckled and he slid to the ground by his truck. He put his head in his hands and was about to scream when he just prayed the most simple, desperate prayer he had ever uttered.

"Please. Help me."

CHAPTER TWENTY-SEVEN

Pastor Graham paced in his living room for a minute while trying to pray. This was coming to a head. After all these years it seemed as if this nightmare was swelling to some conclusion. Or was this just another sad chapter of his pained life?

First, he lost his brother, Scott, when he was only twelve. Luke had been eighteen and had a wild streak. But not Scott. He was a good kid. He was mild-mannered and respectful. He tried hard in school and didn't fuss about going to church. Heck, he even liked church. Weird for a kid his age in the seventies.

Scott was one of the fourteen kids murdered that summer. All of them were good kids, in fact. Luke knew all of the families. All went to church and were active in the community. It was almost like they all fit the same profile picked out by the killer.

Police had suspected it was a local. An outsider who hated the "all-American" type and preyed on the "good" boys of the town. Luke couldn't think of anyone he knew that would do to those boys what was done to them.

Scott's death had unraveled his family. Luke's dad was a deacon in their church but after Scott's death, his dad never went back to church. Most of the families were the same way. Before the murders, most of them had been active members of Agape Baptist Church where he served now, ironically. No, not irony. Purpose.

There was a purpose to all of this. Luke didn't see it then but he saw it now. After the summer of 1992, he became convinced that there was something evil in their little town. And now Tim McDaniel was on his way to confront the evil that tore Luke's world apart twenty-four years earlier.

He understood that there was a real-world that everyone saw with their eyes and there was another world behind the veil of this world that was just as real. More real, even. When this physical world was done the spiritual world that nobody sees right now would last forever. Folks just don't like that kind of talk though. Nobody wants to think that this world isn't heaven.

YOLO, wasn't it? That's what folks say these days. You only live once so have fun and enjoy it all you can. That is the biggest lie the devil ever sold us, humans. What a brilliant lie though. If this life is all that we have, why not live it up and have a good ole time?

But that's just not the case. The *really* real world is hidden from us without faith. We can't see it because we don't want to. Because once we acknowledge it, then we're culpable to it. We have a responsibility to live in accordance with a higher truth than YOLO. And that's not fun for most. That's why Jesus said the "way is narrow that leads to eternal life and few find it." It's not impossible, just narrow.

And ironically, Christians are often viewed as "narrow-minded" folks because they say Jesus is the only truth, the only way to heaven. Well, in a way it is narrow-minded. But that doesn't make it untrue. Heck, lots of things in life are way narrower than that and we accept it. But put stipulations on who gets into heaven and people cry "foul!"

Luke used to be one of those who strongly opposed the church, organized religion, whatever religious elitism wanted to claim. That was before he saw behind the veil.

Now, he knew better and it changed who he was. He had no excuse anymore to be angry at God for the way the world was. He didn't see this life as the ultimate goal anymore. He lived for a higher purpose now. Because when you see the spiritual world, the *real* world, you are faced with surrendering to the truth you always denied or living a lie of hypocrisy.

Luke always despised hypocrisy. No way he was gonna be the king of it. So, he surrendered to the truth and asked Jesus to forgive him of his rebellious heart. The immediate rush of relief and joy that filled his life was unexpected but amazing. All the bitterness and anger towards God for letting Scott die a horrible death didn't just go away magically but it was as if he had a much better grasp of how things worked – both now and eternally.

He served as Sheriff with conviction and faith. He was fair, honest, and compassionate and did his job well. It was only after 1992 that he realized that his war was not against flesh and blood but against spiritual darkness. Guns and badges had no authority over creatures of darkness.

He had been faithfully serving as the Pastor of Agape Baptist Church since then and he had seen his fair share of spiritual warfare in this little town. He had traveled the world a bit as well and saw the same thing everywhere he went. Man was bent towards evil, not good. There was far more selfishness in the world than there was selflessness.

Thirty years was a long time to be in the same place these days, but he was glad he put his roots down in Barnesville. This community used to have hope but darkness crept in forty-four years ago and murdered fourteen precious boys. Hope had been a scarce commodity since then.

The boy's camp was supposed to be the ray of light that brought hope back to the people but when young Tim McDaniel was attacked and found in the woods the next morning, alive but terrified, hope left town with him. Maybe his return would have a greater impact than he realized. Maybe this young man was an unwitting soldier in this cosmic battle. Maybe darkness would finally be driven back by the light.

Or maybe the evil that seemed to take up residence in this town so long ago just wanted to finish what it started

CHAPTER TWENTY-EIGHT

Liz must have stood there for ten minutes, completely unsure of what to do next. What if he awoke and physically restrained her again? He said he didn't care if she tried the door or screamed, but was that a bluff? If she screamed, would he snap through his restraints again and come after her?

She had to know where her children were. If they were close, she would stop at nothing to get to them. She hadn't heard any noises overhead this whole time so part of her doubted they were there. She refused to believe anything had happened to them. She would find them and lavish them with hugs and kisses and a mother's tears.

But first.

She crept past the sleeping man and made her way to the door. It was thicker than she would have thought and was locked on this side with a large Masterlock padlock. That was why he was so confident. He must have the key on him and knew she couldn't get out.

She found the courage to bang on it a few times and yell, "help!" She listened, more to hear the cries of her children than for a rescuer. Once more, "Help! Is anyone there?"

She stole a quick glance back at the man to check that he wasn't approaching her. Still out.

She had a thought. It shocked her a little. Normally, she was very non-violent but she considered clocking this guy so hard that he wouldn't wake up, then grab the keys off of him. Would that work? Surely she could incapacitate a man who was already unconscious. It seemed like her only option at the present moment.

Her initial search of the room earlier had yielded nothing remotely weapon-like so unless she wanted to drop-kick this guy, she had no idea what she could do. Her eyes darted once more across the span of the room. A candle. That's all that was in there with them other than the wooden chair this man was bound to.

She could set him on fire. Whoa. That was a leap. What was she thinking? Still, he had abducted them. He was dangerous and planned to kill them. It would be self-defense. She would light his shirt on fire, then try to light his pants before he awoke. Then she would watch with delight as this sunnuva —

What was wrong with her? How did a thought like that get in her head? Burn a man alive? She still wasn't even convinced how this guy was doing this? Part of her didn't care. Burn him. Now. Grab the candle and Kill Him!

She was scared. Not just to do it, but because it was as if there was another voice in her head screaming for her to do it. A part of her that wasn't really her. She shut the idea down and backed away.

"I knew you didn't have it in you." The dark, bitter voice said from the still drooping head.

She stood there, confused and unsure of what she should do or say. She said and did nothing.

A demeaning and condescending laugh left his lips. "Killing this guy is the only way to save your kids and you still won't do it. *Pathetic.* The keys are right here." He wiggled his right leg, indicating the keys were in that pocket.

This was all a test, a trick. He wasn't going to let her get out. He was pushing her to see her resolve. But how did he know what was going through her mind? Surely he only sensed her struggle. Unless he had put the thoughts there.

Wait, what was she doing? That isn't possible. Why would she even think that? Still.

"How about if I tell you your kids are locked up in the tool shed out back? That they're alone and scared and crying for mommy right now but you're down here because you don't have the spine to kill a piece of garbage like me and save them."

What was he doing? Why goad her into killing him? That same calm from before came over her again. She would not be fooled by this man's words. He was a liar and could not be trusted.

He sensed her resignation again and it infuriated him. He snapped all four restraints again as he stood, and with inhuman speed was in front of her. She had no time to respond as he was lightning quick. His hand was around her throat and she was off the ground before she could prepare to defend herself.

"You arrogant, stupid woman. I am so going to enjoy killing you after I make you watch me mutilate your children." His words were so hateful, so angry that she cringed. But she didn't give in to the fear.

Though she could barely breathe, she forced herself to utter one word. One defiant word before he choked the consciousness from her. "No."

He threw her effortlessly against the wall, knocking her into a dreamless sleep. The last thought that raced through her mind before impact was, "Please God, help Tim."

The man looked at her with hate and loathing. He took the key from his pocket and unlocked the door. He walked out of the cabin and around to the small tool shed in the back. He unlocked the padlock on that door as well and looked in.

Two small figures were still lying on the floor sleeping. The drugs had been more powerful on their little bodies than on the mother. Chances are they might not wake up before everything got good. He'd have to make sure that wasn't the case.

He'd never been so forbidden from taking innocent life before. That was part of the deal in a fallen world. He was usually free to wreak havoc wherever the Enemy's hand was lifted. But He wouldn't lift His hand from these two for some reason. That was what made His image-bearers hate Him so. That He ever allowed anything bad to happen to them.

After all, how could a *loving* God let anything *unloving* ever happen? How naive. Most of these flesh-wrapped creatures are to blame for their own pain and misery so it's just hilarious that they turn their venom on their Creator the moment someone they love gets sick, hurt, or dies.

The fact that the fallen ones, like himself, were the princes of the air meant that they could woo and entice the image-bearers to do all kinds of evil, and boy did they take the bait hook, line, and sinker. When they gave themselves over to the influence enough, they could even be taken over completely. Possessed. He loved making these weak sacks of meat into his puppets. This one he was in now was a drugged-out pedophile. Easy.

Until the Enemy had taken on flesh and dwelt among them, this was seldom challenged. But ever since He walked the earth casting us out of men, women, and children, even sending us into pigs, His true followers have used His name and authority to do the same.

Thankfully, almost nobody really believed that anymore. This made his reign so much easier. If nobody believed he existed, then nobody was ever gonna make him leave when he didn't want to. Most folks were so *reasonable* that it was inconceivable to them that the fallen ones actually existed and did, in fact, have a mission to destroy mankind until their appointed end.

The Book told them all about it, but who reads that old thing anymore? The master's greatest accomplishment has been to convince the image-bearers that they were too smart to believe the Book. Heck, more and more didn't even believe in the Enemy anymore. They had a version of Him that they accepted, but let something go wrong in their lives, and bye-bye faith, hello bitterness.

But his thing wasn't so much bitterness as it was fear. Delos loved to work fear into one of the Enemy's precious creatures more than anything. Fear is the opposite of faith. You couldn't have hope and despair at the same time. He tempted more of them to fear and retreat than he ever saw stand in faith and make *him* flee.

But this one. This *woman*. She was getting help from the Enemy for some reason. Del would have to move fast if he was going to accomplish the destruction of Tim McDaniel. The stage was set. He had hated this guy since he was twelve and showed no fear. Well, all that had changed in one night.

He had gotten away for a season and fear no longer plagued him. That was fine. He gave him a few years to live the good life with his family before swooping in to finish what he started with him. Tim McDaniel was going to die with so much fear in his heart that Delos was going to savor it for centuries.

CHAPTER TWENTY-NINE

Tim was still kicking himself for trusting that old backstabbing preacher when he climbed back into his Tahoe and started back towards the camp. Betrayed or not, he was going to get his family. As he was formulating a new plan, his cell phone rang.

It was Luke Graham's number.

Tim didn't want to answer it but figured there was almost no point in ignoring it. Maybe he could throw him off the trail with a lie of his own.

"Hello?" Tim answered on the third ring.

"Mr. McDaniel. I spoke with your friend, Detective Peters."

Oh, I know you did. Tim thought. He didn't want to let on that he had seen the news so he asked as nonchalantly as he could, "How did that go?"

"Very well. He's on his way now."

This guy was good. He sounded so sincere, almost excited. Tim was so disappointed that this guy wasn't the kind, caring pastor he seemed to be. What he said next only confused Tim more.

"Turns out he's a believer and had a strange feeling about this case, too. He said he'd come alone. Should be here about the same time as you, I hope."

Tim was suddenly hopeful that maybe it was Peters who sold him out and Pastor Graham didn't know it. Of course! Pastor Graham calls Detective Peters and Peters plays along only to unleash the whole Police Department after him. Come alone. Give me a break. Why would he do that?

"Are you ok, Tim? You seem… hesitant. Detective Peters sounded very sincere when I spoke with him. I can almost assure you that he's on his way."

"I don't doubt that at all, Pastor Graham. I saw a news release ten minutes ago saying I was on my way to you and that I was 'armed and dangerous.' Looks like the good detective took your invitation as a chance to solve the case with me as the guilty party." Tim let the anger drip from his words. He felt a little sick in his gut and wanted to let a stream of obscenities fly, but didn't want to offend the preacher.

"Tim, I don't think that's the case." He sounded very reassuring but he was being naive.

"Then how do you explain what I saw?!" Tim raised his voice.

There was an intentional pause on the other end of the line and when Luke Graham spoke again the scales fell from Tim's eyes.

"How can you explain any of the things you've seen the last several hours, Tim? It's all a deception, a ruse. You're being manipulated and attacked. From what you've told me it isn't too hard to concede that what you saw isn't real, wouldn't you say?"

Tim sat there feeling foolish and deflated. It was obvious now. He almost acted on this information and did something quite stupid. Why hadn't he even considered this before? It made so much sense. The guy working the counter didn't even see the t.v. just like the other times. Nobody saw but Tim.

He wasn't sure what to say. After all the fear and horrific visions, Tim felt the most drained by this. Reality was starting to crumble away. If he couldn't trust his own senses then what could he trust?

As he was about to speak, Pastor Graham began with words of comfort and reassurance.

"Listen, Tim. I know this must be so difficult but there is a way to tell the truth from the lie. There is a way to beat this."

Tim could tell by the tender, grandfatherly tone where this was going. This was the same tone Paul always took when he was trying to get Tim to convert to Christianity. He wasn't offended but he was not in a place to have this conversation.

"Be a Christian? I know. I've heard. That just isn't something I can snap my fingers and believe though, pastor."

Tim wasn't trying to be a punk, but why couldn't Paul, or Z, or any of these guys get that Tim wasn't like them? He wanted to be reasonable, not have blind faith. He was more comfortable with science and facts than religion and faith. He truly believed in "to each his own."

Paul could be a little pushy at times but Pastor Graham went straight for the jugular.

"Son, you're being ridiculous. Faced with all the evidence of the last twenty-odd hours you're gonna sit there and tell me that you aren't convinced in the spiritual nature of this yet? Snap your fingers all you want but the proof is right in front of you. There is a spiritual battle happening for your family right now and you have no spiritual weapons. Zero. What good are you to them?"

Tim was a little stunned. He almost stammered a response but honestly, what could he say to that? He recalled what Dr. Taylor told him about praying for him. He said something like putting his shield of faith over Tim until he got one of his own. He didn't feel alone in this but right now he felt pretty ill-equipped.

"I've got you, right?" Tim wasn't being a suck-up, he wanted to count this Pastor as an asset in this little war. He hated that his voice sounded so scared and uncertain. He was ashamed of his weakness. The desperation in his voice reminded him of times he asked his mom and dad if he could sleep in their room after one of his tormenting nightmares long ago.

"Absolutely. But I believe you're gonna have to be the one who steps up to the plate on this thing, son. I'm in your corner but you're the one in the ring."

After a moment Tim found the courage and the sense of humor that had gone missing from him since last night.

"What is it with you preachers and sports analogies?"

With a good-natured chuckle, Pastor Graham put Tim's mind at ease and brought the conversation back on point.

"Well, they get the point across, I suppose. Anyway, Detective Peters should be here when you get here so just come straight to the house and we'll come up with a game plan to try and get your family back. I'd really like to pray together before we jump into action, Ok?"

There was a slight pause and Pastor Graham felt Tim was going to offer some objection to a time of prayer but after a moment he responded simply.

"Ok."

After disconnecting the call, Tim rode in silent thought for another few minutes. He didn't dare try the radio for fear that another distraction or deception would await him.

But for the first time in the last several hours, Tim finally felt like there was some hope. Maybe his desperate prayer was heard. Maybe all this spiritual stuff wasn't just fluff and stuff. Maybe.

But there was a real enemy that needed to be dealt with. Gabe said a demon. Well, Tim was no expert but he was pretty sure a demon wouldn't steal a car to kidnap his family so there had to be some human element to this thing.

Tim wasn't far now and he was anxious to get there. He sort of assumed that since he had a pastor slash ex-sheriff on his side that he could bend the speed limit a little more but he was still unwilling to be further delayed by a ticket so he kept it at just under ten over.

Without any further bizarre distractions like sign-wielding hitchhikers, false news reports, or some otherworldly roadblock, he should be there in the next hour.

CHAPTER THIRTY

Detective Peters sat there for a moment, unsure how to handle his next move. Jurisdiction was not something you could just ignore because you were invested in a case. Peters was a good detective and didn't want to mar his record with a quick decision.

But he had given Pastor Graham his word that he would come alone. Maybe that wasn't a wise idea. Maybe he should call him back and explain the situation. That would be necessary if Pastor Graham weren't formerly Sheriff Graham. He knew what he was asking Peters to do and the ramifications involved.

Sean Peters was confident that this course of action was the move he *needed* to make. He just wasn't confident in how all this was going to play out. He was a man of faith. A man of conviction. He was willing to deal with the consequences of doing the right thing.

Well, that settled it.

Peters rose with the single-minded plan of heading out without raising too much awareness or alerting too many people. But John Calloway was coming his way and had that look on his face.

"Hey, Sean. You have anything new on the McDaniel case?"

This wasn't going to be a fun conversation. Calloway had a nose for deception and Peters was not looking forward to keeping him in the dark on this one. But he also couldn't risk bringing him along on this. He knew John to be a hard-nosed skeptic, too quick to assume a guilty judgment on someone and Tim McDaniel did not need that right now.

"Nothing solid," he offered. "I'm heading out to run some errands and check up on a few leads on some other cases. I have to meet up with a pastor who has some perspective on a case. I should be gone most of the day but let me know if you come up with anything." Detective

Peters was trying to throw his coat on and hurry out the door to avoid any further discussion but that wasn't going to be possible apparently.

"Oh? Well, I've already done some digging of my own and you're gonna want to hear this." That's what his look was all about.

"Hear what?" Peters offered a wary look, already suspicious of what Calloway but about to share.

"Turns out your boy has a history of mental illness." Calloway let the words drip out as if he were describing a pedophile or psychotic serial killer. He could tell that Peters was not immediately impressed with his finding so he offered more detail to ensure he grasped the magnitude of what he was saying.

Holding up a piece of paper as a reference Calloway said, "When he was a kid, he had to go through some psychotherapy for almost a year after he claimed he was attacked at some summer camp."

Peters finished putting his coat on and looked at Calloway until he awkwardly shifted his feet and put the paper down.

"And?" Peters asked it not with dripping sarcasm but with a dry, lackluster *go on* quality.

Detective Peters knew that if he outright dismissed it then Calloway would think him biased or, worse, close-minded. He had to tread carefully with this and let Calloway conclude that the lead wasn't as solid as he thought.

"*And?* I mean, you don't think it's relevant that a guy who may have kidnapped his family has a history of mental illness and saw a shrink for a year?" It was Calloway's turn to wait out Peters' response.

"Are you seriously telling me that anybody who may have gone to counseling for a traumatic childhood experience is more of a suspect in a crime now?" He let the question hang for a second and then went for the jugular.

"John, I'm gonna level with you. I went to counseling for almost a year when I found my Grandma dead in her kitchen. In fact, almost thirty percent of adults have had some form of therapy or counseling and a shocking number of people, many in this office, are on some form of medication for stress, anxiety, depression, or any number of other mental health reasons so forgive me if I don't automatically see the correlation with this guy and his childhood trauma." He was on a roll and plunged ahead when Calloway looked like he was about to say something.

"I came across that in my research, but you know what else I found? I found that he's never been back since after receiving a clean bill of mental health. He's not on any antipsychotics or mood-altering drugs. He's helped his uncle run his family business since his dad died of a heart attack and he's never missed a single one of his son's soccer games in three years.

"So, again, forgive me if I don't see that piece of paper as the damning evidence you do." Peters had taken greater offense to Calloway's insinuation than even he had realized. He was flustered. He regretted that he had bulldogged Calloway again but being so new to detective work he needed to learn how to separate fact from opinion.

"Was there something else you discovered?" Peters tried not to sound condescending but he knew he didn't pull it off too well.

"I guess not." Calloway sounded defeated and, more concerning than that, suspicious. Peters had to remove any suspicion from his mind if this wasn't going to blow up in his face later.

"Look, I'm sorry, John. I guess I take that stuff kind of seriously. My wife has battled with anxiety off and on and has seen a counselor a few times. I'd hate to think that if something happened to me she would be a suspect because of it."

For a second nothing seemed to change but Calloway's face softened a little and he said, "Hey man. I didn't know that. I'm sorry. I guess it's a little bit of a generalization to connect those dots too quickly. I'll keep digging."

Peters put his hand on John Calloway's shoulder in a kindly gesture. "You're a good detective, John. I know you'll find something we can use. Whether this guy is guilty or being set up in spectacular fashion, we'll figure it out and get this guy's family to safety."

With that exchange, Calloway went back to his office and Detective Peters headed out for the day. He made sure dispatch knew he'd be out of pocket for the day chasing down some leads and hopped in his Buick Sentry. He had a bad feeling about what was about to go down so he called his wife and asked her to be praying for him as he went. He didn't give her every gory detail but enough to have a good idea of what to pray for.

One more believer praying was never a bad thing.

CHAPTER THIRTY-ONE

Paul groaned in his sleep. It was a heavily medicated sleep that should be so deep dreams would not penetrate. But there was a quality to his moaning that made Dr. Taylor perk up. He felt something in his spirit. Something amiss. Something unwelcome.

He stood and laid his hand on Paul's chest gently. He began to pray when something drew his attention to the doorway. There was nothing and nobody there. And yet he was certain that there was.

Dr. Taylor did not move his hand from Paul. He did not run to see what was there or not there. He didn't yell out, "who's there?" as one does in a movie. He understood all too well what was happening. He had experienced similar distractions in the clinics in South Africa when he had gone to pray for the afflicted.

"You have no business or authority here. Go in the name of Jesus." He spoke the words almost under his breath but loud enough that anyone in the room would have heard him. He had no delusions that a nurse would pop her head in and ask, "pardon me?" He knew to whom he spoke.

Paul's moaning stopped. He rested.

He took this opportunity to pray again for Tim McDaniel. He was confident that his dream had been prophetic and that Tim *could be* victorious if he put his trust in the hand of God instead of his own understanding. But that was always the rub with prophetic things. God tends to implement an *if, then* quality to His workings. *If* you trust God, *then* this will be the outcome. *If* you do not, *then* a different outcome should be expected.

God is sovereign and omnipotent, but He is also keen on the free will of man. Tricky, this.

Tim McDaniel could choose to walk the victorious path God had laid out for him or he could choose to believe only his eyes and mind, disregarding the things of the Spirit. This way would not end well.

Dr. Taylor had warned Tim about these things and had encouraged him before he left to confront this evil. But he had sensed in Tim doubt, fear, anger, and disbelief. Disbelief was similar, but not the same as, doubt. Doubters want to believe but are more prone to waffle whereas disbelief stands opposed to truth, unwilling to open the heart or mind. Disbelief is the more rebellious brother to unbelief. Unbelief can be a result of ignorance but disbelief is the unwilling heart to believe.

Jesus had said that "the sin" of man is unbelief. Of all the "sins" out there the one that keeps people out of heaven is boiled down to unbelief. Dr. Taylor had explained this to his students multiple times but it remains to be counterintuitive to most.

"How's that true, Dr. Taylor?" they would ask him. "What about pride or murder? Selfishness or greed? Aren't these sins that prevent man from knowing Jesus?"

"Yes, but all sins are traced back to *not believing* that Christ is sufficient. Pride does not believe that Christ is truly Master. Greed cannot believe that Christ is enough. It is unbelief that always produces other sins, manifesting its offspring. Man is keen on naming all the *kinds* of sin but unbelief is at the heart of each."

If Tim remained in his unbelief, or disbelief, then there would be no hope for him. No expected victory. No happy outcome. Disbelief robs men of hope because they refuse to give themselves over to greater possibilities than what is right in front of them.

"I'll believe it when I see it" is a faithless slogan. Proof is nearly always insisted on with mankind. We are so slow to let go of our skepticism that we often refuse the miracle we pray to God to provide.

Dr. Taylor had once been such a skeptic as a boy. Raised as the son of missionaries, he had not naturally inherited the faith of his father. He had heard many stories from his parents and their friends of Jesus and the miracles that faith in Him produces but he had much doubt. Doubt naturally gave way to disbelief for him.

It wasn't until he was about twelve years old that he confessed this disbelief to his father. He feared the backlash from this spiritual giant at his confession. His father was quiet for a long pause.

"Son." His father had a tenderness to his speech that Dr. Taylor had heard many times when speaking to his mother or sisters. It caught him off guard to hear it aimed towards him at this moment.

"Do you doubt my love for you, Cornelius?" asked his father.

Without hesitation, the young Dr. Taylor responded. "Never, father! I know you love me." He was afraid that he had inadvertently offended his father or had implied such a horrible thought.

His father patted his leg reassuringly. "Good, good. I know you do, son. And I do love you. Very much." Neil's heart relaxed a bit. But his father continued.

"But how is it you readily believe that I love you but somehow have come to doubt that our God in Christ loves you?"

Somewhat confused, Neil stated what he thought was obvious.

"But you are my father. You show me love every day. You speak to me and care for me. You have raised me and are always there for me. I *see* you right in front of me and I experience it."

His father had a coy smile on his face. He sat, smiling and silent for a beat.

Cornelius didn't understand why at first, but then he realized what his father was doing.

"Oh, I see. You want me to understand that our Heavenly Father is the same?" he asked.

"Not exactly," he replied. "My love for you may be more evident to you on a daily basis but that's only because you aren't looking at how you are loved by God. He fills your lungs with air and your mind with the capacity for thought. He provides our food, our able bodies to work the fields. He provides His word, which is our only source of truth."

"But I can't *see* Him. I don't *feel* His love like when you hug me and kiss my head. I've never had good reason to surrender to this faith that you have. I want *proof!*"

"Ah. Proof! I assume you mean proof *besides* the sunrise, the mewl of a newborn calf, the Bible!" His father laughed heartily.

"Please don't mock me, father." Neil protested.

"I would never do such a thing, Cornelius! I am not mocking you; I am laughing at the plight of man evident in your objections." his father lovingly retorted.

As keen as he was for his age Neil's twelve-year-old mind was not completely able to grasp such a philosophical notion but he assumed his father would expound on his statement so he remained quiet, concealing his ignorance. Instead of further explanation his father simply said, "Come, I wish to show you something."

Confounded but obedient, Neil followed his father through the village to the outskirts. They walked in silence for nearly half an hour through a patch of woods into a neighboring village. Neil very seldom went through this village because they practiced a West African form of voodoo where they worshiped a spirit called Lao.

The voodoo priest was believed to be possessed by the power of the Lao. He would tell people their future sometimes, accurately predicting sickness or death. He sacrificed animals to his gods and was sometimes seen running around the woods at night naked as the animals. Locals feared him and many hailed him as a god. Neil had never seen him and wasn't sure why his father brought him here now.

"*Goeie more!*" his father called out in the Afrikaans language in front of the voodoo priest's hut. Then in English, "G'Morning!" Neil was apprehensive as to why his father wanted to see this man. Surely his father wasn't the type to seek counsel from such a man as this?

After a few moments, the priest came out. He wasn't wearing his traditional headgear and didn't look as menacing as Neil had suspected. He looked pleased to see his father and smiled broadly.

"Dr. Taylor!" he called out in very broken English. Neil's father had a Ph.D. in psychology from Cambridge. Neil didn't know exactly why his father had forsaken a career in that field to live in South Africa as a missionary but he honestly had never met a man as intelligent as his father, nor more dedicated to the work of the Gospel.

"This man does not speak English so I will translate for your sake." his father informed him.

"*Hoe gaan dit met jou vandag?* How are you doing today?" his father asked him.

"*Ek ondervind daardie verskriklike drome weer*" he answered with worried eyes.

"He's been having terrible dreams lately about going to hell and I believe that Jesus is going to save him very soon. Maybe today." his father translated and expounded.

"*Sou jy graag meer oor Jesus hoor?* Would you like to hear more about Jesus?" he asked with a smile while holding up his Bible.

Neil noticed the man's eyes twinkle with hope, then cloud with anger and confusion. This man was clearly conflicted.

"*Nee, nee. My gode nie daarvan hou nie wanneer ons praat van hom.*" he replied waving his hands.

"He says that he doesn't want to talk about Jesus because his gods don't like it when we do."

Neil felt a tickle run down his spine. He sensed something in the air. A dark quality that he normally chalked up to living in this part of the world, but he couldn't so easily dismiss after a statement like that.

"*Ek glo Jesus is wat jy daardie drome omdat hy lief is vir jou en wil hê jy moet hom te leer ken.* I believe Jesus is showing you dreams because He loves you and wants you to know Him!" his father explained.

At this, the man's eyes darted back and forth as if he could see swarms of bees inches from his face. He was struggling to compose himself. With forced kindness in his voice, he said, "*No. Nie meer praat. Gaan asseblief.*"

"He wants us to go." his father relayed. Neil wanted to go as well.

"Maybe we should, father. He frightens me."

Neil's father placed a reassuring hand on his shoulder. He had a look in his eyes that gave a small measure of comfort but also made Neil jealous. This man had faith like he had never seen. He had no fear. It was uncanny and unsettling at the same time.

"Remember what FDR told us? We have nothing to fear but fear itself? Well, Jesus took it a few steps farther when he reminded us in 1 John4:18 that '*there is no fear in love for perfect love casts out fear.*' We must help this man, Cornelius. He *lives* in fear."

Turning once again to the witch doctor, Dr. Taylor looked him in the eye and asked in Afrikaans, "Do you wish to be free?"

Neil didn't need a translation to know what he asked or what the man's response was. The unfolding of the next few minutes burned an indelible mark on his mind and spirit.

The witch doctor's eyes pleaded for mercy as he began to nod, but only for a moment. He began to shake his head violently back and forth. He started cursing and grunting, growling, snorting like a pig. His eyes were searching for something but never finding it. His countenance was changing. The kind eyes and smiling mouth that had been there two minutes ago were replaced with a sneer and dark, hateful eyes that bore into Neil's own.

Neil felt his soul and mind being prodded and pulled. He was dizzy and nauseous. And scared.

Finally, the man stopped all his growling and jerking about and fixed his eyes on Neil. When he spoke Neil's heart shrank and his mind filled with terror.

In perfect English, the witch doctor spoke to Dr. Taylor and said, "Are you such a fool that you would bring this unbelieving boy with you to cast us out of this old bag of bones? We will gladly fill his body with the lot of us and ravage his soul before your eyes."

For the first and only time in Neil's life, he saw the flicker of fear in his father's eyes. The quickest moment of uncertainty. But then it was replaced with resolve.

With authority in his voice, Dr. Taylor looked at the man and said, "You will do no such thing! I command you in the name and authority of Jesus Christ to come out of this man and leave this place! You have no dominion here, spirits!"

"Then we will fill the boy!" the man said again but in a different voice. A higher, more feminine quality to it. "His doubt welcomes us."

"No!" his father shouted. "No, you WILL NOT! You will leave this place in the name of Jesus Christ and you shall not return!"

Neil began to realize that the probing feeling in his mind and spirit was more than just fear or confusion. These were spirits seeking a home. He realized at that moment that his refusal to wear the righteousness of Christ as his own was causing him to be a pawn in this spiritual battle.

With a final declaration of authority and power, his father pointed at the man and said, "Every unclean spirit and demon in this man is cast out and banished from this place! By the blood and name of Jesus Christ, I order you to go! Now!"

The man looked as if he were about to explode in anger but then he let out a shriek so loud Neil covered his ears. It sounded like a hundred hawks screeching in a concert hall.

And then a deafening silence.

The man lay on the ground and Neil was sure he was dead. But then he slowly stood. His eyes were kind again, gentle. He was bewildered for a moment then broke into a huge smile.

"*Hulle trek! Ek is vry!*" he shouted with joy.

"Yes, you are free!" Dr. Taylor laughed. But then he warned him with a stern and loving charge.

In Afrikaans, he told him, "You must let Jesus Christ fill your heart now or they will return. The one whom the Son sets free is free indeed, but you must trust and love Jesus now."

The man nodded excitedly and smiled. "Yes!" he shouted in English. "*Dankie Jesus!*"

"Praise Jesus, indeed!" Dr. Taylor said. In the excitement of this miraculous transformation, Neil realized that the fear and probing feeling he had experienced was gone as well. His mind was clear again. He stood there for a moment, numb with the realization of what he had just witnessed.

With the most sincere care and love, his father bent to one knee, placed his hands on Neil's shoulders, and gently asked him, "Are you ok, son?"

"Yes, father. I'm fine."

Though he didn't feel fine, exactly. He felt the weight of his doubt, once crushing him like a stone, now lifting from him. It felt strange but after what he had just seen doubt felt so foreign to him.

"Do you understand why I brought you here today?"

Silent for a moment, Neil nodded. His doubts seemed almost like a dream now. Like they were never his. At that moment he traded his doubt for faith. He believed.

"I believe now, father. I believe everything the Bible says."

"Well, that is truly good to hear. But, as Jesus told His disciple Thomas after dealing with his doubts, '*You believe because you have seen but blessed is he who believes and has not seen.'* There is much required of those who believe, son. Are you ready to battle these evils for the rest of your life?"

Cornelius Taylor looked his father in the eyes. He looked at the joy on the former witch doctor's face. He looked to the heavens.

"Yes, father. I am ready now."

That was forty-eight years ago, but the memory has been etched in his mind with vivid detail. Dr. Taylor smiled at the kindness of God with the doubters like him.

The witch doctor was truly converted and became the senior Dr. Taylor's shadow for the next year. Eventually, he learned English and how to read and write and became a pastor of a little village not terribly far from his own.

His story was the catalyst for a great, but short, revival among the people of those villages. The power of Jesus was recognized and many placed their faith in Him. But the dark ones were not going to give up their territory without a fight. When Neil was only eighteen years old, his father was attacked in a neighboring village and beaten to death.

If Neil had been harboring his doubt then he would have been crushed by the news. Instead, his heart broke at the loss of his father but rejoiced that he was with Jesus. Hope is a glorious thing.

Hope was something Timothy McDaniel did not currently cling to. He might say that he *hoped* to recover his family but the hope of the world is a wish, a *maybe* sprinkled with luck. But hope in Christ does not disappoint. It is an anchor for the soul. If he could put his hope in God, then the outcome of this story would be very different. And regardless of what happened to his family, that hope could not be diminished or stolen.

Again, Dr. Taylor prayed. He would pray all day and all night until this came to its climactic head. As he stood there with his hand on Paul's chest praying, a nudge from the Holy Spirit made him pause.

He needed some other brothers and sisters joining him. Right on cue, Z entered the room and asked, "You think we should be prayin' or somethin'? I jus' feel like somethin' big's about to go down."

"I think you are exactly right, Pastor. Something big is about to go down," he replied with a smile.

Gabe was standing sheepishly in the hall but came in when asked.

"I took da liberty to text some of the ladies in my congregation that are known to be prayer warriors of the highest caliber," Z informed them. "Dey should be gatherin' about now to hit their knees."

"Excellent!" Dr. Taylor excitedly took Z's hand in his and together they began to pray. These weren't the simple generic prayers so often uttered of "God bless so and so" or "Be with Uncle Jimmy." No, these were intense, specific, biblical prayers that rose like incense to the very throne room of the Almighty. These were prayers that were lifted in faith to a God that was not far away or indifferent.

The prayers of a righteous person are powerful and effective, according to James 5:16, and these people gathered in prayer knew that their righteousness came from Christ, not their own goodness. It was this heart of prayer that God loved to move in.

And God began to move.

CHAPTER THIRTY-TWO

Sean Peters pulled into Luke Graham's driveway a few minutes before twelve. He killed the engine and was glad to note that Tim McDaniel's Tahoe wasn't there yet. He wanted another minute alone with Pastor Graham before Tim arrived so they could pray and talk through this thing one more time without fear of offending or frustrating Tim.

Pastor Graham, who insisted on being called Luke from here on out, welcomed him in with a hot cup of good coffee. Black with two sugars.

Peters, who insisted on being called Sean, politely and gratefully accepted the coffee and they were both hopeful Tim would be there shortly. Luke was a man who got straight to it, which Sean appreciated.

"This whole situation is a logistical and legal nightmare."

Sean silently nodded for a moment and responded, "Yeah. Yeah, it is. But what are our options here, Luke? I mean, you've at least got some history linked to this, right? What's your take? Is it the same guy? A copycat?"

"I honestly have no idea. We never caught the guy responsible so it's entirely possible he's back at it. But why focus on McDaniel? What's his angle with that?"

Sean shrugged the universal *I have no idea* code shaking his head but said, "I know that this has yet to produce any bodies and doesn't fit the preteen boy M.O. so the link isn't as clear as I'd like. It just doesn't seem to add up to me."

Luke agreed but still felt the need to state the obvious. "There aren't any bodies *yet*. I think there's a real possibility that there might be, especially if we don't find the McDaniel family. And who knows if this guy only went after younger teen boys or if that's all he did here."

"So, tell me again why you're sure Tim *isn't* the culprit in this. He's clearly unstable and I'm not saying I think he did it but in any normal case he'd be our number one suspect. I guess I'm just curious as to your take on this guy."

Luke Graham was silent for a second then scratched his chin stubble as if searching for the right words. Finally, he dropped his hand and looked Sean Peters in the eyes.

"If I didn't know you were a man of faith I probably couldn't even say what I'm about to say without you chalking me up to having some screws loose. But there was an evil here forty-four years ago that reared its head again thirty years ago when Tim McDaniel was a camper. I sense the same evil at work now."

Sean seemed to take that in stride but rephrased his question.

"So why are you so sure that Tim McDaniel isn't the evil this time?"

Luke nodded as if he thought that was a fair question. He took a sip of his coffee and responded with candor.

"Because I see a young man who is being manipulated and pushed by a sinister enemy that is hell-bent on destroying him. Even in the brief conversations, I've had with him I can tell he's desperate. But that alone doesn't mean he's innocent, I know. Still, there's something about this that resonates with a part of my heart that sympathizes with him.

"Maybe I see Tim like I saw my little brother, I dunno. Smart and brave, but vulnerable. I *feel* that he's the victim and not the perpetrator more than the facts tell me."

It was Sean's turn to take a sip and reflect on those words. Finally, he placed his mug down on the coffee table and leaned back into the cushion of the chair he was in.

"I feel the same way," he admitted. "I guess I just needed to hear you say it. But you're right, if anybody that wasn't a believer heard us talking like this we'd be run out of law enforcement for sure."

"That's why I resigned before that happened. I shared a few of my thoughts with some of the deputies once regarding Tim's camp experience and got the *pity* faces. I could tell they were thinking, *'poor guy is losing it.'* I knew what I had seen and had come to believe and realized that my days as a Christian Sheriff were done. I needed, instead, to be a Pastor with excellent working knowledge of the law."

Sean smiled and nodded in appreciation of his experience. He thought of John Calloway and how he got that look whenever Sean mentioned church or things of faith.

"Yeah, I still believe I'm where I need to be but I admire your courage to change gears like that. Takes a lot of faith to step into the ministry, especially these days when Christians are a polarized lot. You can't win with anybody most of the time."

"The world is no more hostile now than it was 2,000 years ago. We just air our dirty laundry all over Facebook and blog about it these days. We seem to have lost our sense of the calling of Jesus. Like the great theologian, Dietrich Bonhoeffer said, 'The call to come to Jesus is the call to come and die.' Most Christians, especially American Christians, are an entitled group these days. We feel the slightest persecution and we turn into a martyr.

"To be honest, I was never a big fan of politics and I definitely don't like to mix them with a pseudo-Christian agenda. Polarized? Yep. But that is partly due to our own inability to be disliked or mistreated and partly because Jesus promised all of His followers that the world would hate us just as it hated Him. We just don't really like that part a whole lot."

Sean Peters sat there for a moment and smiled.

"I can see why you're a preacher now."

Luke sheepishly returned the smile and nodded.

"Sorry about that. I get a little worked up sometimes. Didn't mean to lay that on you."

"Not at all. We need more sentiment like that out there. I have to remind myself of that exact thing when one of the other officers cracks a joke at my expense or mocks something I hold dear. My fight isn't with that person but with his erroneous perspective on things of faith. And going off on him to defend myself only solidifies his beef."

The two men had mutual respect and a kindred spirit was being birthed in such a short time that Sean felt completely comfortable asking his next question.

"So how far are we willing to go to see this through? To help Tim McDaniel?"

It was a tough question but not one that Luke Graham hadn't thought about already. His answer was concise, but thoughtful.

212

"I'm willing to do whatever it takes. But I have far less to lose than you. I suggest you let me take whatever heat comes from this. My town, my history. You've got a career to think about."

As much as Sean Peters appreciated Luke's desire to protect him from the fallout of this case, it was still his case.

"Well, unfortunately, that's not a luxury I can take. My case, my problem. We're in this together."

There was a good thirty seconds of respectful silence as they both took these truths to bear. Luke broke it when he stood and said, "Ok then. We're in this together."

Sean stood with him and without pomp and circumstance, they shook hands again. Sort of sealing the deal on this new partnership.

"So where do we start? What do we know that can send us in the right direction?" Sean wanted to know.

"The only thing I know is that the location of the old camp has been pretty much abandoned for the last nineteen years or so since it was shut down. We'll likely need to start there. The bigger question is, do we keep this party a secret or get local law enforcement in on it? I know a few guys in the Sheriff's Department that would be willing to come to the campgrounds without having to go into all the details."

Sean considered the offer and nodded.

"OK. I can't say that wouldn't make me feel a little better. We have no idea what we're up against."

"Without being terribly melodramatic I just want to go on record and say that whatever we're up against, I'm not real sure extra bullets is what we need. But we could sure use some more prayers."

"I've got those coming from my people back home. You know some folks you can call?

"Already have. But the deputies I can call come to my church as well so that might be to our advantage."

The two men were done talking so they decided to practice what they preach, so to speak, and pray together. As they were capping it with an *amen*, Tim McDaniel pulled into the driveway.

Both men walked out on the deck that ran parallel to the front door so he could meet them there. He looked exhausted and frail. Detective Peters was almost shocked at the difference in this shell of the Tim

McDaniel he had met the previous evening. From six p.m. to now, a little before 1, Tim had been hollowed out and broken.

"Mr. McDaniel." Sean shook his hand with a sincere look of concern in his eyes.

"Detective." Tim nodded in awkward appreciation of his presence.

Luke extended his hand as well an introduction.

"Tim. Luke Graham. So glad to meet you, even under such dire circumstances."

Tim wasn't sure how to respond so he just nodded politely.

Detective Peters made the mental note that Tim's friend, Paul, had a calming effect that was now absent.

"How's your friend, Paul?" he asked with sincerity.

"Not well, I'm afraid. He was attacked by some wild street person that was possessed or high or something. He's in good hands but I hated leaving him like that."

Luke squinted his eyes as he made a mental note of that bit of information.

"There seems to be a great deal of strange things surrounding this. Are you ok if we talk for a sec before we proceed?"

Tim looked fidgety and eager to move.

"I need to find my family. But if you think putting our heads together real quick will expedite that then sure. I could use a bathroom and some coffee if possible."

"Yes to both. Come on in."

As they entered the home a shift in the atmosphere caught Sean's attention. He felt a small wave of fear and panic at the possible outcome of all this trying to settle over him. He tried to shake it but it persisted.

As sure as God was moving, the enemy was moving too.

CHAPTER THIRTY-THREE

Tim's arrival triggered something in Liz's captor. His head snapped up like a hunting dog catching the scent of his prey. He looked different, eager. He walked with purpose from the basement.

Liz's head ached terribly. The throw against the wall had bruised her left hip and shoulder blade but the worst pain was the knot in her head. She was pretty sure there was no real damage, save possibly a minor concussion, but she would be ok.

That was the real truth of this whole ordeal, wasn't it? That she believed she and the kids would be ok? She honestly could not say why she believed that but it was like the peace of it was being poured over her mind over and over. It wasn't wishful thinking, either. She, for some reason not fully known to her, truly believed that this would not end the way this guy seemed to think it would. She *hoped* in the truest sense. It wasn't a "guarantee" from God or anything. She just felt that optimism and hope were more available to her than despair, and she took hold of them.

She also found herself praying quite a bit. That was new. Of course, many would pray in a situation like this, obviously, but this was a little different. She believed what she was saying because she believed in the One to whom she was praying. I mean, really believed. She had heard of Jesus growing up but she wasn't raised in any religious setting. Her mom was a converted Mormon later in life when she remarried, but that just never jived with her, honestly.

She never read the Bible or took her kids to church either. They were the typical "nice" family that had no need for religion. But this wasn't religion. Something had snapped into place for her. This was real and not giving herself over to it felt simply prideful and foolish. God had gotten her attention in the scariest way she could imagine. And yet she wasn't thinking God had manipulated her through a horrible circumstance or anything. No, bad things happened every day. That was life. This wasn't God turning a blind eye, either. He was there. This was the God of the universe reminding her that this life wasn't the only show, just the dress rehearsal.

She had something bigger to live for now. She desperately wanted her family to know and live this truth. Jesus saves. She had somehow reached that conclusion moments after waking up in that basement after being thrown against the wall by, from all appearances, a demon-possessed man who had kidnapped her and her children in order to lure her husband back to the camp where he planned to torture and kill them.

Not your typical "how I came to Jesus" story but she could not deny that she now believed and wanted to stand in that belief. She wished she weren't so ignorant of spiritual things. She didn't know what the Bible taught and had heard only a smattering of sermons at weddings or funerals over the years. But she remembered one thing that gave her great hope - Jesus is more powerful than the bad guys.

She could have countered that line of thinking with a thousand examples of bad things happening. Things like her rape in college. Like Tim's mom suffering and dying of cancer. Things like all the pain in the world. But those were not the reality, only examples. She knew, somehow, that God was truly good and those bad things happening was no more evidence of His impotence or malevolence than one of her kids falling down, scraping up a knee, and blaming her for letting it happen. In other words, the mere existence of bad things did not negate the good things, or the Source of all good things.

Could she use this new faith to get out of this basement? Did she have any power over the evil perpetrating this act of fear and rebellion?

As she pondered how to assert this faith in her current situation, she felt a leading to just hold on. This was not the time. She could sense that Tim would need her soon, but for now, she had to keep her head down and play ball.

She had such a strange presence come over her and was persuaded to pray a specific, and odd, request.

"Jesus, hide me from my enemy. Don't let him know I have trusted you yet." She was certain she was led to pray that. Then she tagged on in matching faith, "And continue to protect the children. I know this will not end as so many other tragedies have. Thank you that you've given me faith to know that. And if something changes or you don't do what I hope you do, help me to love and trust you all the same."

She didn't want to be one of those Christians who insisted God give them everything they ask for. Nor was Jesus only there to make her life perfect all the time. That wasn't faith. God wasn't a genie or cosmic grandpa who gave His kids whatever they wanted.

Liz had never been a fan of the "name it and claim it" theology that so many Christians seemed to believe. What kind of God was bound by the requests of His children? If He had no authority to say "no" to our petitions and requests, even if we tag His name on the end, then didn't that make us somehow more powerful than Him?

Anyway, she looked forward to finding out the answers to all her God questions in time. And she desperately hoped and believed that she would have that time.

The only thing left for her was to pray and wait. And sing. She began to hum one of the only "Christian" songs she knew - Amazing Grace.

She only knew the first verse but she quietly sang it, knowing that she would have to stop if her captor returned. She had shown a bold side to him and he displayed his power in turn. No need to anger him further at this point. Tim and her children needed her in one piece.

CHAPTER THIRTY-FOUR

After an uneventful trip to the bathroom, finally, and a cup of coffee in his hand Tim realized he had a strange nostalgia in this place. But more than just being back in the camp he was in so many years ago, he felt something else. It was only after the two men, one he'd known for a day and the other he had just met, sat with him that he could put words to what he felt.

"You guys remind me of my friend, Paul, for some reason. Like, you've got a quiet confidence or something. I'm steadily freaking out more and more over here and you guys seem like you've been munching on some spiritual Prozac. No offense, intended." he tagged on the end.

With a chuckle, Luke replied, "Well, I assume your friend is a believer?"

"You mean a Christian," he clarified, "then yeah. Definitely. He's about as chill in situations like this as I've ever seen. He's really helped me keep my head in this so far. It was a rough drive over, to be honest."

Recalling the hitchhiker, the radio, and the gas station he had so wished Paul had been with him. And yet, here he was in one piece.

Sean Peters spoke up, "Seen some more weird stuff, I take it?"

"That's an understatement. I've almost questioned my sanity at some points. Except that I know there's something... *else. Someone* else working here. There's no doubt that this is real, not just in my head. I can't explain any of it but I'm convinced it's real."

Peters and Luke exchanged a knowing glance. It's didn't come across as conspiratorial or anything, it just kind of confirmed what Tim was thinking.

"So you two are gonna be my GodSquad now, huh?" he questioned.

"GodSquad?" Luke made a confused but amused face.

"I don't mean that disrespectfully." Tim asserted, somewhat nervously.

"Not at all," Luke assured him. "I guess, to you, that's about as accurate a description as we could come up with. Detective Peters and I are both convinced there's a spiritual element at work here and we both feel inclined to step in and help any way we can."

Peters nodded solemnly. Tim was touched by their solidarity. They had no good reason to help him and yet here they were.

"It means a lot," Tim said with sincerity. "So what do we do now? How do we get my wife and kids back?"

"I wish we had an easy answer for that, Tim," Peters began. "Sadly, we don't. We have called a few trustworthy sheriff's deputies that are going to come for some backup but we were hoping you might have a plan of sorts that we could discuss. Any thoughts?"

Tim's eyes were a little wide. Luke and Sean assumed he was shocked that they didn't offer a well-laid plan. But he bounced back pretty quickly.

"Uh, yeah, kinda. I'd like to go in guns blazing and kick this guy's teeth in but if he's shown me anything it's that he's no ordinary man. Typical tactics most likely won't work. I say you guys hang back on the road that leads to the path and let me try and call him out or something. I don't want to spook him but if we can get a clean shot on him then maybe -"

"A clean shot?" Luke interrupted. "You're suggesting we lure him out and shoot him?"

"I mean, yeah. I guess. I don't know what else to do to be completely honest." Tim was desperate.

"I don't think that's the way this can happen, Tim. We don't know anything about this guy. Shooting someone like a sniper is not an option. We have to get your family safe and I'm not saying that it's going to be neat and easy, but we can't go in with the intent to kill. That's not how this gets settled."

Tim knew they were right but he was so frustrated at the situation that he couldn't think straight. He suddenly felt a wave of fear crash on him and was convinced that sitting here discussing the option was going to get his family killed. He hopped up off the couch.

"I need to go." He blurted.

Luke and Sean both stood and motioned for Tim to settle down.

"Just a second, Tim. Let's not go off and rush into this. No doubt he's set a trap for you and he's counting on you being irrational about things. Our best bet is to take it steady." Luke tried to reason with him. So much like an older Paul.

Sean chimed in as well. "Yeah. You've been manipulated through this whole thing. Don't lose your bearings here."

Tim saw the wisdom in what they were saying but there was a cadence in his head, like a jungle drum beating, *your family's gonna die, your family's gonna die.*

Just then Luke's phone rang. Then Peters'. Sean looked at the screen while Luke went over to his landline hanging on the wall. Both men picked up but before either could say, "hello?" a piercing shriek came through both earpieces. It was like a woman screaming but at a decibel and pitch no woman could match.

Both men dropped the phones and had to cover the ear that had been next to the phone's receiver. It was a moment of confusion and panic. Tim heard a voice coming out of Detective Peters' phone from the ground.

"Help us!"

Liz.

Luke and Sean were still stunned from the shriek so Tim took advantage and slipped out without a word. He went straight to his truck and was peeling out of the dirt driveway before the men even made their way out of the house. Tim knew where to go.

In less than a minute he was at the former entrance to the camp. The sign that read *Camp Muscogee* had been removed years ago but was leaning up against the fence. This was definitely the place.

As with most things from childhood the camp seemed smaller, less intimidating. Cabins seemed closer together, the cafeteria looked tiny compared to the sprawling mess hall in Tim's memory. He parked at the edge of the path that had taken him down such a dark path of his own years ago.

What had actually happened that night? He still didn't fully know. What was happening now? Again, he still didn't understand.

But he was here. And this was going to end. Now.

CHAPTER THIRTY-FIVE

Tim grabbed the handgun out of the truck. He checked that it was loaded and chambered a round. Even as he slid it into the waistline of his pants, he felt the words of Paul pecking at this brain. *"this is not just a physical struggle..."*

"Yeah, that may be true but a bullet to the head will do the trick if it comes to that." Tim countered as if this were an actual conversation. Surely Del, or whoever this was, wasn't naive enough to think that he would come unarmed. It didn't matter. He knew that he had it if he needed it and that was that.

He made his way down the path, only slightly overgrown compared to thirty years ago. He had to admit that in the light of day this trail wasn't nearly as creepy. Still, it held an ominous feeling as he crept ever closer to the cabin.

Just as on that same night long ago his fear and anxiety waxed and morphed into a full-blown panic the closer he got. Images of his already dead wife and children filled his mind. That this was all a sick, twisted ruse to lure him out and kill him. That there was never any hope of saving them, to begin with.

He should take that gun, put it to his head and end this now. *Kill yourself!*

Tim stopped in his tracks. It was becoming more and more clear that Paul was right. This was some kind of attack on his mind. These weren't *his* thoughts. They were being put there with a malevolent purpose and he needed to be sharp enough to recognize the difference.

Only my sheep know my voice...

What? That wasn't his inner voice either, but it surely wasn't the same voice trying to get him to kill himself. There might just be something to this cosmic struggle between God and the devil after all.

But now's not the time to get religious. This was the time to get real. It was great that people were praying for him. He appreciated the gesture. But even if he wanted to believe all of this was some deeper spiritual battle what was he supposed to do about it? Liz would never want to be some church girl. They weren't like that.

He acknowledged God as good and, if this was some spiritual showdown, he hoped Jesus was on his side. But there was a wall around his heart that even the events of the last twenty-four hours hadn't broken down yet.

He walked on.

His cell phone rang. He looked at the caller i.d. and stopped. It was Paul.

"Paul?" he answered eagerly.

"No, Mr. McDaniel. I'm sorry. This is the hospital calling on Mr. Thibodeaux's phone. We wanted to be sure you answered. I'm afraid we have some bad news."

Tim's heart sank. He waited a moment but before he even asked the caller continued.

"I'm afraid that a few hours ago Mr. Thibodeaux's internal bleeding caused a hemorrhage in his brain. He passed away in surgery a few minutes ago. You were listed as his emergency contact number and we wanted to make you aware as soon as possible for you to make arrangements."

Tim stood there momentarily stunned. He wanted to cry. He wanted to talk to his best friend one more time. He wanted to make the person responsible for this pay. Anger turned to rage. And his rage quickly turned to murder. If there was a time when he would have loved to simply get his family and see this guy behind bars it had now turned into getting his family and putting this guy in the ground. Prison wasn't an option anymore.

But even at the moment that all of these feelings solidified there was a still, small voice that was trying to break through. Somewhere in the recesses of his mind, the warnings of Paul and Dr. Taylor tried to surface. It was weak and fuzzy but there was the slightest recollection that the devil was a liar and that he had to stand on truth.

"Who did you say this was?" he found the voice to ask.

"I'm Dr. Killjoy. And your friend is dead."

How could he have been so easily duped after all the tests and tricks he'd fallen for these last several hours? His mind had become so fragile that reality was thinly veiled now. He had to hold on, just a little longer.

"Ok, thank you for calling." he was about to hang up when the voice on the other end spoke up.

"What gave it away? You just refuse to believe your hero is dead?" it was the same voice as before but this time any pretense of professionalism or actual care was drained from it. "Or are you just still that brave boy you were so long ago?"

"I just know you're a liar. I'm tired of your games, Del."

The condescending laugh on the other line mocked Tim and made him bristle.

"Oh, just wait. The games have just begun! I'm about to have so much fun destroying you and your family. Your tears will taste so sweet."

Tim had enough. He ended the call and pocketed his phone. He might not have the upper hand in this or even a decent bearing of where he stood, but he had to take back control of his emotions and focus. His family needed him to be sharp.

He could see the outline of the cabin through the trees up ahead. Long front porch and sagging roof. It had been so dark last time he was here and he never got a really good look at it but there was no mistaking it. He could see how it used to back up to the lake many years ago but now there was a deep ravine that was filled with leaves and mud behind the cabin that eventually led back to the lake about fifty feet away.

He had gotten close enough to peel some bark off the wall on the left side of the porch in 1992. He was so full of life then. All he wanted to do was prove Del the loudmouth wrong and be the hero. Well, not much had changed since then, apparently. He still wanted to shut Del up and be the hero his family desperately needed. This time, he could not afford to fail. Whatever had attacked him that night he was ready for now. He wasn't some scared twelve-year-old kid anymore.

He made a mental note that there was a wooden shed behind and to the left of the house. This was apparently where the murders had taken place in '78. From this slight side angle, he could also tell that there was a cellar or basement to the house and there was an outside entrance. It wasn't like a storm cellar with two doors that closed down onto the cellar but, instead, was a stone staircase that descended to a large wooden door.

In which of these three places would he find his family: house, shed, or basement?

He considered trying to walk the perimeter and do some reconnaissance but considering his foe, that might not be a wise idea. He wouldn't be easy to sneak up on. He decided to announce his arrival instead.

"I'm here!" he shouted. "Come on out and let's talk!"

"Talk?" the voice answered, but from where Tim couldn't tell. "You think I brought you out here to talk?"

"I still don't know exactly why you brought me here. I know 'to suffer' but I don't know why. Did I really make you so angry when we were kids that you've been plotting this for the last thirty years?" Tim inquired earnestly.

"Are you *really* that thick-headed?" he asked in reply. "Do you *still* not get what's going on here?" He let the question hang in the air then seemed irritated enough to just answer it himself.

"I'm not some grown-up version of one of your little middle school enemies, Timmy! I have walked this earth far longer than you can imagine in many forms that would strike the deepest fear into your squeamish little heart. What you saw back then was only the form I chose for that task.

"But you!" he was angry again. "You had to ruin my fun with your brave little heart and goody-goody compassion. You claimed to be without fear. You dared to challenge me. So, I took you on as a project. I haven't waited as you might think one waits. I am not as bound to time and space as you are, all wrapped in flesh. Unless, as I choose to be now, I am also wrapped in flesh."

Tim was trying to follow on two levels. First, he was trying to make sense of what Del was saying, but he was also trying to follow from what direction his voice came. Unfortunately, he wasn't having great success at either. He also didn't trust that he could fool him into giving away his location so he just walked to the front of the cabin and stood there.

He stood for a minute and decided that he would rather Del take the initiative in a conversation. He needed to steady himself. When nothing happened, Tim got a strange urge. He wasn't sure why he felt so prodded to do this, but he finally gave in to the desire and took a step towards the same wall he had stepped towards thirty years ago. In the same way, almost by compulsion, he did what he did when he was twelve and grabbed a piece of peeling bark, pulling it off.

As soon as he realized what he had done he quickly turned around to confront whatever beast-man might be about to attack again. But there was no one this time. No circle of mutilated children either. But from the porch a few feet away Tim sensed a presence. When he turned to see who it was, he stood face to face with himself, like staring into a funhouse mirror.

CHAPTER THIRTY-SIX

He was looking at himself and was truly taken aback. This simply *must* have been the one who took his family. The resemblance was uncanny.

The other Tim spoke with vile hatred in his tone.

"Why did you do that?" he asked.

Tim realized that his actions had riled this man up pretty bad. For perhaps the first time Tim felt like he had taken some initiative with this guy.

With conviction and honesty, Tim answered, "I just felt like I needed to."

Other Tim hopped over the railing on the front porch and was truly face to face with the real Tim. His dark eyes were filled with hate and loathing.

"You *felt* like you *needed* to?" he dripped with mockery. "Suddenly you go from skeptic to feeler? Spare me. It's too late for you to get all spiritual on me, Tim. That ship has sailed. You honestly think I care if you have a piece of the cabin?"

"Sounds like you do a little." Tim jabbed. "It clearly bothers you that I did it. Does it challenge you somehow?"

Other Tim's hand shot to Tim's throat so fast that he barely flinched until it was locked in place. His grip was steel. It was reminiscent of that long-ago night but this wasn't just a scare tactic from an old, creepy ghoul of a man. This was flesh on flesh. Tim's knees grew weak.

"Do you honestly think you could *ever* challenge me?" he asked with practiced calm.

Tim was on the verge of blacking out when the grip released. It was only then that he realized he was only standing because Other Tim was keeping him in place. Just as soon as he was released from the grip he crumpled to the ground in a heap.

"I prefer you like this. Weak and scared at my feet. This is how you'll spend eternity. You're mine, Timmy." Other Tim was savoring the moment, so Tim decided to act fast.

He yanked the Glock out of his waistline and stood, backpedaling a safe distance away, all the while training the gun on Other Tim.

"Stay right there or I swear I'll blow you to pieces!" he commanded. He made a mental note to make sure the safety was off and the previously chambered round was ready to fly.

Other Tim raised his hands in mock surrender.

"Oh no!" he said sarcastically. "He's got a gun. What should I do, Tim? Should I lie down and put my hands behind my back? Or do you just want to get this over with and shoot me in the head? Better double tap to be sure. I'm a tricky one."

Now given the opportunity to kill this... *man,* for lack of a better word, Tim wasn't as sure of himself as he was earlier. Could he pull the trigger?

"Would it be easier if I tried to attack you?" he asked as if he were genuinely trying to help. "I mean, you've never killed anyone before. You beat that guy up pretty good when he was gettin' hot and heavy with Liz, but that was a real heat-of-the-moment kind of thing, I think."

Tim could only say one thing. "Where is she?!"

Other Tim smiled. "Well, I left the door unlocked. I figure she needed to make sure the coast was clear and then sneak out to find the kids. They're still pretty doped up so waking them and trying to get them on their feet, I'd say she should be coming around the corner any... time... now."

As if on cue, Liz and the kids were scuttling past the far corner of the house when she saw Tim, and Other Tim. She looked confused but still let out a one-word cry of acknowledgment.

"Tim!"

As Tim's eyes darted to his family, Other Tim was lightning quick and snatched the gun from his hand as if he were taking a toy from a disobedient child.

Holding the gun in his hand, he pistol-whipped Tim in the face with it once and said, "Really?"

Liz resisted the urge to run over and stood at a distance from the two Tims.

CHAPTER THIRTY-SEVEN

Liz watched the Tim-look-alike as he sensed something and left. She had to assume her husband had finally arrived. She was delighted to know he had, indeed, searched and found them but was scared for his life at the same time.

At that moment she realized that she didn't hear the door lock behind him.

"Oh God, please let it be unlocked." she prayed.

And it was. She was careful, remembering the last test that he gave her, to listen at the door for a minute. She didn't want to draw any attention to her escape. She put her ear to the door and waited.

Finally, at least marginally convinced that he was really gone, she cracked open the door. Sunlight greeted her with a painful beam. It was afternoon, she could tell, but not with any accuracy to the time. She needed to find the kids. She noticed a shack, or workshop of sorts, behind the cabin.

Carefully she ascended the seven stone steps that led her to the ground level. She was out of sight of the front of the cabin but she dashed over to the shed as quietly as possible anyway. Her bones hurt but the thought of finding her children erased any pain from her body at the moment.

She pushed the door open and her eyes had to readjust to the darkness after being in the bright sun for a moment. To her great dismay and delight, two small figures were on the ground with blindfolds covering their eyes. Her babies.

She silently prayed each was okay, feeling a peace in her heart that they were. She knelt down between them and started to remove the blindfolds.

She started with Caleb.

"Wake up, baby. Mommy's here."

She had both blindfolds off now and was gently shaking her son.

"Caleb, baby, wake up. We need to go. Come on, buddy." She was persistent but not rough. She didn't want to scare them. God knows what they might have seen or would remember from this ordeal.

As Caleb groaned a sleepy protest she turned her efforts to Hannah.

"Wake up, sweetie. It's time to wake up now so we can find Daddy."

As if Daddy were the magic word, both started to throw off the shackles of sleep a little more willingly. Caleb even mumbled a question.

"Where's Daddy? Is it the mean one or our real dad?"

She knew then that her children would not blame their father for this as it was clearly an imposter who brought them to this place.

"Your real daddy who loves you very much is here somewhere and we need to find him. And help him."

Hannah was rousing now as well.

"Mommy!" she exclaimed with her typical heart-melting sweetness.

She was pleased that her children seemed no worse for wear physically. And only time would tell what psychological damage had been done.

"Can you guys stand up?" she encouraged.

They both were a bit wobbly but resilient. Before long they were standing in the doorway discussing the next step. She paused a moment to think straight.

"This was too easy." she thought aloud. "He let me out and let me find you. He's up to something."

Her kids looked a little confused but didn't bombard her with questions for an explanation. They seemed to intuit that Mommy needed to work something out and gave her the quiet to do it.

"Lord, please help us. Keep us safe. Keep Tim safe, Jesus." she prayed again.

Caleb looked at her with big eyes.

"You prayed to Jesus," he stated.

Liz looked at her son and said simply, "Yes I did."

"Cool. I like Jesus," he replied with a smile.

"You do?" she asked with piqued interest. "Where did you learn about Jesus?" she inquired.

"We've heard uncle Paul talk about him a lot. And I've asked him questions about Jesus when ya'll weren't around," he admitted.

"Well, thank God for Uncle Paul!" she exclaimed.

This made Caleb smile. Hannah didn't seem to know fully what was going on but she went with it and smiled a toothless smile as well.

"Let's go guys. Stay right with me, no matter what," she said solemnly.

As they were rounded the corner she was struck with the sight of two Tims facing off. One was holding a gun on the other. From here she had no idea which was the captor and which the captive so she did what any wife might do at the sight of her husband held at gunpoint and screamed out his name.

"Tim!"

As soon as the captor glanced in her direction she had her answer as to which Tim was hers. The Other Tim moved with inhuman quickness and took the gun from him. After slapping him across the face with the gun he held it pointed to his head. She heard him say something but couldn't make it out from where she stood. She could tell that her appearance at this place at this time had been staged for this very moment and she felt used and tricked.

She had unwittingly helped the Evil Tim. Now her husband was at gunpoint and she was clueless as to what to do about it.

CHAPTER THIRTY-EIGHT

"Come over here!" the Other Tim yelled to Liz. "I want you to watch this."

Tim knew he wasn't fast enough to turn the tables as was done to him. He wasn't strong enough to fight him. Wasn't smart enough to trick him. He knelt there, face in his hand, completely at a loss. Broken. Just like the Other Tim had wanted.

"Please." he almost whispered the word. "Please don't do this. I'm sorry. I shouldn't have challenged you. I shouldn't have acted so brave. I'm not brave. You win. Please."

Other Tim breathed the words in again, as before. Savoring them. Feeding on them.

"I'm gonna pop a slug in little Hannah's leg, ok?" he stated as if he were planning to offer her gum. "A nine millimeter will shatter her femur pretty good, I think."

Tim could see that Liz and the kids were hesitant to come closer. In foolish desperation, he yelled to them.

"Run, Liz! GO! Take the kids and go!"

Other Tim leveled the gun at Tim.

"You know I don't need this thing, right? But it's a pretty good metaphor for society. It shows the plight of man. Struggling to overcome, to be the dominant species. This whole thing is kind of an ironic scene. You're literally facing off against yourself! *Facing your demons*, as they say."

Liz didn't run off. She knew that would be a waste of time. She watched from the tree line at the side of the cabin but she wasn't about to leave her husband to face this alone.

Other Tim let the gun lower until it was above his own foot.

BLAM!

The blood and bone in his left foot exploded out at the shot. He didn't flinch. He had just shot himself in the foot but didn't seem phased by it.

"Your little shrouds of flesh are so weak. Even your strongest men bleed so easily. Taking this body was nothing. I've in-dwelt many over the years. Finding someone that looked *enough* like you to manipulate the rest of the way took some time, but as I said, time isn't the same to me."

Tim was still confused about what he was saying but he thought he began to grasp a deeper truth at work here.

"So, you're a demon then?" he clarified.

"Ding ding ding! Give the man a cookie!" he mocked. "Man it only took ole Gabe a few days before he figured it out, too. Started trying to find religion on me. But he served his purpose. I'll finish him off when I'm done with you. I knew he'd be the best link to get you to find me."

"Why all the drama? Why not just show up on my doorstep?" Tim asked.

"Where's the fun in that, Tim? No. Gabe was the catalyst to this little feud back in the day so it was only fitting he help out this time around as well. Didn't count on your pal, Paul, tagging along though. He's been a real thorn in my side."

"He told me how to defeat you." Tim threatened.

Other Tim looked blankly back at him.

"Doesn't take a genius to know that, Tim. But there's just one little problem. You don't believe in that stuff, do ya?" he countered.

Tim could not understand why, in the face of all this evidence, he could still not make himself believe in all of this. He had insisted on bringing the gun. He ditched the pastor and detective. He refused to humble himself to what could be the only option for victory. Why?!

As if Other Tim was privy to the conversation in his head, he said, "It's because you know you deserve this, really. You were a bad son, a bad friend, you're a selfish husband and father. Why would any god save you? Everything you've learned may be true, but what is *truth?* And what does it matter if you don't accept it? You can't be loved, Tim. And if you can't be loved, you can't be saved."

Those words crushed him. In his heart, this was the real reason he had such an aversion to salvation. He could throw up smoke screens all day about the problem of evil, other world religions, and the ultimate search for truth. But if he were totally honest, and at this moment why not be, he didn't believe because he *couldn't* believe that God would love him. That Jesus would die for *him*? It didn't make sense.

As this revelation broke him even further, he looked up and locked eyes with Liz. She had such a determined look on her face. Where was her strength in this coming from?

"I'm tired of this skin." Other Tim declared.

As Tim watched, the Other Tim transformed into some strange Hispanic version of him. But not him at all. This was the host. Tim no longer saw him as the Other Tim, but just as Del now.

"You know something? We can enter into animals sometimes. It's easier to enter a person who has completely opened up to the possibility, of course. But there are times… when the parents have been so neglectful… that we can enter into their children."

Tim's heart almost jumped out of his heart.

"NO! Don't you dare! I forbid you!" Tim found his strength to stand and come at Del.

Even though he wasn't Other Tim anymore he was still as fast and strong. One fist to the chest and Tim went sailing back and onto the ground.

"Come here, Liz. And bring the kiddos. I want you and Daddy to see something."

CHAPTER THIRTY-NINE

Liz stood helpless as she watched it all unfold. She could hear the conversation and her heart broke when Tim's inability to believe was revealed. How he must see himself. He was a great husband and a loving father! How could he not see that? She knew Jesus didn't save people because they had earned it or because they deserve it. She certainly didn't. But if the Bible is true, then it's true for all of us.

She wanted her husband to know this, to believe it as she did now. She stood there praying for her husband to open his heart to this when she heard her name called. She was being beckoned to come down there with the children.

So much of her wanted to say, "heck no, forget that." But she knew this was part of the plan, for some reason. She had to trust.

"Jesus, please protect my children. Don't let that beast hurt them. Cover them with your strength, Jesus." she prayed as they walked down to the two of them.

Tim had rushed at the man and was punched backward at least ten feet. Liz yelled out, "No, we're coming!"

CHAPTER FORTY

"No, we're coming!" Liz yelled when Tim was hurled through the air. She didn't know what she was doing! This vile creature wanted to possess their child. Tim had to stop them but was in no position to do so physically or spiritually.

"Liz, no!" he managed to get out before he collapsed again.

Del stood tall and proud. He walked over to Tim.

"You know it was me who tortured and killed all those boys back in '78, right? I've hung around this town now and then over the last hundred years or so. Found an old drunk who hated church ever since his wife left him. He was neck-deep in some porn and filled his heart with thoughts of murder quite a bit. So I put on his flesh and went on a little spree.

"Lasted a few months. I went for the church kids, mostly. Like Pastor Luke's little brother. Everybody thinks that the good kids are immune to evil. Nope." He loved gloating about his victories.

"Why are you doing this? I don't understand at all."

"Why? Well, why are most of you *humans* so evil, Timmy? I was cast out of heaven because I agreed with Lucifer that we should be worshiped like the Enemy! What's your excuse? I was a magnificent angel serving the Creator of the universe. But once I was cast out I embraced my true fallen nature and began to carve out a name for myself. *Delos*, the spirit of fear." He had a gleam in his eye when he said it. So proud.

Tim had heard that the devil was an angel but he had never really put two and two together to understand that demons were the fallen angels cast out of heaven with him. They were given limited reign on the earth but were still subject to God's authority.

It made more sense now that they would revel in the destruction of mankind.

"You *image-bearers* don't even care that He offers you redemption through His *precious Son*," he said with mockery in his tone. "We don't get redemption, Tim. According to the Book we are destined for the Lake of Fire. But there will be another war! And I believe we will finally overtake the heavens and be victorious. And we will finally wipe every bearer of His image from the face of the earth."

It was so surreal to hear this Bible lesson from a demon. Tim recognized aspects from previous conversations, mostly with Paul, but even *he* knew that the demons couldn't defeat God. So the deceiver was also the deceived. Tim took a little comfort in that. If he was so blind and arrogant as to think he could change the Bible then there was hope he could be stopped here and now.

Liz and the kids arrived by his side.

Creation began to mirror the mood and clouds had covered the sun. Thunder rumbled in the distance. It wasn't raining yet but the atmosphere was thick with moisture that would soon descend on them all.

"So anyway," he continued, "like I was saying. I would take these boys and bring them out here." He gestured around with his hands. "I'd let the old fella have some fun with them and then I'd slit their throats. Then gouge out their eyes. And finally, just to put the exclamation mark on my work, I'd castrate them. Did most of the work with old fishing gear. I thought it matched the motif of the place nicely."

He looked at the children to make sure they were terrified. Satisfied, he continued.

"Serial killing is so much fun because the police are always looking for an M.O. and motive and all that. And just *so many* of them are committed by folks filled with me or my fellow fallen warriors that those stupid sacks of flesh barely know what they're doing half the time. But they're still culpable, mind you. We aren't in complete control at first. They want us to come in and drive and they take a back seat for a while. But once they get caught and go to jail, we dump 'em. Guess that's why a few find jailhouse religion. Once we leave they can think straight again and some are legitimately sorry for what they did. I think it's hilarious.

"I dumped those boys in the lake. You were gonna be number fifteen, Tim. I wanted to pick up where I left off. That night, when you came out here. I was gonna do to you what I did to them." His mood and tone soured. "But He wouldn't let me."

Tim didn't understand. "Who?"

Angry at the question, Del raged "You know who! He wouldn't let me kill you. That's why we're here now. Because your choices have allowed this to come full circle. I wasn't allowed to kill you then but I'm sure gonna enjoy it now."

Tim was still struggling to fully understand what was happening and his part in it.

"So what if I cast you out?" he asked.

"You can't," he answered matter-of-factly. "You have no authority. But Liz here." He turned to look Liz in the eye. "I've been picking up on some subtle signs that she might be developing a bit of a prayer life on me. Can't have that, now can we?" With that, he backhanded Liz off her feet and she fell unconscious to the ground. The children screamed and ran to their mother. They knelt by her side crying and calling her name. Tim stood.

With his teeth gritted he asked again, "What do you want?"

"I want to help you open up, Tim. The best way to kill someone is from the inside out! If I take your body, I can kill your children with your own two hands. How delicious is that?!"

"That will never happen," Tim assured him.

"Maybe not. If that proves to be the case then I'll simply kill your family in front of you and let you live with those images ingrained in your mind. Not as fun for me but still satisfying in its own way. But what I'd really like…" he looked over at the children.

"Never." Tim spat.

Del stood with his eyes rolled back in his head for a second or two. He was trying to do something but it wasn't working. He furrowed his brow and tried again. He cursed a string of blasphemous obscenities!

"If I can't have your children then neither can you."

CHAPTER FORTY-ONE

The hospital room had become a prayer chapel. Paul was still out but Dr. Taylor and Z. were on their knees fighting the good fight. Gabe sat in the corner and watched, trying to pray. Paul was groaning and when one of the nurses came in the check on him she was startled at the sight of the two men on their knees.

"Um, I don't want to be disrespectful but you two will need to go down to the chapel to pray, please. Our patient needs rest," she said sheepishly.

Z. looked at her with compassion but resolve.

"Miss, we in a fight for a man's life right now. Not dis man here," he motioned to the sleeping Paul, "though he was attacked by some evil folks dis morning. Nah, we prayin' for his friend dat's in a standoff against a demon from hell. I apologize if dat's a little unorthodox but he needs us prayin'. And we ain't leavin' dis brother alone cause da enemy wants him outta da way, too. Copy?"

She looked at the pastor and sighed in resignation. "My daddy was a preacher. I have seen evil in my time. Ya'll pray."

With renewed vigor, they hit their knees and tried to call on every angel in heaven to help their new friend. They had never felt such a keen battle for one man's life before. God surely had His hand on Tim McDaniel's life for some reason to do all this.

They quoted every scripture they could about the battle and our victory in Jesus. They could only hope that Tim opened his heart to the truth before it was too late.

CHAPTER FORTY-TWO

Del grabbed Caleb by the scruff of his neck as if he were an unwanted animal and lifted him off of the ground. He kicked and screamed but it was a futile effort. He set out at a near jog towards the water some fifty feet away from this point.

"Noooo!"

Tim was caught off guard but was up on his feet and after him. He was a few feet behind and couldn't catch up. Del was at the water's edge hurling Caleb into the muddy waters before Tim could stop him. As Caleb soared through the air and landed in the water, the heavens opened up and released its torrent.

Caleb was a decent swimmer but he was about twenty feet off the shoreline and the rain was already making the waters choppy. Tim was already down the bank and into the water in seconds.

"I'm coming, Caleb! Swim to me!" he shouted.

"Daddy! Something's got my foot!" Caleb yelled back.

CHAPTER FORTY-THREE

Tim swam as hard as he could to Caleb. He could hear little Hannah wailing in the distance. The thought crossed his mind that Del could do whatever he wanted to her while Liz was unconscious and he was trying to get Caleb. That fear momentarily paralyzed him but he decided to let it motivate him instead. He swam even harder.

Caleb looked petrified when he finally reached him.

"Hands are grabbing my feet, Daddy."

Tim took his son's hands and clasped them around his neck. "I'm gonna swim you to shore, buddy. Hold on tight."

The wind had picked up and the rain was coming down in angry sheets. This was the kind of storm that manifested out of nowhere and did real damage.

Del stood at the shore smiling as if he were proud of his accomplishment. Could a demon make it rain? Tim had no idea what power he had or didn't have. He was ignorant of the Bible except for what he and Paul discussed sporadically. He had learned more about Christianity in the last twenty hours than most of his life so far. Still, he knew enough to know that he was going to lose this battle if something didn't change.

Miraculously, they reached the shoreline. Tim practically threw Caleb onto the muddy beach. In the moment that his son was free and Tim went to stand, small hands wrapped around his ankles and pulled him down.

He turned and was looking into the grotesque face of one of the tortured boys. His eyes were gone, throat gaping open, and his skin was a bluish-grey, mottled with green patches. It was a terrifying sight.

Then, others started to rise from the water. Eventually, fourteen of them.

Tim couldn't break the grip. He was being dragged back into the water. While he still had his wits he yelled to Caleb.

"Go to your mom!"

"Daddy!" was all he said, and obediently ran back to his mother.

Tim was trying to think. What could he do? He tried to kick and swim but the other had started to grab hold of him by now. It seemed inevitable that he was going to be dragged down to his watery grave. He thought he heard sirens in the distance. Guess Peters and the Pastor finally made it.

He looked up at Del and hated seeing the smug grin on his face. How could God let this evil prevail? What would happen to Liz, Caleb, and Hannah? Would his death mean their death?

These questions were drowning him faster than the water lapping at his face. As they pulled him out to deeper water, they simply weighed him down under the surface. With one last act of hope, he drew in a deep breath before being fully submerged.

So many thoughts were going through his mind. Every moment of laughter with his mom before her death. The times his dad made an effort to connect with him. The way Paul was such a good friend to him. Falling in love with Liz. The birth of each of his children. But one thought stuck out to him. One reverberating memory that tied all the others together. One that he had forgotten for thirty years until right now. Right this moment.

He was standing in front of the cabin and had just picked the piece of bark off. He turned and the macabre beast grabbed his throat. As all the mutilated boys gathered close to him and he saw young Del laughing on the porch, he prayed a silent prayer for help.

In his mind's eye, he looked back on that night and as he was slipping from consciousness he felt, or heard, or *both,* a voice say, "No. You can't have him." For all this time he only remembered waking up in the ambulance and had shut so much of that night out. But Del was right. He had been forbidden to take his life.

That means that God did intervene. Why? Why was he special? Tim couldn't help but feel conviction about doubting God all this time. Just because we can't see Him moving doesn't mean He isn't.

His breath was running out. He was free-floating about a foot under the surface of the water and the boys had let go at this point. His death must be very near. All the times Paul had shared the story of Jesus with him came flashing through his mind.

"He died your death so you don't have to." he would say. "Jesus was the only perfect sacrifice that would satisfy God's justice and pour grace out on us." "You have to know that God loves you, not because you're so good, but because He's so good." "Jesus is the way, the truth, and the life and nobody gets to the Father but by Him."

The last sound byte that came to his mind wasn't Paul, it was Dr. Taylor's voice in his gentle South African accent. "All you must do is take the hand."

CHAPTER FORTY-FOUR

Liz was slowly coming around. Both children were patting her face and saying her real name to them, "Mommy!" She was finally able to prop up on her elbow and see out of her left eye. The right one would probably be swollen shut for a while.

It was raining so hard. She could hear sirens coming but they sounded far off still. She got to her feet but was wobbly so both kids got under each arm to steady her. Their captor was standing on the shoreline laughing.

And then he wasn't laughing anymore.

Liz couldn't believe her eyes.

A huge hand was coming out of the clouds and rain. It was definitely a hand but it wasn't made of flesh. It was like it was made of the rain and clouds that were all around. It was big enough that a car could have easily sat in its palm. And it was reaching into the water.

Because she had been out of the loop the last few minutes, Caleb filled her in on the dreadful turn of events.

"Daddy had to save me and now he's in the water. The dead boys dragged him out there." He said, pointing to where the hand was.

Liz didn't know what to think. Dead boys? A giant hand reaching into the water? Was Tim drowning?

"Please Jesus, save him!" was her plea. Literally and figuratively, she wanted her husband saved so she asked the only One who could do it. And at that moment, she was convinced that she joined countless others in that prayer. It was powerful.

But would it work.

CHAPTER FORTY-FIVE

After Luke and Sean recovered from the phone calls, they realized Tim was gone. They decided to call in the reinforcements and head after him. He had a few minutes' head start but they were pretty sure they knew where to find him.

They saw his truck parked at the edge of the path. Both men decided that a slow jog was better than a brisk walk if they wanted to help Tim out at all so they took off down the path. Peters instinctively drew his sidearm. They both knew this wasn't the most effective weapon they had but it could still stop a bad guy and he didn't know what to expect.

They heard the sirens of the backup in the distance. They should be here within three minutes. Hopefully, they could get to Tim and assess the situation by then. About halfway down the path, they heard a man yelling, likely Tim's voice.

"Nooo!"

Only a moment later the sky opened up and liquid wrath poured out. The rain was heavy and thick. It took them another couple of minutes to reach the end of the path but as they came out of the wooded area they saw a woman standing with her small children by her side, the boy soaking wet. A man was standing on the shore laughing at the lake.

And then he wasn't laughing as a humongous hand began reaching down from the heavens.

"You're seeing this, right?" Peters asked in a near yell to be heard over the rain.

"Yeah. Yeah, I am," Luke responded with an awestruck tone.

After a second the men snapped out of their stunned wonder and duty took over. They ran over to the woman and the children, but

Peters trained his gun on the once laughing man out of instinct, not sure what to expect from him.

The woman was startled as they approached so Sean flashed his badge to put her mind at ease. The wind and rain were so heavy they couldn't hear her voice but could see she mouthed the words, "Oh, thank God!"

She was pointing at the man by the lake and trying to say something but they had to be right next to her to hear anything. She seemed frantic and worried.

Once they arrived at her side she was screaming, "Watch out! This man is dangerous! My husband is in the lake. Please help him!"

They eyed the man carefully but he seemed completely absorbed at the moment with the enormous hand reaching into the water.

Luke noticed the woman had some bruising on her face and some blood caked at her mouth. "Are you ok?" He yelled to her.

"I'll be fine." She replied. "He's not what you think!" She was saying about the man again, pointing.

Luke had a strong feeling he knew exactly what she meant. Peters seemed more focused on the man and the hand. His gun was trained on him the whole time.

The man seemed to seethe in anger as the hand descended into the water. He yelled at the heavens with his fist balled in defiance. He looked back at the woman and noticed the two men by her side. He set his anger and rage on them and set off in their direction, seeming to be oblivious or unconcerned about the gun trained on him. Peters yelled a warning but it was doubtful he could hear over the fierceness of the storm.

"Stop right there!" he shouted to no avail. He steeled his heart to fire if necessary.

The man began to run at them. He squeezed the trigger.

CHAPTER FORTY-SIX

"All you must do is take the hand."

Tim could no longer remember why he resisted this so much for so long. Knowing that God had spared him those thirty years ago and that he had not forsaken him or his family even now melted away all of his resolve. Years of hardness began to soften and his heart longed for love. Real love. He knew he was a sinner. Not a "bad person" as the world liked to label it. By all practical standards, he was a great guy.

But by the highest standard, God's standard, he was fallen and broken. But the beauty of that understanding didn't bring him the shame he feared such a revelation would. No, it brought sweet relief. He could finally be honest about his true state: a sinner. Because he knew that Jesus loved him all the same.

Knowing, finally believing, in that love gave him the strength he needed to do what he was always incapable of doing before. He took the hand.

And the moment he surrendered in his heart to the truth of forgiveness in Jesus, it was more like the hand took hold of him. He felt light, free. It was almost like he could breathe underwater. He had no fear of dying, though he honestly knew that was still a distinct possibility. He now trusted that his eternity was settled.

But at that moment, he knew that his life wasn't over. He had work to do. He wasn't saved from his sin just to drown, though that would have still been grace at its finest. But he knew instinctively that he wasn't going to finish his race underwater. So he began to swim.

His lungs burned like fire, the breath he had taken was long spent. He kicked his feet and pulled with cupped hands, propelling himself up and out of the water. The storm was a doozy, but he managed to inhale a huge breath of fresh air. His first breath of air as a new man. It was almost like truly being born again. But no time to be philosophical about it right now, he had work to do.

He made it to the shore in time to hear a gunshot. His heart feared that Del was finishing his family but he stifled that fear with a prayer.

"God, please give me victory in this *Your* way. Whatever happens, I'm Yours now, but please protect them."

As he climbed up the bank to the cabin's flat land he saw Del back-handing Detective Peters through the air and grabbing Luke Graham by the throat, all in speed faster than men can move.

CHAPTER FORTY-SEVEN

He pulled the trigger and hit the man in the shoulder. It meant nothing. He didn't flinch or slow. And he was moving faster than he had ever seen a man move, regardless of what he was hopped-up on at the time. Men on crack, LSD, meth, speed or some new concoction of narcotic might be able to take a bullet and keep coming, but not like this. This was absolutely inhuman.

Sean Peters was being back-handed off his feet, hurling through the air. He saw the man grab Pastor Graham's throat with such speed that the man didn't have time to utter a word. He somehow knew that was the plan.

But Tim was out of the water and standing like a man with a score to settle.

"I command you to stop in the name of Jesus Christ!" he yelled.

And he did. Everything did.

CHAPTER FORTY-EIGHT

Tim knew what he had to do. He planted his feet and yelled in authority, "I command you to stop in the name of Jesus Christ!"

Del froze. But even more astonishing than that, the storm stopped. Completely and immediately. He was reminded of one of Paul's recounting of scripture where Jesus rebuked the wind and waves.

Paul had excitedly told him, "He wasn't just rebuking nature, but when he arrived at the shore he was met by two demoniacs. He was rebuking the demonic storm that drove fear into the hearts of His disciples!"

He knew at that moment that Delos had been one of the legions of demons possessing one of those men. Weren't they driven into pigs, he recalled?

"You're done," he told Del.

Del was gritting his teeth but did not move.

"Let him go and step away, now," Tim ordered.

Obediently, Del let go and stepped away. Luke rubbed his neck where the vice-like grip had been. He, Liz, even Detective Peters on the ground ten feet away, were in stunned silence as they witnessed this encounter.

"You can't stop me, Timmy," Del said unconvincingly.

"I can't do anything. But in the name and authority of Jesus Christ, I command you to leave this man."

There was a new quality to his voice, a huge contrast to the angry, mocking tone he had been using this whole time. "Where are you sending me?" he whined.

Tim looked up and saw a small murder of crows was passing overhead. He looked back to Del and nodded his permission. At once the fourteen "boys" came out of the lake and all fifteen demons shrieked their exits and entered the birds. They flew, as one, into the water to drown themselves, just as the pigs had done two thousand years earlier.

The boys' bodies were simply gone as they were only demonic figments of fancy, but the host of Delos crumpled to the ground, a gunshot wound in his foot and one in his right shoulder.

CHAPTER FORTY-NINE

Liz watched in stunned silence as her husband defeated this evil through the authority of Jesus. He had come out of that lake a different man than he went in. She was overwhelmed with gratitude towards God for His hand reaching into that water.

Watching the crows dive into the lake to their watery deaths was eery, but poignant.

No matter how you looked at it, the McDaniel family would never be the same again. This tragic and horrible day had been redeemed. She and her husband had woken up this day separated from God, lost in their sin and rebellion. They feared for their lives and the lives of their children because they had no hope against evil.

But now they both were made new in Christ. This was the mystery so many had talked about before. This was why Paul would get so excited when he would share about his faith. How many times had they patronized him and pacified him and his "religious talk?"

But now they both saw the light, so to speak. She couldn't wait to hear all about Tim's transformation and, likewise, to tell him about hers. But now all that needed to be said was obvious.

"I love you!" she said as she melted in his arms. The children were clinging to their legs, absorbing the safety both parents brought to them at this moment. Tim clung to his wife for a moment and then knelt down and fiercely held his children. He planted kisses on their heads and faces and picked them both up, one in each arm, while Liz held them all in hers.

Both noticed but didn't bring much attention, to their battered and bruised faces. It had been a rough twenty-four hours.

The policeman was cuffing the man on the ground and the other man was smiling and keeping a respectful distance. She instantly liked him, for some unexplainable reason.

Tim reluctantly put the kids down after a few moments and turned to the two men.

"Detective Peters, Pastor Graham. This is my wife Liz and my kids, Caleb and Hannah." They both smiled and Luke came over to politely shake the hand of each child and hugged Liz. Peters was busy assessing the wounds of the man on the ground and was using the small walkie-talkie on his belt clip to communicate to the backup that was nearly there. He waved a quick *I'd love to come over, but this guy needs my attention* wave.

"I'm sorry I left you guys and came on my own. But thank you so much for all you've done and for believing me," he said to both men.

Peters was pulling the wallet out of the back pocket of the man and announced, "I think Mr. Rodney Peña has some explaining to do. But I get why you did you what did. I don't like it, but I get it."

"I hate to say it but I better say it now among the people who won't think I'm totally crazy. I doubt that guy will remember much of what happened. Though he is still culpable." he said, recalling the words of Delos himself. That triggered another difficult memory.

"Pastor. I don't know if this will bring you any peace but the demon that used this man proudly confessed to me that he had used another man in the '70s to kill those children." he paused for a moment. "Your little brother."

Luke Graham had the best poker face of any pastor around. Tim couldn't tell what was going on behind his kind, intelligent eyes. Then he seemed to exhale for the first time in forty-four years. The weight he had carried about his brother's death was lifted once and for all. The "man" responsible may be long dead and gone but the evil behind the man had been identified, and that brought him some peace.

The calvary had arrived in three John Deere Gators. Three sheriff's deputies and a couple of EMS crew were now on the scene with a stretcher and medical supplies. They dressed the wounds of the still-out-of-it Peña and carried him to one of the Gators. It would be a quick ride down the path back to the vehicles.

After about two minutes of Luke and Sean catching people up to speed, one of the deputies asked the McDaniel family if they felt up to coming into the station to answer a few questions. As much as they just wanted to be done and home, they said "sure."

They offered them a ride in one of the other Gators and Tim was about to load up when Liz surprised him by saying, "Hold up. I want to talk with you for just a second." She took the kids over to one of the deputies and explained mommy and daddy would be right back. They seemed hesitant but trusted her. The deputy immediately engaged them with a tour of the Gator and Liz walked up to Tim and took his hand in hers.

"What's this about?" Tim inquired.

"Well. After all the evil that's been done on this land over the years, I thought it might be appropriate if we prayed a blessing over it or something. I'm pretty new to this prayer thing." she admitted.

Tim thought it a wonderful suggestion and found it indescribably comforting that Liz had discovered authentic faith through this just as he did. He was so worried that she would think him a weirdo if he *found Jesus*. Probably because that's how he'd treated Paul all these years. He couldn't wait to tell his best friend the news.

They prayed together for the first time of many more to come. They tried to redeem what was once worthless. This camp tried to do that once. Maybe it could happen again. Who knows? Maybe now that the evil that had clouded this town for so long was cast out the families could move on.

As they made it back to the Gator, Peters and Luke awaited them with one Deputy. They could all ride back together since this gator had the extra seats in the back as long as a kid was in a lap.

"How's this gonna pan out? I mean, legally and all?" he was asking Sean Peters. He couldn't imagine a neat little bow on this one.

"I'm not completely sure but I've already discovered that Mr. Peña has several warrants out for everything from aggravated assault to statutory rape. He's going away for a long time so kidnapping is just another charge on his list."

"You won't get in trouble for this, will you?" Tim finally realized what a chance he had taken to help him.

"Nah. I got a call from a former sheriff with a tip. I followed it and caught the bad guy. Got your family back. Heck, I may even get a raise." he said with a wink.

It felt good to smile after the last day. Tim also felt so thankful for Pastor Graham.

"Thanks for being a real man of God," he said to him. Then he corrected himself. "Both of you."

"Wow. Something must have really gotten your attention in that lake!" Luke said with a laugh. "You're a totally different man that on the phone or in my living room."

Thinking about the years God had pursued him only to find him at this hour, Tim was glad he was a different man.

"You could say that," he replied solemnly.

Answering questions at the station had its difficult moments.

"So it was your gun that shot him in the foot but Detective Peters shot him in the shoulder? And you say he shot himself in the foot, but with your gun?" the deputy tried to clarify.

"That's right. He was pretty out of his mind at that point. Really losing it." Tim answered.

If you strip away all the supernatural elements of the story, it was reasonably easy to explain: The accused was hopped up on drugs and kidnapped Tim's family. Then, he drove them to this camp but Pastor Luke saw them and called Detective Peters.

When they arrived, the man had already taken Tim's gun and shot himself. Then, he was threatening the family in the yard of the house and threw the son in the lake. Tim went in to save him and by the time he came out of the water Detective Peters had shot and apprehended the man.

Paperwork was about to be filed and they were free to go. Peters made sure he knew that would have to do the same song and dance on his side of the investigation, but not today. Today he needed to get his family home.

So, he did.

EPILOGUE

aughter filled the house. The children were playing and Tim sat with his two favorite adults on this earth. Liz, Tim, and Paul sipped coffee and reminisced about life, love, and the universe.

It had been almost a month since the ordeal had ended. Paul was in a full arm cast from where the demoniac snapped his humerus. A few cracked ribs were healing nicely, but other than that he was the picture of health. The kids had handled the situation with remarkable grace, but Tim and Liz took them to a local child psychologist just to be sure they were processing everything ok. He was highly recommended by a local pastor they had met when they visited a church a couple of weeks ago

Detective Peters had closed the case with almost no issues. Turns out the Tahoe stolen from the gas station they had stopped in had been stolen by one Rodney Peña. There was no video surveillance available but the sweet woman who worked the night shift was able to identify the man as being in the store that night. According to her, he was "shifty and unpleasant."

Even John Calloway came around and went to bat for him. After viewing the new evidence, hearing Peters' report, and re-interviewing the neighbor, Mrs. Jenkins, he concluded that the elderly neighbor was confused when she saw the Tahoe and had only *thought* that it was Tim. Mr. Peña was dressed like him and had a vehicle close enough to throw her off.

It made Peters' life much easier and Tim was glad of that. Tim only left town "under duress" and that was pretty much swept under the rug in the "happy ending" style of this case.

Tim and Liz had driven back down to New Orleans to see Paul in the hospital when the case closed to tell him the good news of their newfound faith. Their stories of grace and redemption made Paul explode with joy, which brought in two nurses to assess the outburst. He was blown away by how God moves and works.

After the initial outburst, tears silently rolled down his cheeks as he listened. Tim thanked him and apologized so many times that Paul finally had to crack another sarcastic joke about the hospital erecting a statue of St. Paul before he was discharged.

The kids hated to see their "Uncle" Paul in a hospital so banged up, but he assured them he would be out soon and over to their house for a cookout.

That was today.

So much had happened in the last few weeks that catching up on it all took a few hours. Luckily, no one was in a hurry to leave. Paul told them that he had been officially put on "sick leave" for a month to recuperate so he wasn't in any big rush. These would be a much-needed few days with people he loved.

The big news of the evening was dropped about an hour ago and had been the topic ever since.

"So, I've been thinking about going back to school for my doctorate. Being back in New Orleans stirred something in me. Plus Dr. Taylor was telling me about a little church out in the bayou that needs a pastor. What do you think?"

They were obviously supportive of Paul following the Lord's call but would hate to be so far from him. Still, any excuse to spend a weekend in New Orleans was ok by them! They knew he would make the best decision and didn't try to persuade him otherwise. They listened to his excitement about what all moving back and possibly pastoring a church would mean to him.

As they were winding down for the night, Tim was walking Paul to the guest room and passed Caleb's room on the way. Remembering the last time he was over he said, "Hope you like the Star Wars sheet on the guest bed."

Paul smiled at the memory.

"You know, I believe the force is strong with this one." he chided while scratching his chin.

"Thank God it is," Tim replied.

"And you, my young padawan," he got serious for a second, "I'm proud of you." He said this with genuine affection. There had been so many serious moments between them lately Tim had to ruin it.

"Aw, thanks Dad." he joked.

"Why can we never be too serious for too long?" Paul laughed. "Are we that immature?"

From the other room, Liz chimed in loudly, "Yes."

But at that moment, all was right in the world for them. Tim hugged Paul gently and Paul squeezed back with his one good arm. The embrace was sincere and unforced. Just like their friendship.

But one thing was for sure, everything had changed. Sure, there was the blessed familiarity of family and friendship, but there was something deeper now. There was a purpose to their life that had not been there before. Tim could sense that with this new understanding and relationship was going to be some real responsibility on his part. But he wasn't going to say that to Paul because he knew he'd just get a Spiderman joke.

So, what were the next steps for the McDaniel family? They told Paul they had visited a solid church a couple of times already and really liked it. They humbly confessed that they needed to get to know their new faith. And they were going to try to be open to whatever God brought their way.

They both realized what a scary commitment that was, but they also knew the alternative. Being a *fair-weather* Christian was not an option for either of them. Hypocrisy, theirs or anyone else's, could veil the gospel and they refused to keep others from hearing the truth by being horrible examples of the love of Christ.

That was the real story here. Love. Love drives out fear. Love makes a man go through hell to find his family. Love reaches down to a man at his lowest point to remind him of his innate worth as a child of God. Love had rocked Tim's world and he would never be the same. Love was a powerful tool and he wanted to use it well to show others what had been so patiently shown to him.

They were all yet unaware, but something powerful was stirring. Before long they were all going to be used in greater ways and for greater purposes than any of them had ever considered. As long as dark forces came against the Light, there was a battle to be fought. Not a fight against flesh and blood, of course, but against the spiritual forces that strive to pervert the heart of man. This is and always has been where the real battle begins and ends.

The End, For Now...

Made in United States
Orlando, FL
15 January 2023

28700775R00167